MW01596408

THIS BOOK IS FOR AMBER FAYE DEROSA REED

to
sarah

Che
Eliz

i

'Rockets Construe Vala'- in 2parts

'My Life Without Rea'
AND
'In A Time Of Giants'
Both were written by
Che Elias

© Copyright 2001 Che Elias. All rights reserved.

No part of this publication may be reproduced, stored in a retrieval system, or transmitted, in any form or by any means, electronic, mechanical, photocopying, recording, or otherwise, without the written prior permission of the author.

Printed in Victoria, Canada

National Library of Canada Cataloguing in Publication Data

Elias, Che, 1980-
  Rockets construe vala
  ISBN 1-55212-872-5
  I. Title.
PS3605.L52R62 2001   813'.6   C2001-911062-6

TRAFFORD

This book was published *on-demand* in cooperation with Trafford Publishing.
On-demand publishing is a unique process and service of making a book available for retail sale to the public taking advantage of on-demand manufacturing and Internet marketing.
On-demand publishing includes promotions, retail sales, manufacturing, order fulfilment, accounting and collecting royalties on behalf of the author.

Suite 6E, 2333 Government St., Victoria, B.C. V8T 4P4, CANADA
Phone   250-383-6864   Toll-free   1-888-232-4444 (Canada & US)
Fax   250-383-6804   E-mail   sales@trafford.com
Web site   www.trafford.com   TRAFFORD PUBLISHING IS A DIVISION OF TRAFFORD HOLDINGS LTD.
Trafford Catalogue #01-0276   www.trafford.com/robots/01-0276.html

10   9   8   7   6   5   4   3   2   1

1. 'My Life Without Rea'

CHAPTER 'A'

1.GALLA, EBBEY'S DREAM

"Cosel Haringif on going to the spider's intercourse amongst the branches-Meadow leaves turn up-turned-A sooth-sayer devises a hypothesis in attentive sophism, Stephanie scowling, bringing her pollex to her temple will segue to the step on intimacy-Self annihilation in the Sacred respects of the physical act of love. Her vulva is Paradisal+a quaint ziggurat +toff pubescence-virtu Moistness-One acting as the sole absorber of. Landing parts on wisp, her Appointed lily. Contofh Lassel on going to the celibacy tree-our Father who provides a difficult text- fructuous attempts-He abandons us to weigh East of our keep-post-bourgeois We will need the next hours to proceed our leave—our Father who would relinquish our quiddity in his pasttime-Our father is only shoal-Will never fall in our light"-

NOW,

"Opens us-despite lack of our consent, NOW Seems sad."
-Drink, Ebbey, Drink-I lose –I lose-I wash my ruff, peel'd back

"EN" solicitous. Hetts Flint downs one other demitasse "This es a change, uh Ebb?"

"Ebbey incisively, out of trouble-nods Hetts a morning farewell. Hetts racks the door-The yard in small gardens, hung with the proceeding Catherine Wheels, a muffle tender over-grown grass, Small planted trees from the home's previous occupants. The Flints have last week moved-in, in less time than last-Ebbey has found the tinge of dis-temperament. From survivingbadtimes-is Ebbey's catch-all. He prays like rhythmic——-alms. This, like a lash from a belt that has forbidden----others ---from --their --own --temptations. From Ebbey's praying comes infectious unplanned cat's Cradles-Regular-For Ebbey-A vision –tinted, all He sees are the Scottish Highlands-He shows Himself drinking the murking water that has gathered to a puddle in the indentation made from a wolf's pawprint." Their intercourse had become a casusbelli-Impedimenta-resonates alphabetically-He takes limp red toy blocks and arranges names of puns that accord to Stephanie's Vulva-He's impatient-the mainland's hoodlum floods-"EFG"-Cut-LABIA MAJORA-he pronounces clitoris like CLIT-OR-ES-In Preentice's room, I saw a robin in the main Spring he played make believe camping in tents, Tarps held up with a collective of fern pots-"HISK"-Transition-"LABIA MINORA", Ebbey is still crying-wet behind the room doors-His room sits smilingly across the hall from MUM's And Hett's–Ebb's Room is still obnubilated-'Cause Hetts only now comes crashing less, less, less-He'll never only serve as the obtruder-Hetts had a funny dream of himself ending his Family-life , still being a father to his KID- Shall any be looking? Hetts had later a funnier Dream, where MUM could feel each alphabet Letter.

"Ebbey, from now on Hetts name is Magus!"

Stephanie's belly-now in its second trimester, A roundswell-or earthball)&(floatingglobe=to Rub it; the outjection of her bellybutton protruding- Mugwee has photographed once during this, her second pregnancy=Steph lying naked on her side- A bed strewn with satinpillows, In Picture1.She supports Her body by resting on her right elbow(bending her arm)- In Photo2.- she's covered her face, leaned downward, Obscured, supporting herself with both arms. Mugwee's pictures of his wife were taken with a boxcamera, a fixedlens-Her bloom will when long since after this life, he hopes last on pictureplates. In their privatepicture, Stephanie leans back in a Fatherschair, minus clothes-Spreads her legs. The picture is like a loft that in anyorder, order Confuses me on which part of it to put my eyes Onto.

<<>>TOPOFTHEPICTURE<>Stephanie's<>halfsmile.<<>><>
<<>> CENTEROFTHEPICTURE<>bust<>pregnantbelly. <><>
<<>> BOTTOMOFPICTURE=her vulva<><><><><><><><><>

Little Soanotra awakened this nightagain by the sirens, is rocked to comfort by Emma Betts-, she slept in the samebed as her granddaughter ,through the war Glasses rock forth&backon the cardtable, which is top covered in golfcourse lawngreen felt-aproblem, aleg of the table is much by an half/inch short-so's this uncenteredness and the problematic shaking of any droppedbombs,the glasses crash the floor.each glass's shatter inflashed relays to Soanotra's MUM'S unborn- Stephanie's & Mugwee's referral by name to their next-born is as firebug& lightfly; eachtime the fetus kicks during dusktime, Steph's belly ignites a glow, as if't were an electriclight.

CUM splashes, that CUM has the appearance of an Egg yoke-sickeningsexsent dark yellowCUM-Deep-----WhiteCUM almost blue if we are readily approaching The whiteCUM's color quality-Hetts wrote this,

---

        NOTEBOOK&CHART
    SPELLING 'B' =PEN'TRATION
        FEAR,
        IMPOTENCE,
SEXLY,REVOLSION?=ARISE=STEADMOND'S FACTOR -IS FEAR? S-T-E-A-D-F-E-A-R "HETTS LOVELY NOTES" 2 HAPPY/SAD/MASKS/ZIG/ZAGTHECLOISTERED/CURTAINS, STICKY FROM FRUITCANDY;FOOD EATEN ON IN THEM-INSTEAD SHOULD BE, I THOUGHT ATE   AT THE TABLE-(shit, shit,) he became ejaculated ice pudding which entered to through the floorboards.TWO,he often plucked TWO hens, he smeared garlic all over their stubble,he secured them under his armpits with dog collars. Their frenzy by the time it drew to calm-had brought Hetts multiple orgasms.the terrace steps, lawn, patio tables, and lobby were allover redone ,shockingly left fresh, unfortunately by its questionably fled in terror owners-On the steps that lead to Hetts's room –Clear, regardless of day's in&out quests, a waterpuddle gathered over the corner closest to the wall on the second step-No matter how he scrubbed this up-it without doubt reappeared in the coming day. Hetts replied " You look as if you have seen a ghost!" A little after NOON, Hetts down through town's center was attached momentarily to an artist, sorts' a Magician likeall gave 'is tricks for considerable donation- Never wanting to be a participate, Hetts looked off and Could relax at being just an onlooker-A wand casts Monster cloudform bubbles, these turn the Magician to Stone-his suddenness cracks ringing from the thin stone shell, it'd left a sticking gue on his collar. His marvel Is while partaking in an Indianropetrick- Rope castup in through sky, raps once-and any guest lookeron climbs welcomingly up-Then followed, SCREAMING down a small drizzling blood, pieces of their body scatteringly fall down from our outview-they are next together under a cover&rug , to us happily the guest comes from 'neath un-troubled.

This calm day-Stephanie walked alone, slowly passed those who were sweeping lastnight's blast's rubble from a major portion of one of the tallhouses that in prior stood on the rightcorner of the square. Coat, stockings, brown walking shoes-picking carefully –she supported her walk holding uplong her heavy body-hands on-- her back's archpoints so's not to make nettle with her stomach's yetgiven trespasser. If genetically trite, these relations from her neatly styled neurosis tied with her idea of her interior crumbling 'long with the town's   "BEING BLOWN TO BITS". Mugwee said, "Don't take this out on yourself, not with yourself in this state, you've got to keep your health and all."

Rumbits-- hung about a walkway, they'd -- follow, NOT ONE ? Stephanie seats herself gradually on a Bench-peering over the city that is to her at times (and she felt-- it to be again?)the greatest proclamation of what anyone can & does hope to make out of their life-nearing and to her likely a tranquillity amid this city in its dusk-secretly Stephanie partook a passageway in her scope of reelment-meandering a look at last, of a place & a very little time alone, needed when starving of her own companionship & and of letting yourself be killed before ever telling your friends how to make sum of you after that departure.

Stephanie has that in mind-she'll have to... Luckily can see to be more of a solitary person –probably not knowing of what's coming onto the/her friends.

5

Ebbey lie in bed-without any pillows-His neck arched to a slopepoint-his Breathing increased fastly. Cursed drowsiness made watch, Himself knowingly not slept for much Other than in segments for the weeks Since in 'NEWHOME'. Ebbey made off thru sleep in a Badly worn nightgown+sure as That+he everynight did not consider Sleepattemption before pasting his Face in a thick, thick white(cream)Make-up-placing this even carefully too+ 'round his eyelids,below his sockets-then wetting his hair back- the quickly dried make-up made even more stickout his wetswollen vividly red lips-they seemed large in proportion with the rest of his face-They crowned over his small teeth, though the slightly crooked lower bridge glittered in the bedroom setting. Also in his bedroom was a large orange sofa-'times on nights a sleepoverer might favor this to the floor-and the sofa's proudly solid armrests are known to considerably drive one to dreams-Just as Ebbey told guests,

" 'Cause you'll sleepfast, 'cause..your the while tryin' to forget your uncomfortability". During lightningstorms, Ebb himself slept on this sofa-a redquilt serving as his warm covering-The seconds he counted between the lightning Flashes +peering across the room to the tallmirror-During each lighting of the room+he saw in the Mirror his soft huddled freshform revised to himself In the likeness of heavily sagged flower petals That moresothenever handed directly to him A lesson plan for his witless self —obstinacies. He shuddered, brought the quilt up from below his breasts to cover him upto his cheeks. The lightning rolled 'gain over, Ebbey quivered, realizing his mirror likeness this time as a small ruby. In darkness's seconds he envisioned his body Stretched, snapped and then held in place so tight He could not in any way move-Ebbey felt somekind Of ornaments placed in the gap from his ears to neck+The lightning strung-up, he rolled free+gaining his reflected 'figuration as this time a ruby which concealed in it a hungdown silkcoated yet thoroughly speeled self-infamy.

CHAPTER 'B'

Home as staged from its propers, the outchart- Where being they'd make there, & exactly Less than awhile prior to dusk-they'd parked off from the Side of where the road stops Thrown some shrubs over it, liking It would be not-so-in notice- He takes her hand , making sure that She steps over the riseup of the footbridge, not wanting her to Trip- The bridge had been madeover, appeared to've been recently rebuilt, his feet he'd remember as feeling the still slick tops of the Whitepainted wood- The bridge comes to its ending at a walkway Which stretches to the appeared-to-still-be-operating tavern-

Remember, She entered first, while he'd held the door for her-The place, open though empty of patrons- a rustling is heard by them, coming probably from the tavern's back- A girl enters in from out of the backdoor, a child actually, 7 OR 8years, maybe- He would first think much too young to be incharge of this, the child OR something of whoever is incharge the girl climbs atop the counter, standing above them, her hand on her mouth, gazing strongly at Them without ever saying a word, he was startled, too much at a Certain misunderstanding, to had said anything- They left the tavern, inexplicably, he remembered he held the door on the wayout, too- walked behind her on the footbridge while still holding her hand- Again, to her as inexplicable, they would spend the night in the car-Though this decision seemed one without much option, " Were We to Sleep in the tavern, what else could we have done" he said, " We should Have at least waited to've seen who was in-control of all of that", she said in the tone of very much being irritated, " Not this time, that I don't think I wish to do, only a night here", BUT she was insistent upon going backover to the tavern. He found himself sensibly in her agreement after realizing the significant discomfort he'd have to face while it was-- that his legs were too long to stretch fully out over the set while lying down and that he would have to sleep crouchedup-So again they were over the footbridge and, not-at-all-hand&hand, entering the tavern, finding it still empty, the littlegirl was out-of-sight and they could hear nothing of the sort which would've led them to think she was still somewhere in the back of the tavern? He had her wait in the front, as he proceeded to venture to the back of the Tavern, thru the kitchen, it seems to him that no-one's to've made use of Its contents as of the recent-She stood, then sat at a table, thinking that she should sense an essential aloneness here, she felt mainly her understanding that here there could've occurred matters of importance amongst others-He came out from the back, saying he could not find-- the sign of anyperson being near- She was restlessly undecided- He decided they'd may-as-well stay here till someone comes, or if not and that meant staying the entirety of the night till the planed catching of the boat in the early morning, then be so, still better than the car's uncomfortable interior-AND better than what of her complaints(and his aches) he'd be surely barraged with. As rains propped down on the tavernroof , they both knew now they'd surely spend the night in the tavern, and in the hours that had been brushed away, it seemed that nobody was arriving there-She grew tired, he brought two tables together so she could lie on them, his coat served as a blanket , her purse when emptied was a barely feasible makeshift pillow- As she was now sleeping, he preferred not to, somehow this visit was a preclusion to the evident unknown which they would tomorrow face, so this kept him eager and amusing himself psychologically putting himself in parts of the tavern's construction, and dosingoff-completely for 15or20minutes-reawakening slightly 'fore the bursting of dawn-knowing this by his watch's hand positionings-His 15minute doze at 'round 3:00 AM had he now realized lasted for about 3hours-- 6:00 , he shakes her awake-Lifts her off of the table-puts back on his coat-opens the taverndoor For her-as they step onto the boardwalk between the footbridge and The tavern, a boat, small and being rowed by a sole person- is approaching to the dock at the bottom of stepcase to the left of the tavern, Although still sleepy, He realizes this is their boat – he quickly leads her hand&hand down to the stepcase to the dock-they step on the dock's wooden planks at the same moment that the boatman reaches his hand out to pull the rowboat closer so that they can step on safely free of the common first time mistake of the current's lapse shaking the dock and one missing heORshe's step into the boat, and landing in the water-the boatman begins rowing them away from the tavern's dock immediately upon his insurance that they are both entirely, limbs&all in the boat- The boatman's silence, dis-lodges their justices-configuring the wordless rideaway, He puts his arm around her with their backs to the boatman, they observe as the distance from the tavern becomes farther&farther.The distance to the island&destination was rowed in an hourORso, The boatman places his hand on the island's dock, pulls the boat closeup to it, HE shakes her awake, as she had fallen asleep on the ride over, and in his arms. They step up on the dock, HE asks the boatman of what is the time that he'll return here on the nextdays, in the first words the boatman had spoken to them, he says he'll arrive here in the partial darkness--- in--- the---- early----- AM of 2days time---- from-- now-He--- begins--- rowing--- away as the last words come off his tongue----They---- turn---- from---- the--- dock to land- The----- island---- has---- little sign of people-From----Rightoff- their—walk—onto-----land-there--- is a road which led into a heavy wood- A weather beaten sign which he sees works as the island's map&marker- shows the roads which will lead them to homes of the inhabitants, Stephanie being among those, god knows has been the only thing that could of carried them this far-They start onto the road into the wood, she keeps herself very close to him, they walk as quick as they possibly could-keeping in caution of this place which they have never been to- As they come deeper in thru the forest they start to notice the dirtroad leads to darkness, their surprised to've found the light in the forest fading so quickly, being that when they started in it was and still is early morning- A few more steps down thru the forest, the sunlight is gone completely- they've come to see that the wood is lit by streetlamps, yes those from a City street, metalposts, lightbulbs buzzing thru the forests natural sounds- A relief here&there an awe they'd not likely admitted together in many times-Then a sideroad which leads off from the mainroad that they've thus Far followed, is to their right-There also is another singmarker /map- he Reads it and figures this road is the faster way to the houses, she follows His lead upon his urging-this road too is walked by them in darkness lit also By streetlamps-sooner than they'd thought they would have, they've   come to the first inkling of others, A small footbridge not unlike the one which led them yesterday to the tavern-is laid over a small stream- it leads to the homes- She this time doesn't wait for him to lead her, starting off ahead of him- but from her step down off the bridge discovers herself sinking, the earth giving in, he hears her screaming, rushes over the footbridge to her- Thinking she's stepped in quicksand-Finding this luckily false-she sinks only a foot or so- It's that the earth here is missing its top layer, and the 2nd layer mixed with the probable rainfalls together have created a thick redclay soil, From where she sank they can see the homes, they've got to strut thru this misery they go about that by falling down getting up, again falling, first screaming about this filth, then laughter rests as the best solution- Thoroughly walking thru the last of the clay, from head To toe immersed in it- Standing sideBYside before the houses, realizing the unusuality of what they look upon- The homes are constructed into the sides of mudmounds, seeming like they've come nearly as caves, the plumblingpipes are in ways, some not being under the houses running down from the sides of the mudmounds, all visible-A bit startled, Both knowing the next thing-to-do is locate Steph- To just Go   knock on doors, even that would be fast, seeing that there are So-few-occupants- He prepares to –walk –up -to the first house, slight Embarrassment , he can not-in-a-shot-in-hell make himself the least Presentable- Though 'fore his walk-to-the-home's-frontdoor- He notices Stephanie standing atop one of the mudmounds, "Father, Mother", she. Yells down cheerfully- She stands there in a nightgown, barefoot, the thick Clay draws under her toenails, and between each of her toes- She walks Down from the slope to the mound's side to be with them- She smiles Radiantly, "You found your way," she laughs, " So then come with me", They follow her, Father helping Mum up the mud incline, still slipping But more-mud-on-them at this point doesn't matter- Stephanie tells them to undress 'fore entering her home- A sheet has been drawn aside the home, 'fore being that one was to often take off their mudcovered clothing before going inside- She says that she has some clothing that they can wear, 'til she has time to dry and wash those things- She goes inside to find the clothing First soaking her dirtyfeet in a waterpan put by the door for that- Father And mother undress behind the sheet, Stephanie watches from inside, Their shadows made from the streetlamp glow, their aged bodies were Outlines On the white hanging sheets, Stephanie aughed, "When did I last see my Parents?"

Stephanie rummaged in an upstairs bedroom closet, Accomplishing how she'd set out to find the clothes for-father-and-mother-They're standing still 'hind the hung-sheets, see Stephanie About to step there with them- They didn't even feel a Little embarrassment, " Our daughter…, is there a…" Father(thinking)- Stephanie, not either uncomfortable- smiling.. still, streetlights made the smallgaps between her teeth have a candescent yellow , father saw in her smile.. remembers cake between there too, birthdays ago, and there they had this appearance-"familiar, nothing to get use to," father(thinking)- Stephanie gives them both mens trousers,------ and buttonupthecenter shirts- 'fore putting them –on, they hand

11

Steph their filthrags- holding them out to her-She takes them- (snickering)-taking them to the washing- Now behind the hungsheet, seeing MUM and dad- as silhouettes- Stephanie putdown their clothes, put her hands together-thought of honor, somewhat- Wondered how people manage, this thought brought-on by seeing two people almost helpless- Drew her hands apart picks the clothes back up off the ground- Strolls to the door, deposits the clothes in a washbucket-Again putting her feet into the water pan-Looks down the water 'comes murkier, Put her hand to her breasts, She remembers once being in a large flat, cold, had been a factory(probably) once- Was in a blue openbacked dress, its sleeves stopped after coming over her elbows, her hands- then entirely unblemished, having never at the time done physical work-sat on a cot, pictures were taken, behind her- and the dress came off a little, she had more wrapped it over her breasts then worn it- Her back, shoulderblades, she bent her body in an arc-from excitement ceased shivering- laid out over the cot now-a picture taken of her lookinup,smiling, taken&lost, "lost",
Stephanie (thinking)-then outside, after this, In a beautiful morning, some time in Winter-a partial eclipsed spot-where was she after that-Morning- Kind-of wants to look-up then, and so does now too- Stepping out from the Pan, wipes her feet with a smeared cloth- goes in to wait on MUM And father- Hears them speaking something when approaching her house- hears them then, inside-

-DINNERTIME-6:30-PM –Was budged by father about why anybody would want to be here-

Stephanie- "Still though.. You know, I have to do this, at least now.. I will not leave with you, this is something more to me- I can not , at least now tell you how this means MORE,so..."

EVENING?- Stephanie-"The streetlamps are on for Nearly 24hours of the day other Than here&there shutting off For conservation"

AN EVENT-Stephanie took father and MUM from Home to a "Significance, for the while being here" ON a footpath behind the homes- It would lead them To resting-grounds-As on their trudge to it, gone past Other homes-inhabitants gazed freely from their windows To MUM&father&Stephanie-

Stephanie- "It's that there've been no other visitors Here, they're surprised, probably wondering How one has been convinced on getting here, maybe who's a person that'd drive People to coming-over"

'The footpath has been grown-over in several spots'

Stephanie-"I'm the one&only who's bothered on coming Here, that being rarely isn't enough for it To be clear and+the raining" -
They comeup to the small gate, Stephanie reaches Over-lifting-up its latch- taking MUM&father in-Father found himself surprised in there being a Cemetery on the island, he'd not known that prior To during war, it had occupants, Stephanie told Him once a time&place ago there'd been other homes& People,-it—had-its-own-small-war-These-were---its-soldiers----- graves- in wanting to show them it's something to Her-she tells them the soldiers specters provide the power To run the streetlamps, their souls are manifested swirling atop the lamps- she figured he could quiver at the thought-remained purely without vantage of realizing this shrugged grimly- they trudge back over the footpath their next (lastday) day had a whole solemn -quiet, MUM penetrating it at points with a story of what

13

a person they'd known was now doing, taking deep breaths in these recollections-AS had been planned MUM&father made their next Morning departure, Stephanie DID NOT walk to the Leaving dock with them- bid them away at the footbridge Before the homes-She turned away from them not even knowing if they'd be sure to find their way out, being short for time- EXIT ONE-

NOTE-and she also didn't look back, and it is known long As cliché for the longing in one to grow as those Leaving grow fartheraway from one's field of sight-

2.CIRCLES OF LITE
'EBBEY DREAMS, AGAIN'

He can create his desired privacy out of Hung sheets, curtains, towels, 'else of all To scavenge 'out makin' way out of the BEDROOM- 1.EBB' got'a plant growin' from 'es head-Soil and't 'rutt' chosin' the newplace from 'es   previous hair&scalp- 2.He insists to 'emself, "THIS 'ES RARE ONUFF
                                        TO'VE BE SPRUNGED
                                        FROM A PROPBOARD"

(AND)
    His plant-he calls to-
        A Nova Scotia Rose Fern
(AND) then he insists that it'd sat
        'side a DYNASTY-
(AND) He insinuates its former
        plantlife was in incarnation
        of a Venus Flytrap-
(AND) succeeding to brush out from

what he thought couldn't be seeming
like self- repetitions-
(AND) EBB screams of not speaking of
'so'afters'-

3.DISTRACTIONS-
He'd hung mobiles of nine planets in The room-WAIT-
era/military fans blew In the room, EBB's great attempt to
Capture his running into drying sheets On clotheslines, paying
childlyexample By falling from his feet,brungdown the sheet
Lines-BACK, AGAIN to before- He pulled Down the specific
planets(for Him) with A claw/grabbing mechanism, he
deliciously Observes them inches infront of his face-
"THIS,.. SATURN? "-"THIS, ...JUPITER?" Sheets get caught
over&over in the fan blades-Soon there ain't very much left of
'em   EBB angrily has to unplug the fans, with   His littlehands
dis-serts the stuckensheets-Setting their remains on the floor,
placing "THIS, ...SATURN" & "THIS, ...JUPITER"   there
with'em-Toying them for a second or a little more time, maybe-
With out longer regarding linears,NOW tellin' His truth "OUR
SUMMER'S IN THIS HORRID HOUSES,IN OUR MATERNAL
LORD...BLOODEDFATHER!!!"   Takin' his mattress from the
Boxsprings, and   placin' it in the leftfarest Corner from the
onlydoorout/onlydoorin/-Not   leaving   the   BEDROOM   for
96hours 'planned to sleep these entire hours-96, On what's
contrary   to   the   up-end   of   the   Bed-
EBB(onemoreforus)"GAINING ON YOUTH WHEN THOR-
OUGHLY   GETTING   DREAMT   THRU   MY   FEET"-
Thinks he WAKES the firsttime /after 92hours-HE comes to
find this false-'fore First conversing to a tent he found in the
Backyard-In there a woman sat entirely Nude on carpets, EBB
was to first attribute Her nudity to the igniting summerheat-
SHE tells him her name is Ermadun, that His father has
presented to her clearly that She can stay for the summer's
longremainder In the backyard if keeping 'clear of THEIR
HOUSE LIVES-She asks of him to make a Delivery,   giving
him a small envelope and telling him to take it to a specific
parkinglot-EBB nods his agreement, when stepping From her
tent, he in moments has found the Day drawn to nighttime-

Visible when His eyes oddly took a sec' ta' refocus in a Parkinglot-Horriblebarren hissing buglights, Send him a continuous audio bleep in the As far as the eye sees empty lot-4 young Men approaching from behind him as he turns 'round, they ride unicycles, waving themselves with orange green Hand-fans that have the designs of Japanese mountains, girls in kimonos illustrated on them, EBB sees that for the moment that they're between bringing the fans away from their faces to freeofthought wave them again--The boys Gather round EBBEY, they pedal together in a continuous circle ,so that he finds himself in ifyouthinkofit a circular cage-- There is about a 2 second gap in their Circle, EBB knows that this gap is his Only freebreakingaway chance-The Boys cycle several more times, silently, The only sounds they emit are that of the fanspressingthrough the air, and the roll of bikes 'gainst pavement, hits the blacktop lot in little singular flips which turn momentarily eerie in them being the center of what EBB'S known as in a daybustling-EBB prayingly leaps free of them but very badly, bringing them down with him like dominos in his jump from their circle-

Thinks He WOKE for the firsttime, After 94hours-Wiping the sleep from his Eyes, he still is short of any sense of place-Finds himself in a single longroom-it only Contains a small bed with badly wrinkled sheets , and a TV set overonthefloor-so that you'd be looking down if you were to sat/lay on the room's sole furnishing- He walks steadily to the ONE window at the farthest wall-HE realizes he's above very highly-though he's able to see over to another window, being that the room would seem to be in a highrise building, He looks upon a neighbor's window, but sees only part of a woman's unclad body-He thinks he can tell from the breast, pubic hair, and vagina(when she rises her abdomen a little)that it's the girl from the backyard tent, the one who led him to this predicament in the firstplace-Now, hears behind him a loud cooing, he knows there's another person or something(fear tells him) in the room-He-- sees a woman(again nude) wearing a birdmask, the woman who's face though concealed, would from her nude body appear to be 'tween 60 to 70 from the looks of her breast which sag half down her chest and her gray pubic hair, and ruffly aged body. She spreads her legs and caresses her C-L-I-T-O-R-E-S, moistening her vulva, willing EBBEY thinks at least, and acting on the whim of his enormous erection, to receive him-They lunge awkwardly into coitus- EBBEY'S preorgasmic penis begins to liken her minora in feeling with the resemblance of masturbating with a rottenpotato- Their climax is drawn out thru EBB'S TIDAL ejaculations made more and more significant to him by her cooing that is now loud enough to shatter glass-SOME-THINGWRONG-The woman sees to silence in their post coitus-EBBEY tries shaking her awake-in his attempt he soon realizes is frivolous, She has died, obviously. EBB begins sobbing, he runs to the ONE window, the girl's nude figure is still visible, he Motions to her, but she does not lookup his way-

He hears a knocking thru the walls, a pristine white Covers the room-Seeing a door out- EBB runs to it But first peers thru its keyhole-A man stands outside it –He insist that he knows EBB'S in there and that if he knows that which is best, and doesn't wish to cause a stir, will quickly open this door, EBB sees not any other option and so follows his orders-The man enters, looks around 55 , has wettedback short hair, wears a darkbrown vest over a longsleeved shirt, had a monocle for seeing from his righteye-He directs EBB, telling him to wrap the body in the tissuepaper looking rug which is all the sudden on the room's floor- As EBB does so, The Man Cooks What smells like chicken soup in the kitchen, though EBB never sees, hurried in panic of justclearingthisover-The man tells EBB, "Goodjob, BOY" (AND) "Don't Ever fucking do this again"

"Get the hell out of here, Boy" WAKES at the calculated 96hours,
+EJACULATING+

CHAPTER 'B'-2

THE INNOCENT CARD

Then be more I needingly longed to've
Made the crimson folktaled kisses
Abel told a femalebody nude1. From
What than other 2. Female atop resides
Atop her male body 'neath her
What days far apart in pelvic striding
The malebody nude has obscured
The anger of the femalebody's
Participation as still being the
Receiver when even assuming
The malebody's dominant position
   They made love in the morning at the
Minute of their waking-experimented
Within drastically different arousal clauses
Sometimes each morning anal, vaginal
Simultaneous stimulation of both of
Their genital circumferences thoroughly
Oral- there the needing of a child arose
5 penetrations were the takeplace of
What made much over as a joke that knew
Their course ridden in implications

The archer took an arrow from his quiver, Drawing it back on his bow, aiming at the Apple that the Goat of Mendes had just placed Atop its head-The archer desired to accomplish That the arrow would enter the apple, the arrowhead Would imbed into the trunk of the tree behind Mendes, With the apple still on it- He letgo the first arrow, entirely Missing the apple though deflecting off the treetrunk, making an indentation so slight that one's face would have to be just inches from the treebark to even then barely see it-the archer being set on this desire, letgo arrow&arrow all were misses, each deflecting the treebark so much that after the count of 50 they had split the treebark entirely- the archer now finding his quiver empty, walked past Mendes to gather the arrows which lie on the grass below the tree he gazed closely at the split trunk, when looking inside the tree, he discovers the manifesting drudge appearing this time as a sego lily and taking this in his hand finds that it has a constant excretion of salt coming from its stem, putting the salt from his palm to the tip of his tongue, it's tasteless no sweetness like he'd anticipated, turning to face the Goat of Mendes, questioning him of the nature of the tasteless salt, the Goat of Mendes replies by meagerly saying

"One who measures the depth of water prior to diving into a lake, is rarely the one who measures the distance from just below Earth's surface down to Hell's entrance".

The type of star placed usually on top of a Christmas tree, Ebbey sees rotating above the Sphinx, He got sand in his Boots in such great amounts that he kept stopping often To take them off, shook out the sand while holding them Upsidedown, hitting hard on their bottoms till thinking the major doses of sand are freed from their insides- He discovers an oasis, a small pond, grassy banks circled around, a very tall fruittree, which he sees dropping pomegranates from its branches, seems like one falls for each closer step he takes towards the oasis. On his arrival he plunges into the water, washing the Filth which had irritatingly blemished his face-takes A long breath, and reaches for one of the glistening Red pomegranates that's fallen on the grassbank in an-Arms reach from the--pool to the foot of the tree, before

He's able to place his hand on it, its colors bleed out forming a map of valleys a course off from the desert which Ebb is now in, a splashing in the water, Ebb looks behind him where Anqet sits wearing long trousers that she'd rolled up to her knees to put her feet in the water- he goes to her open arms , grasping him firmly as she lowers him in her arms to the sand by the bank, he rests his head on her bosom ,she pushes him down to her waist. Drawing off her trousers, finds his face sniffling her pubic hair, pushes her inner thigh to be looking directly at her vulva, as he puckers his lips in a kissing manner, a red comes over his field of sight, he blinks , reopening his eyes finding himself inside an enormous seashell where he lies shoulder to shoulder with a Venus who smiles at him silently. Isis hovers above them in a red Christmas polonaise dress There he discovers himself in a family's living room on a Christmas morning- children scurry in dressed in silk bed- Robes, Ebbey levitates upward into the arms of Isis, she holds Him for a moment and then lets go, he lands on a stone Staircase, begins out of instinct heading down it, the discovery Of a dagger in his right hand , surprisingly at first to him, but he swings in a repetitive motion at the winged smudges that flutter before him, these have not form , Ebbey realizes them to be darkened illusions, he thinks a precluding fear. Ebbey was a passenger on a travel bus which leads daytrips To the pyramids, as he looks from the window's curtains that Are in place of what should be glass, sweat is dispensed heavily From his temples, he placed a veil over his face to conceal his complexion from being a mess of flybites. He is there, dwarfed--by the Sphinx, he ignores the rest of the tour, walks up to the Sphinx, begins climbing on one of its paws. A failed attempt, The bottoms of his tennis shoes are short of the tread which He would need he if were to gain traction on the sandy stone. He looks back up at the Sphinx, still seeing that star, He doesn't drop his veil BUT through it this time he sees The star trying hard but realizing its failure at glowing.

21

THE AMERICAN CARD

The western society came to think of celibacy
As an unhealthy expression of sexuality
Not deeming them to've wanted necessary
Explanation of its potentials if carried out correctly
Celibacy is thought of as a mountain
The preparation of celibacy is like that of climbing a
Mountain in the way that the planning of it is as important
As the act itself
Arguing that the westerners have denied this its
Properly deserved dues
Or at least considerations
Harmfully this is closed- the unavailability of
Materials to give one the knowledge of its
Benefactions is clearly sad
In the hope to come to the point where celibacy
Is taught of and thought of as a 'healthy' expression
Of sexuality is farther off than the eye can see
When they except the idea of the inner sex as the
Fertilizer of a select margins growth point leading them
To discreet knowledge-then in the least, this will be the
Starting point for believed advancement and the celibate
Supporters belief that this is the necessary springboard in
our standing and what They consider an evolutionary pause

THE VIRTUE & INSINCERITY CARDS

Ebbey wants to enter an elevator shaft
Atop the elevator & not inside
Saw passengers opening ,closing & holding
Its doors for him, but finally he's unable to

Get there fast enough, his approach is
Over&over again stalled, each of his steps
Seems to've been proceeding him back from
It, not closer as he wanted

A boy carries a message for Ebbey
Made him verify who he was, before he could
Leave this card in his hand, a florescent lighting

Bursts from the carrier's mouth, enabling Ebbey to
Read the tiny letters scrawled on the back of the card
In the more so dark passageway,
THE POSTCARD WAS STATED AS HAVING SAID,

-DO YOU KNOW THIS PERSON-
A TINY PHOTOGRAPH IN THE
BOTTOM LEFTHAND CORNER OF THE
CARD, SHOWING A GIRL-SAY 15 TO 16
YEARS OF AGE, FRIGORIFIC HAIR &
BLUE FLOWER PLACED BEHIND HER RIGHT EAR.
**********3:3O AM TO 5:3O PM*************************
-A WATCHING SOMEHOW HAD TO HAVE BEEN
VALIDATED,IF JUST TO PLACEDOWN ITS
FACTUAL STARTINGPOINT************************
He as first finds this faded, declares its points entirely

Nonsensical-holding the card barely an inch from his face
The girl's picture sends a whispering into his head, now
Replaced " A WICKEDNESS HERE " , Ebbey plainly

Thinks- "YES. YES I..."**** He remembers the girl pictured
On card-" Alice, an Alice & where" –Then closes his eyes-
    " ALICE W.., ALICE WIM..B...L..Y, OR E.." then strains
His thinking and recalls " ALICE WIMBLEY"-but
Hardly smiles for rethinking her- Then reknows a day-
Says this by creating a name then,
    " TOO CLOSE TO THE SUN",
He stands on a beach, shore, the sands are redder, crimson

Sparkling- had walked faraway from the vacationer barrage-
THE 2ND BEACH, Alice waited lying out on blanket near
Pitch dark stone that appears as jaggedly laid out as ripping
Spikes, and when its visibility is swayed another way in the

Sunlight's illusion it appears as softly sticky as a running tar
Pool- Sat down by her, saw three boats(he thought) nearly
Hit the shore- an interlude where the Mayflower signals him

Asking where they are, best finds his feet, wants to see an
Ark dock as biblical pun, not explicitly-what of the USO or
Was that USC –underwater space crafts, no skill in this.

Repellent, he felt " NO ME IN THESE NONSENSES", not
Lightened to spend the day in interior dialectic in-jokes-
Left Alice lying there, walked back to the crowded beach

Keeping his eyes alert for something exciting- over there
From looking off the crowded beach he sees a violent
Splashing a ways out from where most of the swimmers are.
" DROWNING, DROWING" thought that immediately
As he watched the person's scurry-without-
Below&above the water. Ebbey looks for a lifeguard,
Thru the crowd he sees only one at the beach's opposite
End, did not understand this first, in the time it would take
Him to step&nudge cautiously thru the crowd to the
Guard's post, get the guard's attention and for the guard
To swim to the soon-to-have-drowned-, understands he's
Got no time to realistically carry that out, he would have to
Himself swim out there, if there was to be a chance of
This vacationer being saved, " DROWNING, MAYBE" ,
Distinctly paused unlike he'd ever before done,
" THAT'S ALL….MAYBE,MAYBE,MAYBE" .

Instead went back to the 2nd beach, laid down
ShouderTOshoulder with Alice, they slept there under a
Towel they slightly dampened with water until the
Evening- He woke once under the towel and looked over

At her face, really couldn't figure any reason to tell her
About what had occurred.
During another vacation once, he was staying with his
Parents in a expansive hotel, he was drawn to an
Exotic garden which had been planted and grown

24

In the hotel's court. He walked to it thru the hotel's halls,He
kinda of thought he saw people float past the
Windows during his walk, one of them must have been
Alice, she kept motioning for him, at least it looked like
Her, she kept bouncing against the glass but was
Unsuccessful in crashing thru to be with him-
Ebbey easingly strolled past making a clearly uncaring
Sentiment.

***** A CIRCLE CHANT**RECITED BY EBBEY FLINT*******
NOTE-fools gold marking the EAST&WEST circle points
&dame's rocket marking the SOUTH&NORTH circle
points**************************

EBBEY-"A prophetic dis-assemblage, spores This,-giver-Car-
een, wouldn't thou for Most of all be built in that, spheres
emun-ciate Careen's pauses, Bolly O' Ragal has shaken
Careen's attention, got it 'fer 'emself- The blanket Careen spent
the night in was decorated with the Designer planets &rockets
laid for these boys- And Bolly dreamt of stars a'course their
great riddle Careen, 'You'd may positive in her constellations
,Did thou eventually learn their positions Thou owing their sky-
map -important, this 'es What they mean-together-as-their-
greatly----acocked"--'GLASS'—"A----high note pure ,pure-
Flinges a wetguppy head if't is Sifting- Bolly O'Ragal one-none-
only Dream- Was't to've entered a warm wet vulva 'GLASS' Its
con-tet-tin-tickle-THE townhomes locked And't-Lodged The
people-UP-Came the sunrising in there- AND'T -let 'She Rise-
Trance psalms, extract-the little leopard Scanned the morn'rise
valley- Careen – the sweetest Loli-pops 2 men kiss with them
in their mouths—Their---wet-tongues lap them back&forth-
Azrael rode Throughout the pastures in a horse Pushed-to-
Wagon-The plains miscues-He discovers- the cannot'ations
To've wherein the Body men don't leave- If he saw Hands,
fingers sput in a wax- And't-piss purr out-of his Canyon- HIS
sizing understand? WHERE Bolly O'Ragal wrote our blanket
Rhymes- EARTH BLANKET-Jezzy lost in the fields was not
found By a person, dangerous solicitations Could anywhere in
a sec' lay her final not -wrote-in-time-of-death WILLS"

EBBEY, HERE & PARTIAL

WHAT IS THE NEXT PLAUSE OF REA

I HOPE IT TO BE BOTH DIALOGS AND'T-RECLAIMED
FRAGMENTS PROBABLY OLD PAINS
THAT ARE AROUSING WHEN FRESHLY REOPENED
I KNOW WHAT THIS STORY IS REALLY ABOUT
I WILL SOON REFRAME THIS NIHILISM " never a pain
Like this one" ***********THE LATER EPITAPH****************
Ebbey FLINT STEPS FORWARD AND'T RELODGES HIS
NIGHTMARES HOLDS A HALF MENTAL LENGTH
HALF PHYSICAL LENGTH THE THROWN CLASSICIST
TURNS COME MORE THE FLOUNDER SHIPS
   -TODAY-
   -AWAY-
   -TODAY-
WITHOUT THE FEATHERS THAT FELL AROUND US
THOUGH OTHER THAN MYSELF I BELIEVED NONE TO BE
AWARE BUT I'VE PLACED THE STONES AS SAID TO BE
LAID ABOUT FOR THE RECOMPENSATION OF MY
SHADOW'S BOTTOM-I DO NOT LEAVE FOR NOW AT
LEAST ONE ONLY WRATH'S CASING DOESN'T LONG
LONG REALLY ESPECIAL COLD, THESE GIRLS IN
SLEEVELESS ROBES WHICH FLOWED BEHIND 'CAUSE
THEY FELL TO THE GROUND BEHIND THEM-DRAGGED
ACROSS THE SAND-THEY CARRIED TORCHES- SOME OF
THESE GIRLS MIGHT STAND ASIDE Ebbey AS HE WALKS
THRU THE CENTER OF WHERE THE MAGICK IS
BROUGHT OUT OF- WHITE MAGICK IS GOING TO BE THE
MENTAL IN THE AIR THIN ESSENCE- BLACK MAGICK IS
GOING TO BE THE PHYSICAL ESSENCE THE STORM,
PISS, SHIT, BLOOD,SPERM , THIS MAKES A PERMANENT
CONTACT WITH THE CIRCLES ROOTS REMEMBER Ebbey
Is inaugurated in a place taken from roman empires-------A
fragmentary superimpositions of what they've said to us are
New infancies "this all happens to've occurred righthere" A
Lilith, an denials are PASSIFICIAL ? THE WISHING REASON
SPEAKS THOUGH WILL TEND TO BE HEARD AS WHAT IS
OUT OF THE QUESTION-"REA, THE PRESCRIPTED
CERTIFICATION OF OUR LIVES TOGETHER"

THE PLACINGRATIO THATS BORE AS THE CERE-
MONIOUS FACTION'S DISSOLUTION ON NOT WHAT DO
YOU GET HIM WHICH TASTES SWEET A ROUSING
STINGY SUGAR PURED ONTO RAWLAMB – " la, la, travels
alone upon the river's banks, pluggs, la ,la," – Ebbey-" What is
the harm?" Ebbey-"Is that my hate?", Ebbey-" Is it the
standingstone to Broken thoughts?" .

THE BLACK MAGICK ISN'T GOT TO BE LEFT
IT IS ALWAYS THE WAY HE FELT SOMEHOW AGAINST
HISSELF AND'T-THE WORLD'S BLOCKINGS OFF-

"Combinations are just the same"
MORE OF HIS INVOCATION, ASSEMBLAGE

THE DESPAIRINGLY IN THE ENTIRETY WHICH PERSUMES
WHO'LL NOT HAVE CHANGED THE PEOPLE LENT
EVERYDAY FOUND MY KEPTGONE KNOWS PLACES

THAT SEE FINALITY OF HOW PRECIOUSNESS DOES NOT
HAVE A PLACE WHEN SEPARATE MATTERS ARE
RULINGLY SCOURAGING THOUGH THE FILLING IS
SUFFICE COMPENSATION FOR LYING IN THIS EPILOGED
DECAY, THE SPECTACULAR ASSUMPTIONS ARE NOW
ASSEMBLED ASIDE ONE ANOTHER AS E.F.'S LONG IN
WORKING INVOKINGS OF BOTH HIS MAGICKS.

SOFT CIRCLE CHART(a reel)

****EXIT****		****ENTER****
(ILLUSION)		(ANDALUSIAN)
	LINEAGE	

	CANTERBURY	
	*************	
	GIRFT	
	WARLORNED(ARROW)	
	************* ENGLAND	

	SOLIDLAND	
	MEET, WE'LL	
****EXIT****		****ENTER****
(ILLUSION)		(ANDALUSIAN)
MEET, HE JUST DID NOT WANT THE CHANCE OF		

	-BEING HERE-	
	E.F.	

Ebbey DOESN'T EXPLAIN,
" THE CIRCLES BLEND TO STIMULATE NEWWAYS TO RE-
ENACT A COMMON VALUE, SO EASY THE ONE JUST
EVERY LOSE BREATH"
" the sporned comaterall, an arrows gauze for he, they weren't
voids, (stronger) they w..e..r..e..nt voids, the traps fixed ontop a
swing we 'n' ever for mmm…possibly..mmm…distinctly certain,
(furious) how can I hate him not knowing what he's told,
(CHANGES)SHARED THE MISHAPS IN WHATS STUFFED
FRIENDS-IN LASTFOOL, THEY'D HAD WALKINGHATS
200+201+ROSYMINES THREWN 'N' THREWN TALED
REMNANTS,(LAUGHS)THEY'D-----HAD--------WALKINGHATS
(LAUGHS)- THE SPATIALSHOAL CURRED MATTERSLESS
AND'T-WASTOO, IS KNOWING THAT IT WAS FALSE
ENTIRELY THE CORRECTION, IF I CAN POSSIBLY SELECT
TO--BE--IN--THAT--STANCE,--THE----IMPOSSIBILITY,--------I
PRESUME-----PUTTING--SOMETHING----ECONOMICAL TO-
GETHER OUT OF FRAGMENTS, BUT THEN NOW THAT
THESE FRAGMENTS ARE ONLY ONCE A YEAR AT THAT
EVEN ALL POSSIBILITY IS DISSOVLED IT WILL STOP
HERE AND REMAIN TO ME EXTREMELY VIVID AND
STRONG MAYBE NOT TODAY FOR ME , JUST ME TO RE-

HAVE IT- "but if Rea must remember this, how? If she's not considerable for nullifying its worth."

CIRCLES OF APPLES & ORANGES EMPTYING
*********************MEMORIES OF MAGICK BLACK
*********************& WHITE*********************************

{Feature 1.}   {Feature 2.}
{ CIRCLE }   { CIRCLES}
NORTH** Salt,   NORTH** Rue,
*   Amethyst,   *   Daisy,
*   Pearl,   *   Pine,
*   Beryl,   *   Oak,
*   Selenite,   *   Acacia,
EAST** Geodes,   EAST** Primrose,
*   Coral,   *   Maidenhair,
*   Pumice,   *   Strawberry,
*   Obsidian,   *   Blackberry,
*** AMBER,   *   Orris,
SOUTH** Onyx,   SOUTH** Rose,
*   Sardonyx,   *   White Heather,
*   Holed Stone,   *   Bay,
*   Tiger's Eye,   *   Mustard,
*   Sapphire,   *   Tamarisk,
WEST** Opal,   WEST** Bladderwrack,
*   Onyx,   *   Pomegranate,
*   Sardonyx,   *   Seaweed,
*   Pearl,   *   Burdock,
*   Beryl,   *   Violet,

        Ebbey Flint,
          (Midsummer)
             June 21

A**VISITATION**********

Felt to've then fell'an 'mongst the 'COMESTOGETHER' EBB-"Don't believe,..Don't Believe" EBBEY-" I need,;;I want a chance_ it's just a craziness…saving, we're kisses, more into me" Ebbey lowers the adjoined horns that were covered By lawn grass-Striking them on the mare's head+She's down, Ebb indenting her, There-EBB(puts his hands together)-" We prays fer the Andgels , we plays My knees, THE ANDGAL…hail to Retrieve the public abode-pressed 0:#:3:0044$"

NORTH
Orange,
AMBER,
Sapphire,

EBBEY,A bit more,NOW-"Bastet, Home..sun's light Ah sees findin' the new In thru me_____ I forget Day, Gave me a chance To,"
LAW'S respected with POWER'S REASON+ EBBEY'S luck lands him here, RIGHT?(EBB), Righthere 'sides of this circle-You've never lived In Its lucklest 4 directions= EDDEY Gotta say oncemore-"NORTH,
          EAST,
          SOUTH,
          WEST,"
-Bent over to be in center with the ground, and laping (nowords), dirt against the rufftop of my mouth-
EBBEY FLINT, Towards the beginning of AUGUST-'Lughnasadh' -EBBEY FLINT, I, Felt gluttoned in the War round HARVESTS- EBBEY FLINT(when I say)
   "BYE SUMMER, BYE.."

*********VISTED, IN THOUGHT…PRIOR FALL******WAS A FAILED FALLTHRU***********

EBB, 'bout now to've been gone-on with what little light is left in the day-"I'LL TRY AGAIN",+the grief made to vapor+ EBB crossing a point to've been knowing at this standing(he'll enter)- IT abides useless 'tivity+"COME SIDE…BY, BY & WE GREW BETTER"-a small murmur-" LIGHT SHYS.. I DON'T NEED THAT,SO" Sits nude, then starting to shiver, as the excitement goes its brought the cold, you've got..alright -

Ebbey has got to play a minimum of notes, a wood flute-+he's got alot more waitin'-"I NEED TO TAKE ONE… THEN MENTION…YOU, IN A CHANT"---'PRESENTING' THE POSSIBILITY OF ACTUAL RESULT, in all-this-
So, Ebbey waits, felt a slight momentary stirring-In his groin, feels part of his sex retract,"I'M GOING OFF..I'VE GOTTA REPEAT..THAT MY STANDING IS NEARING ITS DOWNPOINT" that he spoke-
-Then not a thing-All he says now-is that He afterall figured that There'd be nothin' from the Start of this, to here&onward-
ENTERING home, HE was concealed in a longcoat-STANDS there, at a counterspot, dribbles a laugh or two, reflecting evening as just silliness-Then leans backout thru the screendoor- From the porch he viewed lights wrapping up, they came as cinders, & as ashes from a fire upward in recount-Felt an outright stirring momentarily oncemore in his groin-The speck whirlwind wrought-to-arousal-
-LAUGHING-
-LAUGHING-
-LAUGHING-
NOW he at-the-least may have actual results, THE specks make a myopic 'mergence to be at Ebbey's pleasure as Woodsprites-SAT on the porch, LAUGHING, LAUGHING, LAUGHING & then for What remained of the evening he had the aspect of a conjured, "GOODTHING" & the marksmanship to Prove the point-in-ability- of LAUGHING,LAUGHING, LAUGHING.

DEAR EBBEY,

Jewel in the heart-the other side of a thresher-The growth of a great parameter-Dead/unclean-Through an alphabet and stars in parts of themselves Cried into the sordid valor-and private detachment creeps Along for a mile of a brief canopy-to be heard in all ports Of melody-after morning hide separate blows to a host where mercury shown thru-brisk-not so tempted but a failure-the recognition would come clear to you early on-and never when going far would you forget or forbid it- you can etch a symptom of your first meeting with her-the crass structure of her confession keeps her weighted down-when you've entered those conversations for the first time in your life-a response I hardly figure-a lucrative/substantive summary of the years so far-this cannot be put down-it has a courageous place as for all-you've gathered yourself and keep a startling reflection with a great likeness to the giant steppes from the rewound past-all roots are torn from the ground and they find their end at the shore where they've left danger-The clown climbs abreast on the abbreviation of AngloSaxon interludes-where it finds its wake and ripples with the meager gleams of all tarnished spurs-hence forth detects an irreplaceable communication to heighten a figure of speech & to seal it with its once in a lifetime correspondence with a sparkling chainletter-Thou have slept-have poured a careless in to the wayout-MORE, if I have not wept in all chambers of the Dharma& in all resurfaced violence- Probably a place we lived, I remember the smile from the hornets of a simple Heart- the anagram of an interior fluctuates to Violate composure, if then by chance thru some Instinct pressed in a roofbeam, reach towards A collective voice that marks as to've been tarnished By the apprehensive cleft-a day of no errands, spent Comfortably in a nocturnal irony-daft provisions heap rolls the heard horns , the day has drawn too close the once cherished dearest company-a proper invasion since became what it's known for&for leaving: to have gone home-Immensely simple casualty- I knew, I understood everything till the last part, I will not try to change a thing-this time it has become abruptly clear, in here where there wasn't any suggestion of keeping within the bounds of a time frame-to've held all that can be counted-to've held all that's lost when

34

brought together-so much of what has been, does come to pass-some of what halts when your are to have knelt before what it is you think of as being greater-if that would have come earlier it would have not been understood-then now to turn to the foremost accumulated agony-I knew I had felt apart from each conscious that has been presented to me-being for the exile of a stanine surprise-the regular color ,I can't even smile for the luck that I wish it-there, to've been lucky enough to've looked upon that-rightfully told and told more after there isn't apprehension to weigh a focus.-

AGAPE

A group of young boys sat unclad 'neath a Tree of apples which is at once ablaze, it Combusts as its branches are swayed upward with The gusts of air caused by the wind, As the wind lets up The flames also cease, its branches hang there being drawn Heavily downward by cinema reels.The reels unwind on their Descent to the earth, wrap like a flood 'round the boys at a fast enough frame rate to divert the boys attention with precocious flickering movements- Feet away an assailant (amongst-other-possibilities) strikes a straight razor quickly down&up on a stone-preparing-The boys quiver at the sight of him-dressed in a poorly constructed stork costume-wings made out of newspapers not even painted over, the headings can be read in moments where he stands very still-puts on the headmask of the costume, a long beak with a grapefruit wrapped-up and hung from it, resembling the bird bringing a lucky newborn, cotton balls stuck with clay lend an aimless imply to what should be the stork's feathers. The assailant steps to the boys and draws a chalk X-mark at each of their feet, tells them to crouch here on their knees. When they do not listen, he pulls one of them, pushing Down forcefully on his shoulderblades--has him resistively Placed on his knees at The X-mark. Commands him to now Be-as-still-as he humanly can, The assailant's thumb stretches the boy's foreskin over the Chalk X, in one gentle strike it has been severed, the boy falls back in shock, our assailant proceeds to the next boy, who resists less after having just witnessed the only outcome, the same is carried out on this boy too, in shock is placed aside by the assailant, arms resting at sides, foreskin strewn in the short bounds of the chalk X —EBBEY flinches even though he's only witnessed this thru binocular lenses,

"How in the Suburbs?" wondered EBBEY. He observed this while standing on the deck of a sailboat that's been raised atop a large mound of dirt in the far-left-hand-corner of his backyard. Hetts moved it there in a bulldozer he'd rented, the dirt mound-He'd raised the sailboat atop of it with a hand- me-down-equivalent of ropes&pulleys- LATER in the summer , Hetts moved the boat to the far-right-hand-corner of the yard- on the sailboat's deck he installed a permanent binocular system which costs 25cents for a nearly 9-to-10 minute view-ONCE that summer, EBBEY brought enough change to watch The entire suburbs for ONEWHOLEHOUR- The highlight of That was discovering the ZOOM feature on the binoculars Side- In a window of one of the homes, he saw a life size Windup doll,

" They'd need atypical entertainment, here if You figure-out the situations.", EBBEY knew-The doll, EBB Thru-people-came-to-know was a SHE. With flexing joints like that of a REALHUMAN-BUT then EBBEY Laughed – " if be there any here!" If wound tightly she crouches below desk lamplight her face shines voidless of any features, a mercury resounds therein the facial screen, SOMETIMES, EBBEY was told that a bluelake and a flurry of cranes Was played on the facescreen, if she were wound tightly And commanded to " Play a better place!!" – ONE Could even speak a monologue and she would repeat It in a selectively faint whisper. STILL LATER THAT SUMMER, A neighbor played EBBEY a recording of Her voice, supposedly-" _____ to've had again. forget yourself its imprints".

"PLACE ITS JUSTIFYING ____WORMED INTO DEEPER SPACES" " THIS TELLS US HOW IT IS THAT THINGS HERE MUST TAKE THEMSELVES A WAY A LONG A HIGHEST CENTRAL REGARD,____ THAT IS WHAT I AM LIKE I UNDERSTAND I WISH THIS SHOWS- IT FELT TRULY HERE NO LONGER" "that is, everysingle possibility and Defeat encountered." "HERE HAS BEEN ABOUT, NO THAT IS TO ME, THAT I WILL WANT THEM TO BE ABOUT." What about what we faced too, yearsago, could've Have never/ where that stands, what it faced?" " IS ALL OF THIS THE SAME?" -EBBEY thought immediately that this was a treatise about the suburbs, BUT Hetts argued it was about highways being built thru the Rain-Forests.

Imperial slope/ Stork brought the newborn but.....?

(THE TERRIBLE TRUTH ABOUT REA)
1.This said that Rea ran to be by a fruit tree it dropped apples on her head one after another- and then roses fell down in bucket amounts. The tree caught on fire, and Rea watched it burn down To a small pile of cinders at her feet, as they were carried With the wind into her eyes, left the black dust on her face SHE knew her true love, more of knowing what it is, really.

Rea decided to write an interpretation of "The Scarlet Woman" It still didn't change things, though Rea said in glee 'BEACAUSE THEN BECAUSE ISN'T!'-KNEW- TRUE LOVE'S-KNEW- AND'T-HAD NOT OF BEEN HAPPY, ..HAPPY IN A LONGESTTIME...-

KISSES THE RUNE WHICH IS SIGNIFICANT TO AUTUMN

That was drawn with permanent marker on a man's testicles Has got to lift his penis up a little, he's lying down- And in order to get her lips on the center-

The study has got a painting of the resurrection hanging On the centerwall-Dogs playing poker on the leftwall- Nymphs&Satyrs cocktail on the rightwall—Remains of Jigsaw,

B___-" I can see it now, as a silky black, no- Icy, the wetness made her bathing suit Seem as if a frost was dripping slowly off, And't-her breasts were still firm, she was--- All of 16 years, .. At the time, I'd"

Middle-" So write as plain as you're recalling here-At least a GIRL, not a woman closing in to be In her 40th year,"

B___-"No actually it won't be written down, a number of Reenacted stills, but the girl's face isn't going to Be visible, all the shots framed right below her Shoulders, though the other characters which are Placed in the foreground are entirely shown to Who is seeing the photographs."

Middle(struggling)-"This goes on the back, the trick is that It's looking the same in its cutout But just needs flipped over And't-Placed accurately."= KISSING THE RUNE SIGNIFICANT TO AUTUMN =He doesn't obtain a hardOn during her caressing of -- His testes, he keeps his cock limp- She lies her head on his thigh, fondles the head and shaft Of his cock, disappointingly –settles—for—drawing-- the Rune significant to projection on his foreskin-

Rea knows now the dream MUM canned as 'LITTLE FISH' - The rope/the hanger formerly a restaurant of class You'd of needed to confirm to a dressing code To've even had a quick brunch- He languishes, " I thought one more Fall then We'd probably close this place", "At least You will have done, somehow a startTOfinish Action, even if that wasn't a triumph, it is good still." Rea says to him********************************The rocks splashed allover, and Rea meandered And in-a-little-bit followed the trail next-to-the-traintracks-The little spot, not the hanger or the restaurant, the rope Still hung there, Rea who is inquisitive by her nature, began Climbing up the rope, pulling up and pushing with her feet, She came out in the rectangular room, runs over to all the Fish tanks there, reaches her hand in, takes a handful Of littletiny fish out of the water, needs a bag filledup With water if she wants to take some of them out of there with Her, MUM asks about then-" If you'd have done just that Would you have had a 'SATISFIED' adolescence?"

O' REA IS'T TO DIE, O' EBBEY IS'T TO DIE, ARE WE TO BOTH DIE IN THE SAME LAP OF SUMMER? THEN, WHICH OF US IS TO'VE SEEN THE OTHER DIE?

Rea got her stuff off last, And nobody was looking but one boy- The scar on her back starts on her shoulder Runs down under her bra-strap, ends a little Above her waist, is a deep red mark- must have Cut so deep that a tissue layer is so very red that-it looks like a new burn and not a cut- She feels the boy standing there staring at her body- "WHAT,WHAT!!" she yelled, -__"UM na'thing" and he ran out, left by herself she very quickly took her bra off and pulled on her sweatshirt.

On the landing out from the study during a break From the jigsaw's muddles-
B___-" She would be closer and closer She'd have grown more and more every Day, her smile flips you off, and is a day& Night."
Middle-"In the picture that we show her face, how about the Last one, be it a prologue of sorts, she's got to Have her hair about to her neck, a clip keeping----Her bangs to one side of her face, she's standing Against a wall leaning her head in a

downward Position, so----- that--- she- is looking up at whoever
Sees the picture."

B___looks down at his feet, and sees a small black egg, He
reaches down, and stands back up by Middle, holds it Out to
him, and they see how it reflects color from its Blackness the
same as if it were a clear prism, the colors obscure their views
of each other.

MEAN WHILE THEN<>

Towards the middle of summer, Hetts began Lining the walls of the Flint family home with velvet reproductions of icon paintings. The floor too, he covered with rugs which Explicitly detailed human bodies twisting among flames In a imagineless hell, " Imagine I'm swimming," Said-- Hetts at the dinner table, but was not understood or Rewarded for his decoration of their home. Though, Ebbey walked about the halls filming the Decorations with a video camera, carefully doing this With an in-camera-edit, the result had a slight similarity To the finale of Tarkovsky's 'Andrei Rublev'. Hetts continued his home designs, NEXT he placed a Pieta in a shallow fishpond in the backyard, he put it Together with a bell that rings when he slams the Base of the pieta with enough force to send the bell To the top of the pieta, he does this with a sledgehammer, Rewards himself by reaching into the pond and putting a Fish in a plastic bag, carrying it inside and talking about a 'Specialty' for the day's remainder.

O' PLEASE, PLEASE, & PLEASE

It was in a bookstore, yes, that he first saw her, Ebbey kept looking at Rea while he hid behind a shelf Carefully looking at her as she was opening books, so that she would not take awareness of his marveling. Finally talked to her about simple books of metaphysics, Luck he had to find her in a section he had a previous Knowledge of, if not he'd have never had a RIGHT word to Utter. Impressing, he paid the change she was short of for the books, He's at her home more quickly than if he had even hoped to be with her in private. Clenches his teeth over the coffee table where she asks him to stay the night. They'll sleep in the same bed, Rea pulls down the blankets And reveals that she lays out newspapers on one side of the Bed, for boys who sleep nude, so that they can if-they-do-Nocturnally discharge, the sheets won't be soiled, they'd Need washed 4OR5 times a week if not for the newspapers, With the rate that Rea had boys over.They went right-to-Sleep-first-supposedly Rea implied that's what they'd do & nothing else first. Ebbey tosses his body around on the newspapers. "LESS EXPENSE IN COLORS FOR LOCAL WOMAN" * A local artist has become particularly fond of- using her own body fluids as hues on her canvases. Ms. Worels told us during our Thursday visit to her studio, "Shit, urine and even blood have become more proper for me at this point than any oils, at this phase in my painting 'cause I'm trying to discover the-from-the soul link between artist and art, so I feel that the tools that go into it must come from me literally". Ms. Worels assured us that she takes utmost precaution with drawing the blood.*

Ebbey tosses to the other side half asleep, an erection stirring. The head of his penis is rubbing Rea's thigh-a tiny bit Of Cum sticks to her skin. Ebbey looks over at her, Her eyes tightly shut and her lips smiling to him from A clever dreamstate. He slides his body a little more to The edge of his side of bed, hoping the excitement doesn't Cause an orgasm, It does, he came allover the papers, Assuring even thru the embarrassment to have his -CUM-IN-PRINT.

"DISAPPEARANCE,REAPPEARANCE&REDISAPPEARANCE OF LOCAL WOMAN" The life of Mr. Lurry & Mrs. Eldora Ford has been one of much interest as of lately. On a June Morning as of now nearly 10years ago, Lurry gave his wife their usual morning goodbye, He was planning to see her that night, as he did always after the workday. On that evening to his surprise he returned to find their home empty, undisturbed, after there was not a sign of Eldora in the following days, he filed a MISSINGPERSON report. His search for her was prevalent for the following 5years, but drew to a close after a succession of false leads. Mr. Ford had given up hope completely on his wife ever being found, as he returned home one night from the workday to what he stated as the "The Dullness of when she's not around", to his surprise he found Eldora cleaning the kitchen. Oddly when being question by Lurry and the case's investigators, she had no awareness that she'd been gone for the last 5years and she behaved just as she had on that infamous June morning When Lurry had stepped out. Lurry, who was just glad and astonished to have her back could not see any reason to have her questioned further. The Ford's returned to their usual life for the next 3years. All seemed well when Lurry- left- one morning, again biding Eldora farewell.

He returned again that night to shockingly again see that she was not there. He waited this time 3days, hoping the best about his wife, Then filing another MISSINGPERSON report.

ELDORA FORD HAS NOT BEEN SEEN OR HEARD FROM IN OVER TWO YEARS, ANY INFORMATION CONCERNING HER CURRENT WHEREABOUTS WOULD BE GREATLY APPRECIATED, AND SHOULD BE ADDRESSED DIRECTLY TO HER HUSBAND, ALONG WITH ANY INQUIRIES REGARDING REWARD MONEY.

Rea awakens, puts her hands on Ebbey's chest. Smiles at his red face, sees his CUMSPOT. Touches His penis, aroused again- She climbs atop him, placing it in Her vulva, proceeds to laying him. This being Ebbey's realfirst And a similar –in-camera-edit is rolling in his mind while being Fucked. The entirely so-blue calm sea waters. The piercing screams made notably by seagulls on the tall whitecliffs which surround the water, At Ebbey&Rea's climax this picture becomes only just a monitor hum and a series of lines void of anysuch distinguishable colorsORshapes.

PSALMS 44:19 THOUGH THOU HAST SORE BROKEN US IN THE PLACE OF DRAGONS, AND COVERED US WITH THE SHADOW OF DEATH**

O' A LIFE OF REA

"He sucks blood?", Lays out a reproduction of the surgeon's photograph on a dinner tray, while he sits on a toilet embroidered with images of ferns. Gets excited by the shadow that might be only An upside down sea otter, or a bird diving to the Loch's surface-"This is the realthing"!- He exclaimed while stroking on his shaft- Masturbating-himself-to-orgasm-the fruits Of these labors intertwined with R.K. Wilson's Picture- that-though-proved-to-be-false, created an enigma.

ISAIAH 35:7 AND THE PARCHED GROUND SHALL BECOME A POOL, AND THE THIRSTY LAND SPRINGS OF WATER: IN THE HABITATION OF DRAGONS, WHERE EACH LAY, SHALL BE GRASS WITH REEDS AND RUSHES*********

45feet long, 75feet wide and 45feet high. A window was constructed around the top. How in the world were dinosaurs fitted On? He took them as 'KINDS' in less of 200. They came from eggs, so-to-start-are small-Beasts didn't rip flesh 'til after the flood.

MALACHI 1:3 AND I HATED ESAU, AND LAID HIS MOUNTAINS AND HIS HERITAGE WASTE FOR THE DRAGONS OF THE WILDERNESS*********************

Jean Chastel, loaded a gun that belonged to another
On an evening In the June of 1776
His shot that he fired entered the beast
Too took it down, Relics were discovered about
When in its cut-open chest. Its huge corpse was
Taken through region-to-region, in way to indicate that
The horrors were brought to their finale, the season's heat
Too rotted the corpse 'fore its examination
'Twas laid to its rest in the earth of France

MICAH 1:8 THEREFORE I WILL WAIL AND HOWL, I WILL GO STRIPPING AND NAKED: I WILL MAKE A WAILING LIKE THE DRAGONS, AND MOURNING AS THE OWLS*************

Rea constructs a bomb from metals, screws, nails. Intends to plant it in a logcabin deep in the wood. Carries out her actions.

She finds a gratification while watching the thing burn. She runs eagerly thru the wood 'til coming to a warmspot, walks under an arch into a paradisal garden, she hugs a huge furry cat, who has all the colors of the rainbow within his matted fluff. In time Rea grows deeply distant from herself while living life in the confines of this paradise. She knows she must take leave, sadly even the warmspot has come to sum up a cold one. She waves her fluffy friend farewell. Walks back thru the forest, now in the depth of frost. Stops as the burnt remains of the logcabin to find THAT, "Was there in the months flown bye?", Dispassionately she'll have to make another long wait to know but now more of the waiting suspense is made more venomously being that she has only herself as company, not the growth gardens of a splendor which she how long made past shoal.

JEREMIAH 9:11 AND I WILL MAKE JERUSALEM HEAPS, AND A DEN OF DRAGONS; AND I WILL MAKE THE CITIES OF JUDAH DESOLATE, WITHOUT AN INHABITANT***********
Frances had fallen in the brook while playing with the Glen's Fairies, Elsie insists that they take her father's camera in order to photograph them, using a single glass plate, They returned claiming to now have proof of the fairies, tiny winged women danced in front of Francis in one of the photos, another photo shows Elsie looking at one of the fairies, the image is blurred, as it appears that she was moving her head as one of them flew next to her face, does this indicate that the fairy was genuine and was in the act of flight as the this picture was taken, another photograph showed a small man, apparently to me an elftype figure with Elsie, their photo taking was made into a foreboded act by the adults, Photos debated, faked, then if so, how? They'd stuck to their designs that they had seen fairies in the brook<>
ISAIAH 51:9 AWAKE, AWAKE, PUT ON STRENGTH, O' ARM OF THE LORD; AWAKE, AS IN THE ANCIENT DAYS, IN THE GENERATIONS OF OLD. ART THOU NOT IT THAT HATH CUT RAHAB, AND WOUNDED THE DRAGON?****************

REA'S PUNCH&JUDY- She'll ride a go-cart on a safari-Holding a butterfly net in her hands, trying to bring down Tembos. She'll wear a mask made of fogged clear plastic Just to blur her beauty a little.

JOB 40:15-24 BEHOLD NOW BEHEMOTH, WHICH I MADE WITH THEE; HE EATETH GRASS AS AN OX. LO NOW, HIS STRENGTH IS IN HIS LOINS, AND HIS FORCE IS IN THE NAVEL OF HIS BELLY. HE MOVETH HIS TAIL LIKE A CEDAR: THE SINEWS OF HIS STONES ARE WRAPPED TOGETHER. HIS BONES ARE AS STRONG PIECES OF BRASS; HIS BONES ARE LIKE BARS OF IRON. HE IS THE CHIEF OF THE WAYS OF GOD: HE THAT MADE HIM CAN MAKE HIS SWORD TO APPROACH UNTO HIM. SURELY THE MOUNTAINS BRING HIM FORTH FOOD, WHERE ALL THE BEASTS OF THE FIELD PLAY. HE LIETH UNDER THE SHADY TREES, IN THE COVERT OF THE REED, AND FENS. THE SHADY TREES COVER HIM WITH THEIR SHADOW; THE WILLOWS OF THE BROOK COMPASS HIM ABOUT.BEHOLD, HE DRINKETH UP A RIVER, AND HASTETH NOT: HE TRUSTETH THAT HE CAN DRAW UP JORDAN INTO HIS MOUTH. HE TAKETH IT WITH HIS EYES: HIS NOSE PIERCETH THROUGH SNARES. (OR WILL ANY TAKE HIM IN HIS SIGHT, OR, BORE HIS NOSE WITH A GIN?)**

"For a cigarette?", But "Will not to've frained" This disinfectant-That leads with force to A favorite among plums-"SEE?" and With dosage that would bring you down to A wetspot that couldn't have possibly acted The deed which left the impeccable wrought Over a period-history- Might have went some Other place-Maybe wasn't spotted- Or a finger Ring that presents a squall bowing once in Its summers dress-"Let you pass, buddy."

O' Rea might have gotten in a trap by the bleeding Of her female parts***************************

Alll of 371days draw to a close. The boat came to rest not on a the very highest peak but above the 10,000 feet mark somewhere atop great Ararat. But las' what drew all the world's creatures to the ship at the start of its functionary lineage?

PSALMS 148:7 PRAISE THE LORD FROM THE EARTH,YE DRAGONS, AND ALL DEEPS:*****************************

The smile from her was the first grace I've heard spoken,My Galla that I waited my life for, Then this clads my Tassel, what confronts you, only yourself, therein to've Rolled-up, all across the daylight, why don't I ever want Leave, like ever I've done before, it became, how you've Gone, just because, give me freedom of your hand, the Smile from her was the first grace, keep a journal of all Thing that-do-, not that you love. Change(may I) I will love you, we're my frantics, Is't a moon t'night, is't a t'ardropping, for't night, Thereset n't a moon, we're... is't lathe, figure the darkest Peers, we're.. a younger girl.. is't allrise, allrise, allrise, "SOME WHISPERS IN MY SKULL"-for't is that I take hers and is't that I do, told you to make sure that I am allhere, therest that I've cri'd, when is't the day's wholly loss always we're treasured, not here, not here, what is't her pass, what does here mean, the classification of the seminal glass, here, The names, I'm protected, I'm, the blown mussel, never the Lather naught 'fore the vile stanza is breathed o'er, I told you To makesure I'm allhere, is't we're the funless end for't

Prism waking a bema, the deadpart-"ITS COSTOMARY TO STAND"-theirs, so left a little-theirs, closed so left-a-left-he's Talented eventually-Travail, Travail, like this aviary hit I can see Them all scathing the hoistcoop, What? The blue scenery Talents the suspension pasts theirs, raise a trough, got their Claws in us, The deal not about the smaller castle guessed with The princess, you'll be happier and all, it's accosted, took off to The rate of winter up-gone the cloven foot, arc of the land and People, cement coast, no rail over water, bravo hint fraise, the Licking bulb slashes the scars to prove continental worry, Galla Takes us back a few epochs, the fraud of what the christened girl In the stars & stripes veil leases on as saturated milk from her Bosom, Awful-Or-Beauty-Or-Between, places her hair in a snood, The bare trot, you're the waddle prom, he too is the fair, though known thought threw paramnesia, kindly idium jabbing with great success at the fovea centralis.

Ostentatious rhapsody, savory her sneap, the measurable Corset is unfastening my disbelief: sheltered underneath a Tympanum, zephyr in the set, Tippled-Cum-Love-Winnie-Points-Dressing her tuft, coating her folds, what's his flower, Wirra wintry, to be oral about its bloom, the satin root, Tippled-Cum-Love- Your mantle, patience like the jolted soli That brought profitably that such mantle, parturient if I'm the Spoof or loved when made, Paschal Full Moon Bite Sir, Paschal Full Moon Bite Sir, Getup there I'm waifing your Partizan, you can not hear the Mem.. O.. Ry.. you can not Hear the M.. Em.. Ory.., Pasquinade, I did so mirthy for Emiline, the rein circles that heir expand the needed conjure-pock,Then we're the small boys that've needless to say, got the regnant, rejoicing the old girl, but.. but we're doing it in the sheugh, I fearfully approach the last pines as were stationed therein the maps as the clothing near about where the stars 'O MY HEART,

JOB 41:1-10 CANST THOU DRAW OUT LEVIATHAN WITH A HOOK? OR HIS TONGUE WITH A CORD WHICH THOU LETTEST DOWN? CANST THOU PUT A HOOK INTO HIS NOSE? OR BORE HIS JAW THROUGH WITH A THORN? WILL HE MAKE MANY SUPPLICATIONS UNTO THEE?WILL HE SPEAK SOFT WORDS UNTO THEE?WILL HE MAKE A CONVENANT WITH THEE?WILT THOU TAKE HIM FOR A SERVANT FOR EVER?WILT THOU PLAY WITH HIM AS WITH A BIRD? OR WILT THOU BIND HIM FOR THY MAIDENS? SHALL THE COMPANIONS MAKE A BANQUET OF HIM? SHALL THEY PART AMONG THE MERCHANTS? CANST THOU FILL HIS SKIN WITH BARBED IRONS? OR HIS HEAD WITH FISH SPEARS? LAY THINE HAND UPON HIM, REMEMBER THE BATTLE, DO NO MORE. BEHOLD, THE HOPE OF HIM IS IN VAIN: SHALL NOT ONE BE CAST DOWN EVEN AT THE SIGHT OF HIM? NONE IS SO FIERCE THAT DARE STIR HIM UP: WHO THEN IS ABLE TO STAND BEFORE ME?

'POLLY'

" GLADLY I HAVE SETTLED IN THE NEW PLACE
-GONE ALL RIGHT-
 -HAVE NOT RETURNED-
-HAVE NOT RETURNED-
  SO I'VE TAKEN A CHARGE-TREES & GARDENS
  DONE NEWLY-UP-
 -VERY NICE PEOPLE-
 -NOT TOO MUCH TO DO-
 -VERY NICE PEOPLE-
  -NOT TOO MUCH TO DO-
  I WRITE PRESENTLY GOOD BYE,
                 FROM YOURS VERY TRUE"
    'POLLY'

THURSDAY THRU FRIDAY

WETTEST&HEAVIEST&COLDEST SUMMERS
WHAT'LL BE MADE OF THE DOCK FIRES
11:OO PM- SEEN DOWN WHITECHAPEL
12:30 AM –SEEN LEAVING A PUBLIC HOUSE
1 TO 2- " ASKED WAYOUT OF THE KITCHEN"
2:30 AM- SEEN EAST DOWN WHITECHAPEL
3:15 AM- NOT SUBSTANTIVE FROM 2 LOOKS
3:45 AM- "COME, THERE'S A WOMAN!"

'POLLY'

" LEAVE THE THOROUGHFARE OPEN
LEAN DOWN THE SAME HOUSES
OF LOCALITY HIGH, HIGH WALLS
SERVED-UP OUR BIG MISTAKE"

ISAIAH 34:13 AND THORNS SHALL COME UP IN HER
PALACES, NETTLES AND BRAMBLES IN THE
FORTRESSES THEREOF: AND IT SHALL BE AN
HABITATION OF DRAGONS, AND A COURT FOR OWLS.

E.F.+ April 30th- put the tree, potted if possible, In the circle,
This time he fills the bags with Ivory- bending down to whisper
into the bark-Puts a piano key in its soil- Places a worn
costume Jewel, that painfully fake, is appealing 'cause of Its
large glazed plastic---- sparkling--- emerald- Stands--- on--- his
toes----Believed-- to've--- spoke--- barely--- Above ---a whisper,

"A Queen, straightenup, then Will need to be unified in draping our precocious Night?"

'SIVVEY'

ENTERED DOSSET, SATURDAY SEPTEMBER 1ST
THOUGH MAYBE THE LAST FEW DAYS IN
AUGUST-HALF A PENNY-
-YOURSELF LUCKY-
-YOURSELF LOVELY-
-NOMORE-MADE-HERE-MONDAY-
-SEPTEMBER 3^{RD-}
-YES, HOW DID,CHEST?-
-CAN I GET PICKING BOOTS?-
-FRIDAY SEPTEMBER THE 7^{TH-}
-THRU SATURDAY SEPTEMBER 8^{TH-}
-5:00 PM- SCENE AT DOSSET WHERE-
-THEY PULL TRADE-IS NO USE?-
-11:30 PM- GONE HOME TIL 1:00 AM-
-1:35 AM-I'LL BE SOON, I'LL BE LONG-
-OFF BRUSHFIELD THEN SPITALFIELDS-
-4:45 AM- SEATED FAR LESSLY OLD -
-ORDINARY-5:30 AM- YES, YOU WILL, -
-YES, YOU WILL, A SHABB, NOT AGAIN,-
-YOU WILL?THE ARM THAT'S LEFT OVER-
-BREAST, PULL OUT THE LEG, THEN? -
-HANBURY'S EIGHT ROOMS, HANBURY'S-
-GOT TWO FRONT DOORS-PATCHED -
-IN THE BACK,THERE IN STONE, DIRT -
-&GRASS-YOURSELF LOVELY IS OUT-
-OF JUST OLD 'SIVVEY'-

DEUTERONOMY 32:33 THEIR WINE IS THE POISON OF DRAGONS, AND THE CRUEL VENOM OF ASPS.

E.F.+ Imbolc- "I've not seen nothing like this." Where Ebbey Professed the sufficient renewal-Discourse, discourse- Having been brought-up Sloth in form, a lifetime, his is short-in too long the youth-basking the small gas lamp-Takes like a broken heart- It reminds him Of being fresh not separate for that- So, he'll make it as much a wish, " Not sorry?"

REA-"THEY DID NOT BUILD ROME IN A DAY, THOUGH THEY HAD PLENTY OF THE DRAFTS DRAWN IN LESS THEN NO TIME."

Sandra Mansi's photograph- moves from out of the water-comes from underneath the surface and is not moving along the top while seen this time-close to 70some feet when put there in comparison with the waves-

REA-" ENOUGH FOR ME TO'VE GOTTEN A REAL CIRCUIT WHICH CROSSES OVER HUMAN NATURE."

Rea places her lip on Ebbey's knee, lying in wet grass- puts a white sweet cream around his lips and at their edges, felt like she burnt some type of bridges while she kissed him with that being on there-Put her tongue in his throat and felt as she were sailing off In a blanket of colors-Then she was to ask," What fills this world." But she hasn't ever gotten an answer for that question .In the still crossing point from midsummer to winding into The late part of August, it was then which Hetts began to Receive these dispassionate correspondences-Rings on his phone, that when he answered on the other End he heard a loud hum that fused into an angry crunching And banging to a light wail, and finally a voice which proclaimed to hex him-Oddly his work about home was not stifled in the Least by the frequency of these calls, instead of tracing them to The directly guilty parties(still as of then unknown)- He reversed all that and began to live specifically for them- he could expect Them at least a 12times in the day if he were lucky, Upon Hearing the ring, he'd drop whatever he was doing and scurry To the phone, hoping to get there by at least the third ring-Fearing he'd miss one, and have to wait longer, his worst fear Was that they would stop coming, Happily for him they lasted 'til Late into the Fall, the most assuring aspect was as before stated, Not-Knowing-The-Caller-

"I feel you must tell us, no, it is that you must at least make it clear to me, to hell with all the others." The web gains my reliance-was first learned by seeing a muse as more than a kindling sprite-This, and protected so easily, isn't it, if let on as an absurd vice which in its comparable means took me over the unclenched hollow- Then be to've been inclined by its perfectly shaped face-To sleep there on this sweat soaked summer dress, drawn Over my face to guard the spreading morning light that if it Could, would eagerly wake me Just-A-Little-To-Early- That, I don't think is at all the worst disaster.

The face beautiful, and a masculine garb- May pressed-Sold important, no-body's old color- There's not fashion-In the forming of chest- when I'm led to believe is going to Look, and does to me from where I see it, as a gauze Yellowish, my way of welding that as a tanned carp-Where it was that the harder light which in its ability to Hold out the marks like charts of cause for cause places Where I can't be, I found to've got to the way where I pass Off by holding that within, and argue of how it would all be Laid entirely different if lit therein a soft light. The conclusion I see as little pauses, and leaps, they are not a manipulation!-

REA-"I WANT TO COME BACK, A LOT LATER IF IT NEED BE, I WON'T BE ANYONE, BUT I'LL SEE YOU'VE UNDERSTOOD."

If formality will for a moment coincide in a joint effort with disintegration. They're knowingly bye, saying if they're to tell me any at all is justification. " Hum' what's ever slushed in our shape, he'll to've came in a stature, it is a novelty led with exceptional dither that can open their transcendence as the knot which so suddenly upon being untied leads us in the outer tail of our predictability." A seam more to the lower half when She'll , "hear it now," "hear it now," ruse. Coursed in the damn conglutinations whether rests her therein a lacy conglomerate, She'll , "hear it now," "hear it now," wants to've hung her stockings on the ice cuddled star-

Rung water wants to open the door but warned of being unable To push one through, " the road by home, gone to be there enamored by a stickle of shells, gone to be there waving on the lower half below the population estimate," -"good god!",

" gain hither made, he said pasts the post-elemental mark, but he reemerged with the hope of making that his point." Then why are you afraid to touch us, when you so much more Than have got us at the tips of your fingers, my lips move and Are gone to be there, nicely, then move with my help the most fickle dampness dripping its way on down my inner thigh. Then, never excepting the annoyance of reaching my lip on The cress of the bodily functional sanitation.

And doesn't this feel rather good? And I found my spirit Diplomatically repressed by being coined a phrase for its only stake that measured in merged fluids sipped as writhed if we're supposed to've said I'd pissed concrete. And been suckled like a mirth, " isn't that me," "isn't this me," " here I am looked after, here I'm pretended as being a self-reproduced sexuality, you know I am and will say too," "you were there, and doesn't speak in turn what's this that supplements how my body's been hung and remember its flattened and how's That any single representation, a shit that hoards me, dis-passionate in a recompensated fund."

The differentiable sexual identity, the episodic escape, the Episodic loveliness, " and the reason's collage I'm not kidding Couldn't be true for being beneficially presanctioned as Receptively Penetrable, the muse herein stands by itself as

being non-verbal If the case at hand is subsided violations,
"look no hands, look   No flavor and so well, do you think intruding is like sniffing somehow a solitude catching fire, a legislature that dibbles a non-such sparking?" "This secretion can write a thank you note, and do as you will in the prior margins, that lap congratulates before the post-mortem warrants that it is here too, and was introduced, is customary to stand and address your guest, heaven rinsed a purple muck from me and is gone to be thoroughly nit-picky in if it does or does not decide to give me over, knowing about that its destination is well-kept, and wants to reach me in, bubble to a yellow, rise me on a slender sift and too, now different brushed all in a planked chalking , so too , when I wanted not to think myself as rare, fell boringly eaten- out."

JEZEBEL'S 14th POURED MURDER

Found them there in the moor in a bit of a scrape. "please try," "now, please," "please, you're…going to have to try," . It looks utterly hopeless from where I stand. "take you in sky,"- Well, there's just not a chance of that, not anymore, he pretends but he hasn't pointed a stab of will out in the hurry forth weariness- "OK, bird", "OK, bird" , - The chorus comes on 'fuckin' crazy- " All right turn the lights down and leave here alone, MR.- is that just how things are done around here, if I don't, I leave, and let on to that prior to departure-Some of their mothers said even on the fourth they can't hang A flag in the backyard 'cause if for the best of their health, It were to fall to the grass, degrading a characteristic that some People's lives are centered around, 'sides there is younger people here and they might not(at this time) need to hear this. Stephanie told me all about you, I've meant you once, for you? YES, I will consider the exception! — STARTS' THE LEARNING-
Is there, is there. Wines no questioning the blanks. Don't recover then, shit. HE really said a lot of the Differences on how they'd felt, he could barely clip it Off at the half a mile mark, A dusk trip- It needs to Be said alone, taken from the heap, Sometimes…. Glistening, sweet lapses in to a bucket with a foamy Broth on its muzzle, hold him down in a leader's bonnet Long enough to get--his teeth around the tight spots-Of –The--- biggest--- apple, a-big red heart, a complete no-one.

-STARTS' THE LUSHING-

Stephanie....Stephanie...Stephanie..., MOM? I wanted her+ being lonely, Why should I be Treated like a don't have to partake in being there In that, a puzzle, fastens the smarts, all, I got nothing Lending this to me. Stephanie took me over around the Lots where the homes are antiques in themselves. Kind Of slowly pulled back off the rug when my legs fell to Sleep and hurt when they snap at the joints as I had to Re-lift to walk-up again-Dis-believing the least now to See that I was drawn to this cubic box, I kept shying A ways from her smug face, Rather large nose and Kept calling, " blue-eyes", "Blue-eyes" , " Young-woman". A crackling kicks downward on the upstairs floor slightly To rouse where we're sitting close, by her lapse comforted And can lay rest to annotations, "What was that?" " All!" A loud crash from the upstairs," -that interrupted us for The ONCECHANCE of being buried, one more cloister,
     "is difficult, even though, more of these friends,"-GETUP-
     "Again," –a bunch of playingcarddecks fell off a handmade book shelf in the masterbedroom's closet- "HUM" then can't find a ways backing to get forward, This, you see with Stephanie?, "at least in my case with her can only work on, if I got planned in stellar detail."-

SOMEWHAT OF AN ALLUSION TO AN AMERICAN NIGHT-

Capsized where this is plucked as a gift from the Delicate top layer a longtime past my bottom. "how would you kill an overdue," "dared feeling like he was freed off the love, the love that smacked in his tonsils and never managing to give the crowd a laugh, so we decided together that it were like the taking of a wafer in the narrows," –That was disgusting to the innerspreading who found us dis-quieted, "said our hearts got un-tuned with the low humor of the young. "who is the man that doesn't leave," " They got us on that, you cannot get a perfect boy, they got us that we'd come into him right after we'd mistrustingly blurred him from his youth, saying if we'd watched with discontent throughout his sleep," Polish his cock by letting his wings outspread- "Who in the hell goes thru that to take away privacy, but remorse is the only mistake, when these factors   tend to blend," – in hell boy- any other things you wanted to ask me before I go on to the several desires-

" To tell you..OK – friendlessness," –staunch in a whole but I put him up for that, take the piss off the records- " It's as a mathematical lesson(though I hated math)," Put these boys against one another in their systematic Auras which are about then coming out of them-Then I Walked out of here in a peacefulness, - from that place and after I could step over my own feet with both eyes closed, past, past them, brushing the other check of desire- As easy As at least settling for a 2nd place finish, even being this in all a pivotal tournament, I think it would be great, if The next time I see, NO if I never see them again, I can Remember them all as good friends- Each served their Purpose as a pointing inclined band on the wake of What I'll respect as wake of my life thus far- "What would it be like if you see him again," " I think it will be great(confidently spoken)," " Why then didn't you stay there," " substantiate in all respects, I'm always one who's going, and not here, then I go There,"- "if it helps you to leave them back there in your Conscious as friends you made and kept in spirits, then I'd So-much try to believe that," "You speak too much like the Goner in this all, but you aren't going away, I assume?"

We'll move far from here? And in an earnest to get together There, didn't have to be before we got to there? " I will-in a gray coming over, " "Bored legacy which got itself off thru inserting superficial swinging in its large, large dry spells," "And for the first time in its life it gets to move out of the way- all the while knowing how to partake in its plans that cohere to its lusciously craved and skillfully honed ability in the self climatic urgings, Then watch it on its back moaning out its burdens, tensing down to relax after subsequently having just burst."

REA SPELLS RHINOCEROSES

The whole prong that's got a wrought sift. "I'm young too, sign out,"-Plays the heart, so she'll tip the brim of her straw hat, and breakout with a sobbing, "Prodigiously solvable hurt before, real double sod," says Rea when asked about insecurity. "Pre-oviposition, like I loved if eggs were on isolation, pretense, they fall to our little flat, like an omen," "Yeah, he can't tell you what to do,"- Then Rea sought to've warned all wearing gratuitous attire, "Looks here's one and another," says Rea protruding her witch's finger- "if love ain't there, then she don't adore no-one, who can say she'd let-on to the idea of being in love with being in love?" "Does a luge on your vulva make you sleek them off more quickly?" " Dewclaw, switch, hock, pinbone,!" –if you ask her sounds funny,- (Partly my own fault that I need a courageous piss subsequent to ejaculation)-

I can almost hear her knickers rubbing- Then I turn to The wall, kept quiet, "tension, right," Runs from me down the Road, clad by a sarong, On one shoulder hung a waterbottle, Hung a cabbage wrapped-up on the other, With herself, With herself, " Why do you do this," Rea says back to all the People whom she does not know, "I can't find nothing," Breaking a stick takes more discipline too, then the Dreamy things too go straighter, I remember sobs when, When thinking of her not being here, See her in slacks carrying A black parasol, upside two more boys who step into a Un-identified structure in a white morning, Me, looking there For a best, best friend, Rea says "That too is nothing,"-

 "Get this right on the day 'fore the awful," Somewhere under an uneventful loom, don't go see her, It took a lot to ignore that sounding that constellates past friends about like it were a horn crying so to bring the news of a terrible war   blossoming. "I once get to surround," laughs Rea. "I'll own-up to it, bit a lovest currier," laughed Rea subsequently."You ain't got no damn proof," – "Now I will swallow-up little boys, canned if gulping a fountain's spray shot in great height,"-"That's all that if we're to fail, parts the remainder of our worries," –" We get that you'll be a droll who don't know, 'til he hears bright l ines that blip thoroughly in concession with his heat drawn pulse,"

57

"You'll get to figure that it's truelove if you regurgitate on   a pismo clam,"- "If she can coax me on Tuesdays, Rea willingly barrages my thoughts with the truest meanings of all my selfish flaws,"-

REA SPELLS MORDENT

The repertoire does now list these days to make sure That one concludes their day on un-planning each idea They'd just conceived for tomorrow-That's when Rea Said to me, "Nothing at all lasts, tormentor,"-" Plain old Lights out, to serve your half,"-Wherever she filled-up a Gashing brandy-"Wherever you are, it's easy to lift this And say naturally it was done for your best interests,"-"But then I got worried when she was in danger,"-and Just this…- Make yourself properly taller, grows-up High in her JACK&THE BEANSTOCK routine- But.. She does that without making us feel as if the thunder Is the naturalized animalistic Maybe-so that makes us The corner brush,-"Robbed, no-matter who you are",- I just told Rea- gets yelled as " The firstlife, the firstlife," By someone who's been taken out of their grieving by Rea's risks,- " For the works I'll still tell them off in that Very cottage where Rea referenced to've been brought From her Mum's vulva."-

Lots plan the deafgames. "Then I'll know,"- that I been the Farthest person from her, under the oppressing costs of Her telling me I'm the closest-"Go away!"- I raised thus Numerous sickly children, and so god bring a few more from me-I never thought you'd hop donw&up whispering- " Nice gone, nice gone,"- I've taken all the impressionable rides where you gotta stand in longlines on heat smoldered afternoons,-"how long should a visit be, even if one is lonely?" —Take the long move, and she sees a cycle of wrists brush her nipples, said up against a busted fence, "I don't arouse you in the least?"- God, backup.- Scrub her back in the hungry baths, utilizing a 'worsh' cloth, "Not to make summer impossible,"- Asks that you tell her about what living in the earth is all about- " what's a rinse on a wethead, a swampy margin, that got mugged in its   easy on&off pre-spurt,"-"Oh bye, you, Oh bye, you," – Take a turn in the buffalo feeding, in a trapping for the humming   bird's in air suspension thus is trying to be a person such the extraordinary thing, or would it be a lease in this passage-

I knew that Rea likes to say- "Beautiful worlds,"-and flows That to speaking, "Beautiful world's have always kept learning,"-I got to know where she borrowed that from, this wonderful face, she points at two hills and speaks of correlation between the human facial formation and the peak's cress, not differing much, like her blush and a spot of grass, " Hey not yet, I'll get to there if you'd give it a second,"-Gets the advantage of telling me smoke rising from a ravine is a blissing allusion to the laughter about to guzzle my abdomen- turns my on my side be kicking my shins and a few pickup stands on my feet-" And I did stay, when you see how it pours into more of the distance after it is not full enough to get over the hillsides without the lose of its grouping," Rea siad this most winsome when describing a porcupine entering her sex, laughed that it would have its own showmanship as a clitoral aversion.

REA SPELLS WELLS

Saw the juicer as what it really was, the discovery. She sits out 10 potted lilies on a tarp, pours sand onto It to serve as the workbase, gets costumed as a The Statue of Liberty, in a gown, blue smooth muck on what skin is visible, And a flickering torch, "A shadow covers my bottom, tell me will this if timed correctly cast it out?"- is waved by the people in a time-to-go fashion- insists that she's rehearsing community, A little girl who walks hand&hand with her father, asks, "Are You Jesus?"- insinuates that ,"I never in least wanted to get those kind of responses from this,"- It's OK for only me, that she is not in a suffice home feeling 'til getting thisout- Rea says that when someone avoids discussion of the elements that she structured who-she-is around, that it's an offense as grave as rape- "tip the collection-can 'round, stranded if your going to end your life if nobody puts their lifeblood in,"- Lift my arms off the ground as wanting as ever before to put them around her, I feel that if this has not lessened after all that we've put each other thru, than it is to forever be so- Sea demons carry kitchen knifes to cut the bride's corset- Rea, Why don't you see that farelove?

REA SPELLS MOORS

My side of town, so we stop, just like that to drag to a   Clearest false awakening- Humorously putting our eyes   Tightly closed- More queer to be without nothing, when She used to wear layers-but Rea assures that other people Have put together something less in their ruff squabbles-Then home's siding collides along with her writing out each Piece of her life that lead her to preclude the closer of Every situation she'd found her life to be at that point Dried in the rite's mosque, " I just didn't want to get in the Way not that I was at all disinterested,"- that is one thing that I should have said- Cancel the briskness her bottom sulked To, is that the right word- " It looks that you're without help, But she might drop-off nicknames for the chase that Mentions dreaming like a fool who waits to go forward."

Open the beyond of the bending venture, if that's what   You're going to say,- then living without a prince causes a   Trite filled existence circled in slow traffic court- I wondered   If any others actually do this,- nothing is wrong in a may-say- Total-sensibility, just that there are no breakfree bows- I handily sought her, I find milk and I do not hand it to her-Come on a darling who crosses bracelets to her in stealth Magnetism- Asked if you heard that with your ears- It is Better to be sung to sleep, your dreams being a blank Image but having the gift of a montage of sounds that came Off on the way from the back of mentalscapes new enough To possess familiarity not ones that were hid somewhere For years- As always with Rea's singing, it isn't too long before the listener visualizes Naked men, Rea sees that it's excepted prior to the serenade to know that no apology will be required.

REA SPELLS POWERS

A prodigal softshell turtle stood off by the dusts Is just a drag down-they said won't firsl, then they Made it to be that it was your wrong doing-You have Too, it is just as simple as that-Fetcher of learning tool-Had hexes out on all the girls who meet his fancy- All the ones he every put eyes on specifically-Were the Most completed letdowns-the jest of what they want to know(Is though unknowingly to them) everything he'd never want his life to made of-it is not that they'd every notice, they peer in out of minutely fascinated curiosity-Said as I want to do my life in my time, taken asides from the crowds,-Yeah, they always come with the refusal of playing the radios on anything framed to've been misogynistic—"Whew, come see that, O' dues we're asked assuring, Whew that's to standup the dues asides, O' you don't tell him the reasons why, after doing all of that, O' gone to be for a longest time,"-

And I have to tell him, the parade's date falls parallel to the His birthtime- I'll swing them for all it's worth-In the world At the best 'X', not me I got you-The costumes require 5 People to give illusion that they're dragons, "you should Know that for yourself"-"What are you waiting on, now"- "if you can't change yourself, something else, depending on this being easy,"- You've really made something from this that I could've never- Then they come out speaking, - "I will NEVER do this again..."- O' the hardest times, you all right, you all right, and I can't leave with it, I just feel worse, tonight and nohow,-O' I feel him In the mirther's protectionary devices, O' I still haven't Ever come to live, and I can't leave the goodnight, and I can't leave the wild scythe,-O' all right for you to remark On all you've done in the way of traveling,-

With its own hardy flux-all it wants to do-dropout-Impulsive Dane-Who goes there, is what they say Of my hand shaded face when I arrive in the sundown's subfusc-I get to return myself in home, later, half of who'll be with me in the long trueloves,-"Might they get at calling you mine, when you've been with me,"-"Please, Please, really done against you more that I'm sorry on your in-store staling with your-come-go-plays-if-, O' then that's that, that I count loving the awful shit I did against you, O' then the marigolds in my groin that resume the ether when their fingers take a perfectionist's sense of caring in peeling my foreskin back over my cock,-masturbating me,- and leaving me on the floor-I say sorry to my semen not getting its so deserved distance Step, after it has run in a lapse when the hood makes earnest Amends in catching its goodtimes, serving the purpose of an Alarmclock's birdy, gets called the painful awful's surf"-

Rea was claimed to have said, "You're mine now forever," She had a tire swing in the backyard of her childhood home, Strange for her to see that it's kept there, and long after she's Gone, she thrashed a segment over that expired prevalence- Before she does she, she feels a little sickly, and so is outside, back, "O' GREAT DAYS"- Sees the pads of her own two feet being rubbed in the soil- the frothing of the spring near the flowerpots is what she'll choose to there so cleanse them in, "Rocks&Skys,"-"the soft bodies gotten lit awhile breathing motel room bed sheets, where outside authentic decay," – She rocks in the swing wearing her short dress, flings us a gust of her underpants drawn a little down exposing her bottom, the way she crouches inside the swing, and kind of wraps her feet 'round it, leans her nape back, her hair falling. In summers, the backyard's source of illumination comes from a motion light- flings on when Rea comes closer into its range, riding the swing-"you're still here, why are you still here," I have a good taste to not leave the taste of work alone, down the small streets to town hall, get there or bust- My compensation for the plain and simple, and to get to be laughing by Rea sleeping with me,- But a growth willed a massacre, wasn't any longer a girl-O' I was protected, The tire vessel, when its faster swinging ceased and Rea Came down from it, She wanted to sleep that summer every night in a tent in the yard,-O' that if go-and-find-yourself-became the pure-summer-that-fell-to where it was used once and twice over of its innocent child,-But wasn't nobody else's forgiven friend that turned me lose,-There at dawn's verge, the crickets step back in phase and Rea's eardrums widen to the sound of bird's calling her,-When one wakes in a tent it is usually 'cause of the voices that stem from the incased rousing heat that gathers in

62

it, making it by mid-day impossible to not awake, and usually the times that you'll wake prior to dawn are the times where if you try to fall back asleep, you end up discovering it to be an impossibility, maybe even childhood makebelieve excitement doesn't keep one clear of the discomforting jabs from stones and cramps from the uneven earth that are all brought,even when placed over with heavy padding, 'cause one is after all sleeping on the very earth itself,-now the younger-girl-Rea to contrary slept 'til the smoldering afternoon,- Woke up in need of a long pee,-walked half asleep inside home,- Stepped back out relieved, didn't enter the tent but plopped Down to the grass with fresh sleepiness in her eyes,- There She felt a magick begin to fluster, -"I, for the longest time Got the most extraordinary feeling in my finger tips, if they Were all about an object, the surge could bleed Its way Down to the tips of my toenails," -little Rea after lying in The morn's wetgrass proceed to the backgarden in pursuit Of the meadowsprites, hoping to gain the satisfied vaining Of admiring them in their rite-"What, did I crawl to there On my hands&knees, No, actually felt I gained a reliance In myself in the 'all/worths' of that summer's mornings"

Our friend Rea found the sprites she-so-greatly-Wanted-Saw them carryon 'round her silhouette-Making their way to her brow, forming a looming Halo- They made bite marks on her mouth's Corners- swooned her eyelids-"For the month's go, Uh', Which of those presents the outdoing of Rea's Mum's silly season,"-"O' my darling they think they're so damnable in a clever hypo, they'll see what's the way that never leaves the top un-bored," – Then in the hidden garden, Rea after a sprites game, partook to her drowsy season,-"I'm talking to you, I'm taking you in for a coherent wallop"- Rea's slept amongst the garden's shadings,-"I knew you've had that ability, the thanks this awards me in the pretext,"-then he affords a lot of other callings, " cohere in for the wallop, one which is –a-must-of spreads 100s and me gone to you- Rea awoke there crying aloud from a polished dark dream, this was an irregular occurrence, our girl hadn't much been exposed to the verybad fears- She remembered the dream of some person opening her heart cavity, take out the obvious-holding it to her, she is much too horrified to scream in the actual dreams placing, so that clarifies the wail she let out upon her awakening- Those dreams of one's death are said for to some to be a premonition- But this child couldn't know any way into that- She just felt a mis-placing, her fear had caused the garden's shadows and sprites to be a place void of familiarity- Rea got that- for her even as a child to not under mind the emptiness that was to not long follow, made her in her young age the more blissfully precocious"- "The sun where they aren't suffering, twisting up from this all be," Says Rea's Mum, knowing what the girl's imagination(not yet hinged) would see that place as-THEN Rea gather herself in enough time to get swiftly from the garden, right then I can't see how this could become the girl who makes the point of what does&doesn't concern her emotions, and does that with much bigger immediacy than the scared one who ran with what seeing back now, was a delight not a fear, from her garden- The catch, she returned that night to swing&tent-slept so less soundly this time- Waking in what seemed to her to be every few minutes, as-soon-to-sleep-as-to-awake, A tall grass that got swayed against the tent created a scraping noise, which upon its-ever-so-milliontimes-moving across the tent, made the fear in Rea to be the most amazing sensation, this was unlike the garden foar being that once she discovered its cause she awaited as the substitute for a hypnotic-in-effect-tickingclock that gave her an idea of how much it would take for her to get a sound rest- The coming day, that made little sense to her, The grass's sway had been stifled by the heavy rainfall that With it also brought a coldness that drew Mummy to rap Upon the tent flap and bring Rea into home-"There's some Type of a melodic effect that recalls the innards of that Summer's seamless ruse, just the pounce of stiff fingers on frost etched panes."

CHAPTER-'C'

STEPHANIE JOURNEYED TO THE PERISCOPE
AND THIS IS WHAT SHE FOUND THERE

'JUNA ISLAND', THE FIRST PARADISE-

And may friends whisper hello, they'll have their
Rains seasons 'til they've gotten basked in the 'morse
Otherwordly? There Stephanie moves up on the whiter
Sands, another time she'd have brought a map-
This one paradise if seen from overhead is a perfect circle-
Not one blemishing seam that'd impair its circumference-
Exactly two rings, the outer one, and then Stephanie's
Core Gift. The outer ring is made of burnt bristled wood-
The remainders of the pieces of this tropic that've been
Tarnished-Some of the wood chips protrude, serving the
Place of spikes, Stephanie sees that if one were to pierce
Her foot-The split would be caused by the climate to quickly
Rise to infection, probably end with her meeting her death-
Stephanie has got to pick her steps carefully through this.
While lifting herself over some of the bigger fallen tress
She sees small rodents peek from out their nests,

Stephanie is careful not to disrupt them, taking special
Ease in stepping over something which appears minute and
Inhabited.

At least getting closer to her Gift Core, she sees a flaming
Arch. Thinks quickly of stepping around this, not under, the
Singe might ignite the hair atop her head, using the bow she's
Placed in it as a fuse to carry the burning to the rest of her
Body-Taking sight of her Core Gift comparatively in that it's
Apprehended in an oasis likeness-Core Gift is more a marsh
Than the tropic Stephanie figured on-Moving aside the foliage
That obscured the direct pathway in-The steps that she takes
On the rock laden path turn to more of a bounce after a few
Moments-Though the path in no time leads to an empty
Clearing where Stephanie begins likening this venture to a
Trek thru a thicket of scowls-Then now, enter the blissful
Incarnations which while presenting their quality of a
Magick that will certify Stephanie's disciplinary division of
The truth between self-worth and selfishness-Then now,
Core Gift's marsh becomes auditorium for a merging
Assortment of nymphs- They carry small harps, are sneakily
Unclad, scuffle about the air, the size of full grown humans-
     " O' the fairy people"-Then now, they come to the earth and
Lift up Stephanie in their arms, momentarily flounce her out
To the squishing earth-Then now, what is more beautiful than

To be made love to by sprites that plod you onward to a
Climatic fervency, who've taken on human form for just this
Occasion-The intensified plucking is pulled on the harps,
Where Stephanie lies dripping on mushy ground to gather
Herself in the sense that the fairy people have departed-Then
Now, she'll rouse herself to make way from Juna's Core Gift.

The now, let Juna sink to the sea's bottom after the
Closure of Stephanie's paradise-Then now, its remembrance
Can be just the meagerness fizzling awhile being sunken.

A SECOND PARADISE-A CINEMA SCREENING PLACE

Stephanie-"An uncovering life,"
Then now, some placing, a South African home-
Stephanie sat in the corners of the house's rooms-
Finding that they were the coolest places in the house

The windows laced in a netting to get riddance of some of
The insect species-Somewhere, Stephanie places her
Hands on the spots on the floor where some of the insects
Gather in more immense groupings, has some of them run
Up her arms, weirdly puts them on her thighs, brushes them
Off when they get uncomfortably close to where she doesn't
Want them to go near-people arrive at the front of the home,
Bringing duplicates of valueless things- magazines for
Things she can not obtain, things she'll not at this time have
A chance at seeing-Stephanie-"A scene therein,"-then now,
Stephanie becomes the receiver of picture cards that have
Gotten an unreadable scrawl written on them, regardless of
That-She'll see the lights, and then the friends who'll take her
Into a city of huge parades, costumed participants, O' given
Regards for the value of colors, you know if something is
Bright___ it has got a godliness here that has amongst itself
A splendid concession of "What Makes Us Very Happy, And
It Does That In The Time That We Need It Too,"
There Now, in the city Stephanie nearly gets killed walking
An intersection with poorly functioning lights-turns her head
One way and just to see the traffic on-coming in a hazy
Boom-stumbles out of that luckily still keeping her life-------
Meets a boy somewhere in town, asks him for directions-
He gives them lacking substantive know-how----------
She feels a little in danger when two local boys eye her
Funny she gets out of their sights when it would seem to be
That they're about to accost her--------------
Then Now, finds the coral gardens, steps and walls that are
Risen high, constructed out of the varnished reef-
Led down one coral tunnel to find the discovery of a
Screening room, A motion picture projector which is also
Constructed from the reef—dangerously flickers the images
Upon a pull-down screen probably proportioned for the
Exhibition of 16mm prints-shown in a classroom setting-
School desks and chairs, are placed in the room, the
Audience consists of maybe 3 other people, 4 if you count
The projectionist, who appears somewhat embittered-
Presumably 'cause of having to screen the same 3 films

For the length of their exhibition lives until the prints are
Beyond 'exhibition quality', he is then supplied with 3 more
Films which he will also screen for their entirely short
Exhibition lives-Always films from the crossover period of
When sound was replacing the silent films-preferably Lang's
'M', Eisenstein's 'Alexander Nevsky' and Bunuel's ' L'Age-
d'OR'. Stephanie's purchases a ticket, and takes her seat
During the Battle on the Ice scene of 'Alexander Nevsky'-
Finds herself startled by how Prokofiev's score replaces the
Sounds of battle which she'd anticipated.
Stephanie is the only female in the audience, Two men
Who were sitting close to the front of the room
Have noticed her sitting in the back of the room, alone.
They've slowly made the progression there too, going
Desk-by-desk-, attempting to create the illusion that their
Dis-satisfied with their view of the screen-Stephanie's lost
Deeply in the film, not taking notice of them-they are
Soon directly next to her, one to each of her sides-
Stephanie's face is shining, granting a proficient glow
Towards Eisenstein's irreplaceable gift-----One of
The men places his hand on Stephanie's knee, moving
Slowly up her leg, when his finger is nearing her groin,
She brings her legs together, he takes his hand back-
Stephanie profoundly startled, stands agile, turning over the
Desk, departing with agility from the screening room-
Followed by the two men-Through the coral tunnel,
Down the court's winding stairs, enough speed to not
Sense the evident entrapped feeling that is present due
To the height of coral walls around the courtyard-------
This she may sense if not-in-run, maybe if their pursuit
Was more a cat&mouse one—Stephanie even though in
Fear, remembers the way which she'd entered, and is
As-fast-as-her-feet-can-carry- to've made her way out-
Entering the silently unoccupied streets, still moving
At a steadily quick rate through their half-dark/half-lit-
Passages—The city looms over her in an encasing state,
    "A trap, a trap, and you've become a part of it too,"
Stephanie-"An uncovering life,"

There Now, at home-still being the receiver of the poorly
Scrawled picture cards-She reads the backs of them sitting
 In the house's coolest corner, turned them over to see that
When placed correctly they form a picture----like the films
That while enjoying she was harshly interrupted-This Now,

Is the safe chance at the stakes of a moving image—
The scrawled cards on their tops show the image of a
Man lying on a hospital table, forced to swallow ants
And watch their passage down to his stomach on a
Monitor-mid-point- the image fades out-fades in with
A montage of maps of important Eastern Pennsylvania
Cemeteries--------Stephanie-" When I'll go, Is that less
A guess at wearing peoples favors," is this putting the
Flowers at the graves of friends, and this is about the
Peacefulness of not getting a companion—
Stephanie turns the cards over on their backs she wants
To reread them to see if she can probably make some
Sense of the hand-writing- maybe it's another projected
Image-one that can be viewed here safely and happily-
Free of any such conscious interruptions.

NIGHTINGALE- PARADISE, THE 3RD

Over the western embankment a bleeding is done
While dry lightning flashes towards the pre-thought
That our minds are precious and to keep them guarded
Off a leaking of salty tissue remnants, resembles the
Possible ending of where making-up well known thought
Of her in the leisure of a camera prism, setups, setups-
    "There isn't a feeling along the east," – the orb glided
Aglow beneath the water, emerges to form a lifetime,
And Then, the face of a girl whom it is required to be neatly
Seen-THE CLASS STRUGGLE SPOKE THUS____
Endlessness, lights, switches, systems, And Then-
Parades that are the streams, the freedom's epoch-
Awhile moving along the city's streets- And Then too,
The lifecycle's epoch-The city's entire distance across,
And Then too, out to each of its ends-This all was viewed
Through a Plate Lens, a flat camera that can glimpse-And
Then, stride out like a tracking shot performing a continuous

Take-And Then, brought out the rippled flecks in the night-
And Then, awaited the grandeur of each of the city's edges.

The audience for the Plate Lens comes-to-see-Stephanie as
She strikes a match to illuminate the writing that's been
Scrolled on the whale's belly's walls- In the mucus of this
Behemoth's interior Stephanie uses a miniature campfire
Lantern to illuminate a small portion of the beast's belly's
Floor so that she can have a quick game of jacks—As the
Ball that's required in the game's rulebook is bouncing
Readily, the tickle this brings causes the beast to roar,
Spewing forth Stephanie, she comes from her great plunge

To fall freely upon a tub of yellow, red, purple, 'Balloons'-
Popping a suffice too many-leaving a scant remainder,
Awhile regaining herself she discovers that the
Kaleidoscope she found in the behemoth's belly is
Still in her overcoat pocket-Stands up on her own-two-feet,

And then, experiments with the kaleidoscope's possible
Visual transformations-Finds a particular pleasure in the
Structural prismatic of the kaleidoscopic verge that in
So many ways displays a ruby colored suit of armor being
Penetrated by a stave which shoots a flaming bolt-

A curtain is closed over the Plate Lens, the audience have
A reinforcing awe along with an "it's over all too soon" in
The finality of their last gasps, And Then, was that all the
Valuable ½hour that their admission secured them,
    "it's all over too soon"-And Then, the room that the Plate
Lens is situated in, its lighting dribbles downward to
Seclude it amid a deep, deep black-The broker clenches
The teeth of the lock together, And Then, After the Plate
Lens is assuredly amid the deepest, deepest safety,
And Then, behind that the room's 'audience entry door'
Is too Locked&Shut-

A shroud is swept through the lowerlands of the
Farthest Northern embankment. It has got the
Face value to prescribe a certainty that there has
To've been a human figure laid-over-on-it.

THE PLAYER PIANO

Hetts discovers that he's been granted the ability of

70

Flight-not with wings, just as he is, when it is desired
He may leave the ground and remain hovering in the
Air- Time is needed in honing his new-found-freedom-
At first he'd smash very hard into walls, so he'd have to
Write off indoor flight- And Too, knowing that if he was
To partake in flying outside, and where anyone might be
Able to catch sight of him, And Too, thinking of the attention
That this would draw-to-him. And Too, the dissatisfaction that
He might-not-ever-get to realize the possibilities of his gift.

That Fall he takes a teaching position instructing adults
In G.E.D. courses-the classes are held twice a week, at
An olderhome in their suburbs-Still a house but where one
Of the rooms has been coverted(And Too, rather poorly) into
A makeshift classroom-By sitting out a few desks and chairs,
Hanging a blackboard, and drawing yellow white drapes over
The walls to give the pupils more of a 'homesunshine' feeling
That they'll need to have when wanting to keep learning Across
Their stumbling blocks- Hetts has got to determine Where He
Should start each student off from- after giving them A sample
Quiz which determines the grade level they were at Before
Leaving proper school- All he's got to do then, is sit at The
Painfully wobbling cardtable that's been rigged as his desk And
Occupy himself with something, 'til one of the pupils Requests
his assistance- Hetts is class is a meager 8pupils, Was 9pupils
'til one of them left at the midpoint- after a Dispassionate
interaction and failure on Hetts part to explain More complex
algebra-

Hetts finds it gratuitous that out of the 8pupils there is just-one-
Female. And Too, for his luck she is in a traditional sense
Unattractive- And Too, that she's only once-in-the-semester
Requested needing him- He leaned over her desk to explain a
Simple scientific formula question- Showed her how it was
Done-Let her try it by herself the next time to see if she was
Onto how he was explaining this- His eyes strayed from her-
Hand-on-the-paper to shifting down her nape, which was
Uncomfortably laden with blemishes, Hetts bit his lip-And Too,
Saw thru this to somekind of 'physical lusts value' in his pupil-
Before she'd finished the test primer's example- He saw
Himself draw his hand down to the seam of her buttocks, And

71

Too, hoping that he could slip-in-one-of-his-fingers- All This,
'Fore she asked if she'd done it correctly- A bit flustered he told
Her she'd done it correctly, without even really checking-it-over.

Returns to his cardtabledesk to get himself back to drawing his
Plans for additions he's planning on making to his home-Gets
The feeling as if his kneecaps were spinning under his skin
In a 360degree motion-Drops his sketches and is carried
From his cardtabledesk up-over his pupils and hits hard
Into the room's opposite wall- clutching his left shoulder with
His head's skin split dripping blood on the classroom's floor-

And Too, lifted up-over the pupils, sent out of one of the
Classroom's windows-In the air he loses all gravity and falls
Straight to the lot below the olderhome-smashing thru the
Windshield of a pupil's car-
Has glass between his teeth and throughout his scalp-Seems
That most of the bones in his body are broken-Quickly
The pupils hurry to the olderhome's lot to where Hetts
Has fallen-They're startled to see that he's still alive-
Two of them lift him from out of the car's windshield-
Place him there on one of their coats-And Too-in a
Quickly forming pool of his own blood-in the lot-
One of the pupils goes back inside to call for an ambulance-
Though figuring that Hetts will have died in the time-It-takes-
It-to-arrive-He miraculously stands back up-Spits some of the
Glass fragments out of his mouth-uses the coat he's was laid
Out on to wipe some of the blood from his arms&face-
Tells the students that they can go home early but not before
Telling each of them what to brush-up on before they meet
Later-on in this week. And Too, tells the one pupil in particular

Whose car that he immensely damaged, that not only will he
Pay completely for the damages, but that he will also offer him
A ride home, tonight.
(The conversation between Hetts and his student on their drive
(To return the student back to his home)

Hetts-" Sorry that we got cut so short, though I can give
        Extra time next class if there's some things
        That you missed this time."

Pupil-"Ah, I might think I'd be able to get those things

Looked over tomorrow, and can have it known by the
    Next class."
Hetts-"Do I turn here?"

Pupil-"Yes, it's just right down there,"
(Hetts takes the turn and pulls in-front of the pupils home
(To let him out, NO words are exchanged)

(What Hetts thought on- the-way-home)

(Starting-up to a bright beam-
Four flibs and a subsequent
    Number of brightly colored strands
      When collected-Form the doing of a
      A color chart)-(If I can't of gotten a
      Measure of taking the siege passage
    That's dis-reputed itself in its own
    Satisfaction captions)-(HUH, I want
My..., HUH)-(A whisper and you
    Start out at just a joyous revulsion)

AND TOO, A BIT LATER ON

(Hetts at a get-together with some friends, A child's birthday
party-But Hetts is most Saddened at the physical state of this
child, Who is without use of his legs and just barely Has gotten
use of his arms-And Too, a mental State a bit un-right. A child
of a friend, it is explained to Hetts that the child was left like
this from the results of a degenerative disease)(Hetts sits with
party guests at a restaurant's patio, on a beach boardwalk.The
actions occurring on the beach are visible from the seat that
Hetts has taken. He observes some children wading in the
water, the tide breaking just up to about their waists, they've
taken a toy sailship in to the water with them. He sees a
women lying on her stomach, who has unhooked her bikini
strap to avoid a tan line.Then he draws his attention back to
the party which is occurring. Hetts gives the child a gift, The
parents unwrap it, a plain red ball, hold it in front of the child,
place it in his grasp, He is not the least roused after it slips out,
and Rolls past Hetts feet, And Too, off the boardwalk. Onto the
close beach, Hetts wanting a moment Away from the
celebration, volunteers his services To retrieve the gift. Departs
from the party, has to Walk to the far staircase some ways

73

down the to End of the boardwalk in order to find himself on the Sand. Looks at his feet during the walk, maybe 'cause of the brightly beaming sun rays. And Too, So just to sense his own company. Down the Wooden steps onto the beach. The ball Has rolled to the water, And Too, if he does not hurry-might-be taken out to the ocean. Slips off his shoes and socks, rolls up his pants legs, carries the shoes and socks in his left hand, fearing that they'd be Taken if he were to leave them on the beach. Hurries out to the Ball, which is luckily small enough So that he can grasp it in the palm of one hand. As soon as he gets back to where the tide mark stops, he puts down the ball and puts his socks and shoes back on. Moving back to the staircase which leads back up to the boardwalk that leads back to the celebration.)

AND TOO, ALSO LATER

Once on a dreary morning-Hetts sat at the kitchen table,
Observing as Ebbey surveyed their yard- Is lifted from
His daydream by the telephone's ring- A neighbor says
Come at once and take your son from our backyard,
Proposing the claim that Ebbey is committing an act of
Vandalism on this neighbor's lawn ornament. This ornament
In particular is a well-fared model lawn-jockey, And Too,
It is the neighbor's accusation that Ebbey Is partaking in
Its decapitation by rapping on it with a small mallet-
Hetts argues that how can he retrieve his son, because
He is within his sight as they speak, And Too, is in Hetts's
Backyard- The neighbor still insists that it is Ebbey.

Hetts final response is to carefully place the phone down-
Without warning the neighbor that he's getting ready to
Do such a thing-Hetts gleefully recuperates back through
Daydreaming, awhile seeing Ebbey take and mistake
Their backyard's layout.

AN OBVIOUSNESS STOCKED

A pristine indecency a magick country summer, is not
That what they've heard of coarsely, high hillsides a
Hotly white crown. All adds to've that they've had, they're
On a endlessness, and that, they've likely known. Now Hear,
This suburb's prospective ambiguities, As Quickly As One

Does, The seats in the House of Parliament, And Too, Youth's
Refinery, has sought them as that they're no more than Ant
Hills, The Parliament's Men have gotten the advantaged
Disinfectant-made-easy, They're for-to-smother-the-ant-hills-
In-a-fixtured-gasoline, which they'll pour-on-the-ant-hills-from
Outta their Tea Cups. "O'VE WEE", speaks one man,
"HOW'S THE DREAM FIXTURED IN THIS SPECIAL SINGE
ON CALLING WINDING ROAD," speaks another man.
The ant hills' ruins are taken out at a dusk, the Starkness
Of the high risen flames against the banal suburb housetop
Skylines is the greenback for the parliament to take their
Places.

And For, Upon the bell that ushers in the Parliament Members'
Mealtime, And Then their seats are taken in the eatingroom.

The meal consists sluggishly of a loaf of bread which is a
Molded replication baring similarity to the likeness of Heads at
Easter Island, It is carried down by a goats milk full chalice.

During the meal the parliament is shown a 'THEME SLIDE
SHOW', the title is 'THE SEXUAL ASPECTS OF
CHILDHOOD', the Parliament Men Learn Something which
Hadn't ever actually occurred to the lot of Them: It is not
Uncommon for 13teen&14teen year old boys to masturbate as
Much as 6times a day upon first discovering masturbation:
Then one of the slides shows a young girl tightening her corset,
Though the next slide is to show the corset positioned by itself
On a large gold platter, And the next slide shows that it's
Swarming with ants. The Parliament Men find themselves both
Gravely taken back and faced with most vigorous offense, The
Decision is made among them that as of this date onward, No
Slide shows can be shown at mealtime unless having been
Looked over by a notary public.

I DO BELIEVE, AND HAVEN'T YET GOTTEN A HOLD
ON MY PRIDE: MIDDDLE REA-

Rea takes pleasantly to the habit of driving to-and-fro about
The suburbs, stopping in front of which ever home she takes to
Her fancy and taking a photograph of the front of it. She's got
To get out of the car to frame the picture correctly, And Too, at
Times when those inhabitants of the home see somebody in

Front of their house with a camera, the first thought which
Occurs is what-in-the-hell-is-this-person-doing-, maybe some-
One-from-the-state-who-has-come-to-tax-them-evenmore-.
Rea Has been fast enough on her feet to get back in her car
Before the house owners can get their hands on her, only once
Has she been caught, an obese man held her arms behind her
Back, took the film out of her camera, said that he never
Wanted to see her face around here again. And Though, on
The luckier times when Rea gets away with a good picture,
Upon receiving its printed copy, she's got a bedroom album
Where she places the photographs, next to them she writes a
Short story that details what her life might be like or for that
Matter what type of person she'd be if she'd lived in those
Homes with different families, finally as a different person. Rea
Loses interest in this hobby after disclosing that it is just a way
For her to delve into her self-hatred. She finds in a matter of
Days a quite different hobby. This hobby involves her
Hiding out by those creek beds and little wooded areas
Which are sometimes in parts of the suburbs, The rules
Are that she can take no change of clothes and eat only the
Food she can scavenge. All she takes with her is a
Small-draw-stringed-bag the type which a compact camping
Pillow is usually placed in-cheating a little by taking 3 things,
A small bar of soap, a tiny cylinder containing toothpaste,
And a suffice number of tampons which fill-the-bag-full.

She spends 3nights around a the creek-bed-spot-, living
Off wet grass, and some hopefully not poisonous berries.

The tender solemn of this spot gave her an urgency to depart
To a new place in less then a series of 4weekdays. She found
Her new spot to be a neighbor's garage, though this went
Directly against the rules of her game, she justified it by having

The children(whose parents owned the garage) bring her food
And water, act like she was a stray cat, not telling their parents
That she's living in their garage. After doing this for 1weeday,
A weekend, 3moreweekdays, she returned to her home
Entirely filthy, out of toothpaste, less then half a bar of soap,
And 4less tampons. Ushering herself immediately to her
Shower. And Too, taking a sadness for the aspect that her
MUM hadn't even been aware of her absence, she thought she

Might redirect her actions towards picture taking, that being a
More congenial hobby, And Though, she was never to carry
This out, having for a longer time to come to a distraction with
The not-leaving- home-simplistic of plain daydreaming.

HOME SPUN ANOMALY

More-Say I, how they're wanting, too- Magick country summer
Is herein to play the bigger part of this. Where Stephanie
startsEach day walking a path down the high hillsides going
through
A deep valley. Losing all impressionability of Their realization
Of how-to-them-she has always-appeared-to-be-.
In the high hillsides cottage, Stephanie keeps the water clock.

Referred to as that because of the likeness of streams and
Waves that've been carved and painted on it-Upon each hour,
It plays an enchanting music and dwarves carrying drums and
Flutes march around it in a circular motion, this ceases at the
One minute past the hour mark.

And Too, contrary to all others' beliefs-the solitude is far
From the downside of Stephanie's life at this point- the worse
Thing is the work, Her having to pick berries, grow a lot of
Her own foods, carry pails to get water from a spring-
The trip for water is the longest hardest trek, she leaves early
In the morning-a path thru the thicker woods to the spring,
Which was grown over upon her arrival in the high hillsides,
Is now again a walking path- She takes two pails, also a small
Thermos that she can strap to her waist-A certain tree catches
Her attention each day-it is sprung from the ground more than
Half way to the spring- Its reasons for attracting Stephanie
Might be the exuberant carving on its trunk-Which details a
City's square on a crowded day-the details have been expertly

Carved right down to the facial features of individuals-
Stephanie takes a peculiar coherency in the idea of being
Reminded of where she came from to get to here, And Too,
Each morning of this task-one of the faces looks implicitly
Familiar- A man Stephanie can recall from some part of her
Past in the city-The Rumbit Walkway-the colossus inscribed
In her look-out-over the city, The Days, Days- Seated on the
Bench placed atop on the lain cobble of the Highwall-

And Too, heard somebody calling out, as they got closer
To her, she realized that she hadn't ever seen them before-
A man in an overcoat, gave an apology for taking her for
Somebody else- And Though, came to ask if he might
Take a seat next to her, she kindly obliged. They both
Sat there on the bench, both got to look-out-over-the-city.

Saying that he thought her to be his niece and that was why
He shouted out, she did not believe him, And Though, acted
As if she did, figured just a person wanting company-
Threw something to the pigeons that landed near their feet-
Spoke of the city, stretched out his arm to point towards
Certain places there, Surprised Stephanie by leaving before
Her, nodded her a good day-
Walks past the tree, after the resonance slips from her.

On the remainder of pathway to the spring the forest's
Foliage is heavily thick atop. If the day is overcast in this
Part of the forest it seems that it is nearly the nighttime.

On a clearer day, beams of light break through some of
Separation points in the leaves of the forest's ceiling.

Stephanie totters with the two pails, the light hitting the
Forest floor has the layout of prismatic camouflage.
She regains her footing, walks the last section of the pathway.

And Too, arrives at the spring. Gets footing on some of the
Small stones which have gathered around the moist thick
Mud by the spring. Kneels down to fill the first pail, and
Afterwards proceeds to do the same with the other pail.

Sits them in the grass nearest the spring's throve- takes
The thermos off the strap that she'd fastened to her waist.

Unscrews its cap, And Too, fills it full-attaches it back to
Her waist strap-gets the pails, steps back upon the path,
Heading towards the high hillsides-

OBVIOUSNESS STACKED-UP

The Parliament Members attempt a comparison.

They've brought out a scale to aid them in the weighing of
Two things, A taxidermic tembo head, And A sparkling
Diamond, Which excites the members all-the-more-when they
Come to Learn that it was once hanging around the neck of
Royalty . The tembo head Is placed on the scale first, And Too,

The diamond is placed on-the parliament members feel a Moment's anticipation, their mouths watering a bit with the Eagerness of what object will out weigh the other-And Then, They've now encountered a grievous disappointment when it Comes-to-be-seen-that the tembo head just barely out weighs The diamond, And Too, they were not aware that the Taxidermist had placed many coins inside of it.

FOR TONITE, LATE TOO(SCENE FROM A KEYHOLE, THE HORRIBLE THINGSWHICH HAVE BEEN DONE)- {1.}- Azre watches his own image on a video monitor as he is taking preparations. He has stood a video camera on   tripod in the left hand corner of the apartment's dressing room-Plontif, who sweeps the floor of the den down to nearly the last blemish-a hotly cloistered apartment-The Den Is laid as such that all of the modern conveniences Have been gathered together, pushed to one side of the room, tightly cramped. After this had been done, the remaining space is filled with the following items, a whale's skeleton, a cartouche, tembo tusks- " The worst even doesn't last that long,"- "it too has gotta have an end,"

NODUS: THE SIDE OF THE FACE & THE APPREHENSION
      FROM THE CLOVEN FOOT-

{2.} There in the den, Plontif watches a video cassette of images of coastal lines—It has been edited so that random verses are sent across the screen, to join-in-part-how-the-repetition of the water's movements can release an incognizant crescive dirge. "The worst even doesn't last long,"-   "it too has gotta have an end,"-" like a sing-a-long to've let time's passing cohere,"- "The meatly stars, pivotal joust- the grand buffet loins have, the pyramid gives pace and lonely quails, too visions,"- Azre lifts they plate which covers the dressing room's door's keyhole-downstairs he can hear a big howl in their building's lobby-telling Plontif that he trust that he has taken the necessary precautions-"O' one of these days, visions too," – closing the apartment door, make-way to the lobby-

{3.} A woman on all-fours, masturbates herself with a Christmas tree angel ornament-A blue river runs around the lobby furniture, -"Take a little lacy, darkest visions too,"- muddy

79

footprints are pointed to the door-out-of-the-building-"Those delicate hoof prints are also made all over the walls and the attendant's desk," –" Here we required the mark of somewhat a satanic abbreviation," "Carte blanche, start over,"-"O' one of these days, too many visions,"- close the apartment door proceed to the lobby-There's a crystal ball, with fuming red hues surfacing inside of it-There's particular sofas that have been covered with plastic, to void spill stains- The Gypsy Princess behind the crystal ball, asks the Azre & Plontif which girls they want, tells them it's on the house- Apprehensive in the facevalue of the two not seeing any Woman, only Our Gypsy Princess, who's got to grant wishes To whoever gets the longest straw,- " Kayo," &-"Kendal Green,"-Closing the apartment door-steps the way down to the lobby-entirely vacant, as ordinarily there is no attendant at this hour-the howling sound comes from a small cube that had been placed on the attendant's desk as a gag, when it's shaken it also gives a cow's mooing sound effect-steps the way back up to the apartment from the lobby-opens the apartment door-closing the apartment door behind them-step the way through the den's course of obstacles to the dressing room-caresses his thumb on the seam of Plontif's jeans- unclipping their top button-Reaches his hand to where he's made his way past his pubes to've got his hand holding Plontif's testicles- Taking his jeans down, a joint effort-Also taking his clothes quickly off-falling back down to The bed, Looking up to see Plontif directly above him,Stretching a prophylactic on-over his erection-commencing There upon a orphic love---"O' on my way, my heart, my heart, O' hide it a way, a love a palea a restitute , my heart, my heart, O' on my way,"-

CHIMERA TEACUP

The best that I can do here, Stephanie is fac'd with trot of the more ordinary lifetime. She's discovers herself as a guest at an afternoon teatime-Wore a pink prom dress, is creepingly out-of-time- flumps a dice like succession of sugar cubes into her teacup and has got to make it through this as the plainly good listener-Has a crumpet, then is goodly excused for her passage to the ladies room-Has got to polish a few blemishes on her nose, using a powder fluff--- finds this opulently implicit-checks b'tween the crevices of her teeth for the remaining crumpet bits- makes the step-passage back to the teatable- nods mostly the answers to what she gets ask'd, happily can-do-so for the evaluation that they're most calm yes&no responses: if she were to verbalize them-Therein the dull teatime margins, she's gotten least 2 sacred glimmers-and the ideal of their occurrences in subsequent file, is her saving grace, visions too,- Teatime's later verses- Stephanie being a bit bored -looks down To her cup, at her tea- happy to've seen a chimera there- Strolling in a crisply flaming landscape-flumping her scaly tail to Stephanie, who perks her lips in a kissblowing motion to reflect a return greeting-she does this in a fastway-'cause knowing it'll be maybe mistaken as malignance by the teatable's sitters- looking up from her cup, and seeing the sitters still bursting, their self-enthralling echoes amongst themselves-Stephanie's mental state is emerged in a thuddle wrought Daydreaming- In the wide windows 'hind the sitters, through The half un-drawn curtains, there she sees a phoenix fly'ng-Therest a emerald green florescence in its empennage- Its breast and underbelly are formed as a fan tracery, Colored by a phantasmagoric assemblage of red and Orange hues-that sparkled to such a degree that it left Stephanie seated alone for a time at the teatable after The sitters had departed, for the reassembling of herself-

TOO LATE, TONITE....TOO LATE

'TREES SONGS'
   -Can't you be as free as the star on its way-
   -O' gain-This more-O' gain-This more-
   -Can't you be as free as the sail on its wind-
   -O' canned for the rustle atop the tree branches trove-
   -O' gain-This more-O' gain-This more-
   -O' can't you be as free as salivated water's urge-
   -O' canned for the rustle atop the trees branches trove-
THE BISHOP'S HOWLACE: WE'RE LOOKING FOR THE MONSTER TRUCKS, IS THIS WHERE THEY LAND THE AIRPLAINS: EBBEY'S GOTTEN ANOTHER DREAMBOW - He places a cardtable(having removed the table legs) atop his head, fastens it under his chin using twine-A group of pixies

play blackjack up there, with their legs folded in lotus position-
This occurs as Ebbey takes an afternoon stroll through the
downtown area-Plans to catch a picture show-" Whats ever on,
and Whats ever looks decent,"-He receives sneers from the
other theater patrons- As He pays his ticket price, and takes
himself into the movie-Luckily for Ebbey that last row of seats
are against a wall, This will enable him to slouch down in the
seat, put the Back part of the table against the wall, give his
neck a rest, And keep the cardtable level so that the pixies can
continue Their game without sliding off the table: if it weren't
level-The pixies disturb the rest of the cinema patrons 'cause of
their Constant glowing, the audience's complaint is that it's
distracting their attention from off the cinema and making them
turn around to look at the back of the theater, 'cause when the
pixies reach a high level of excitability they're known to give a
vastly luminous glow, now this at one point-and deep into the
film's better part-grows so bright that it's like the audience is
watching the film without the lights being turned down-The
cinema manager unkindly asks Ebbey to please leave the
cinema, Ebbey wouldn't usually leave without giving back a
argumentative counter point-Though maybe for the cinema
manager's luck- Ebbey doesn't want to disturb his friends,
them being atop his head and all-So he leaves, and even
without his admission price being refunded-DON'T TIP THE
DREAMBOAT OVER-Ebbey wakes one morning, and attaches
slabs of Meat to his body, on his inner thighs and all over His
chest and backside-This is for protection-What have you, a
makeshift body armor, which he will Deeply come to need
today—"The Alma Matter's Tournament," Ebbey and other
boys from town have decided to hold this in A neighborhood
baseball field, They can see no better place Than HERE to
draw a crowd on a brighter summer day--- The boys will play
renaissance reactivists: "Right here, Today too,"- The squad
gun fires off the starter flare, and the Boys dispense from their
pits, riding on saddled ostriches- Holding staves directly
pointed at each others chest,-Ebbey Cleverly had felt this
premonition of being taken down- And when the opponent's
weapon greets his breast plate, A sogging pluff sound is
echoed back from the meat's Purposed absorbed as that it

were a sheath-Ebbey Commandingly turns the ostrich around, and gaining Speed, now in the turnaround of where he firmly holds the Stave. Severing his opponent's head completely from his body-

Blood spurts from the splitpoint of where the head has been Separated from the neck, in a flooding comparable to that Of a firehose. As Ebbey steps down from the ostrich, the Father of the deceased rushes from the stands, and't is Coming out from behind the dugout, -As Ebbey turns around He receives A Blow from the stone which was held by the--- Man--Ebbey falls to the ground- the man pounds the stone into--his forehead, blood obscures Ebbey's sight, A deep ringing phasing to silence— 3.

RESTFUL PRISONER-In his bedroom he converts a long red towel into a cape through the use of a safety pin- He parades 'round mockingly in the form of a super hero- Puts on an adult diaper, and squats on the floor in the attribution of soiling it-"Ah, the pleasure of shitting oneself in the more adult years,"-A reason for celebration, after accomplishing his task-He discovers when looking in the dressing mirror that he's Taken on the appearance of a New Year's Eve baby, But one whom is the possessor of a hotly rising fecal Stench-pulls of the diaper and places it in the bucket of Seaweed which he keeps beside his bed, thinking that Ought to nullify the stench 'til he can conventionally throwaway-The diaper-"Too bad it's not made of cloth, though in a sadder Moment I will urge it onward to its longer life in some dither-free Landfill, might be lucky to wind its way at the bottom of one of The Grand Canyon's crevices," – Now he continues to his Evening hobby of wrapping a distaff – He marks an hour which He calls quiet time, this is where he tries to solve a Rubik's cube That has been occupying a less/extra amount of his spare time for the last several summers, He gets it down to one blemish, every side matches nearly; EXCEPT for a blue square he cannot get out of the red square side- He gives this occupation only one hour and sometime a little-less, having at times forgotten of its frustration for weeks-THEN he experiences one day during this, A clairvoyant note-It is on a train trip through the western states that he'll come to complete this puzzle-It is there too, that he may search also for a remnant of his summer diaper, though solemnly he will see that it has taken the needed steps In its liquefaction-- solemnly he will see that it has taken the needed steps In its liquefaction--

TREE SONGS- SELECTION NUMBER TWO

-Roast abode the nettles-O' hide-Risen abide the merchant--O' hide-vagrant promenade-Frozen atide the allusion spurts-- Roast abode the nettles-O' festive clam shell-flood the- merchant's steady footing-Risen abide the way which is-shown as were the safety mark in the tree branches trove-Roasted the staunch neither aqua bell--O' too-O' hidden, ---they're shown as the safety mark in--the tree branches trove-

TREE SONGS OF THE ILL BRED PERNICIOUS SOUNDREL

-Aim sour grape staves O' coolly hearted soliloquist-
-Supervenient is not perforated-O' coolly hearted soliloquist-
-Please give thine word of honor- A courage amongst perishing populations-O' offer the fruit laps to the down trotted mother's wounds-And all thine permits to let lose in the tree branched trove-TOO, LET GO, UP I GO-Rea intends to live vicariously. Bridge a vetch to the darker crisp magick. Wearing a haik,-" I'm onto the visual fields,-" "American",- Rea, Rea,- Someone there too, I can put up a big trust, now the night clerk, a place beside, there was no way, a place, asides they're to tower a splash,- Who is this,-{1.} a long responsibility, to be held 'fore substantive halt here hastily to be there too,-it,-can it be two,- and too dispassionate,-"Am I used to where with things raged as people coming off with the easy answers,-"

MYSTERIES

Farther out through the water, Her face isn't Entirely distinguishable,-I did not see it thoroughly 'til she sat on the deck, wrapped her breast, stomach, and back in a towel,-vision is successively reached through a daft tag to the water's top,-In sequence, in kind, is that known,-"Whilom, from time-to-time anything you like,-changes feelings through the whigmaleerie",- -"You don't got to wait",- said Ebbey,-"Not for the time",--Has he approximated the whims, sent the flaws away,--In the clearing he splits open the bag of feathers, douses them there on the ground with his urine,-Non-interruption of the rite,-There is never asked,-"As how can any man say that,"- -The early whim series consists of all of his hates, and his bad tastes,- deliver those off accompanied with a puritanical saliva, and a quantity of tail feathers masquerading on his ears,- "Loss of the hard loss, to shelter in the thicket the life crutch, innocently perfected by long-in-coming-tears moving slowly in the another way an not an impure tassel, it is the long carry over from the act of bride & groom, how slow, slow, slow it took Ebbey throughout the long summer to clench an edible dither in the grommet of this Fall's sabbat,- His fluids let-go in a runnel flooding down his legs,-having covered his body in rosin",- "Here is the sworn return benefit of the wisest practitioner,-A clipping is onward in if his stature, slashing what ever he has thought, felt , and known of his physical and psychological perceptions, states, and stability,-An incredibly harming yet warming flame glows thoroughly underneath his first layer of skin, his pupils are also clouded by a smog which soon ignites to a flame,-his figure aflame from toe-to-head in a Moon illuminated clearing, he is burnt beyond disfigurement to the-would-be-end of his physical state of existence, what remains of him in the clearing is a singeing pile of ashes,- A strengthened breeze rolls them out from the clearing, its gust splashes them to a probably infinity",- A stillness older then time's origins is held for a longtime in the clearing,-In the mess of feathers that Ebbey had scattered and pissed upon, the circumference of where they lay turns significantly damp, from under the top layer of earth a surge of water roughly disperses,-gushing, soaking the entire spot,-A unified fertilization,- The ground caves in, a pond soon takes The place of where Ebbey's physicality had climaxed,-The Light Of the moon beams directly down onto the pond's surface,- Which fizzles, a solid shape comes from below the pond, urged by a force which delivers it directly from out of the water,-A soaked figure lies gasping, choking mildly on water, next to the pond,- it is Ebbey, sent back to physical existence from the spot of his exit from it,-His eyes after not understanding, only half remembering the Transformation which has taken place,- Gleaming pupils Strobed by the moon's lighting,-He is the young man Which had unknowingly taken leave,- But with the skin and Pigment of an infant,-Baffling to him to live once, die and Return, here to see this all again with new eyes,-Ebbey Realizes a danger in the knowledge of a developed adult mind experiencing birth, and in there some how knowing the outline of the life process,-And Too, to've been born through Earth itself,-Reels for the major portion of an hour in the moon Light,-before realizing the chill he's got from having come from The cold earth up through the pond's water,-He thinks he might Remember the way out of the forest and home to suburbs,-

OSCILLATE

The moon's light is bright enough in places for Ebbey To find his way out of the forest,- startling to him that he Even has a sense of direction after tonight,-He finds his Way to the road, a country road, a backway to his home,-Unlike the forest's clearing, out here on the road it is very dark sometimes In long stretches,- Ebbey feels fear, humorously thinks, " for the First time in my life",-'Long the side of road down by a creek bed, he detects a glowing, Upon closer sight he sees there are several men, the tallest of them probably comes up to about his ankle. By watching them make their way along the creek side, he is able to safely make his way through the darker stretches of the road,-now on the main road which runs the way through the beginnings of the suburbs,-A problem,- He is walking in a residential neighbor, unclad And very soiled by mud,- trying to do this a quickly as he Could in this state of mind,-It is unfortunate that he would Encounter a squad car, red & blues awhile strobe his field Of sight,-They've spotted him in their headlights after receiving Calls about a person streaking in the district,-The 2nd time, he feels displacement,-and anxiety,-3 feelings thus for the first night of his 2nd life,-The police not understanding the circumstances, had thought that it may require significant amount of force to bring this man in,-After stopping Ebbey, and then seeing his age: that is thought less-though questioning leads them nowhere,-They wrap him in a blanket, classifying him as a disoriented youngster,-figuring he's downed a quantity Of alcohol or street drugs,-Ask him if can remember who he is, And where he lives, his pupils suffer significant irritation when They're examined with a small flashlight,-appear to the police To be slightly dilated,-He's taken home in the squad car-Looking out through its back window he sees the short Glowing men gesturing to him,-The police walk him to the Front door of his home,-repeatedly ringing the bell,- 'til Hetts Answers it,- He too is questioned and threatened, about papers, examinations, child abuse too,- police depart from Ebbey's home,-Hetts says little, eager to return to bed,- Ebbey also retires to his bed in his present soiled state,-

NOCTURNAL EVIDENCE: DREAMS HAD BY E.F.-Re-vaults, a judgment in the corpus procedure, a uniquely Large tooth is found in the drawing room, a red stepladder Is leaned against it-The steps up to the tooth evidently end Abruptly. On contrary, the tooth's enamel turns to a gel-type film this thus allows the

the curious to enter-finding themselves--------Inside, here, they've grown the height of a taller-city-building- This is known to them as they look down at the fright they give to those of ordinary height on the ground below them-Re-vaults to've one partaking the procedure of a place where One fits in, finally too. Exodus from the birth canal, later discovering in a photobook That his umbilical cord appears to be a candy cane in the Photograph which he is shown-Doors open up in clean air, Sees Hetts step from them, one in particular opens above A peculiarly long red light-Hetts comes from it, down to the City street, and hurries quickly away-walking out later, sees Hetts come up from a manhole, wailing violently, hurries Quickly away-he follows Hetts to a loft which he assumes Hetts has Kept for sometime(unknowingly to E.F.), knocks on the door, is let in by Hetts- Inside he has got many farm animals, Tells Ebbey that he abides the sanitation laws, so he is able to keep these here because of that. Notions to Ebbey to stay for dinner- Serves him a large stuffing filled octopus-Before it can be cut & served-a seam splits open on it, 5 men whose height is to about E.F.'S ankles- run out of the octopus, knocking things from the table-Dinner having been a letdown, Hetts tries to make-it-up to Ebbey by showing him a film,-The film is titled 'Cosmos Proceedings'- It begins as two boys are cleaning their bedroom closet, find a long dark passageway in it, they assumingly walk thru this by holding their hands against the sides of passageway walls, this is an awful part of the film 'cause it is done in a long take, and the viewer must nearly sit through 8 minutes of complete darkness and barely any suffice audio, nearing the 7 minute mark-A small shining light appears on the screen, the camera keeps Moving toward this 'til the picture is completely glared-There's A CUT and the two boys are now standing at the French Riviera. The next segment of film, is a two hour still-life, A reproduction of a Carvaggio, using unmoving live models----This deeply irritates Hetts and Ebbey, they commence to Fast forward through this painfully dull sequence to the film's--------ast passage,-This segment also clocks in at a marathon------Length,- bordering on somewhat of 5hours,- it details---Some------person's----- voyage to an-- uncharted tropic, ---and---- their---- supposed discovery of paradisal conditions, nymphs, satyrs, lush scenery,- for an hour this is delightful, though for the next four of nearly the same thing,-it becomes impeccably trite,- Forcing Hetts to fast forward this, also,- The take a look at another tape,- Titled 'The True Story Of Last Summer',-The fact that it closely follows the margins of the horror genre makes it much Easier for Hetts and Ebbey to cope with,- this picture's plot involves a man taking a job as a department store Santa but losing his position after biting a child's ear off,-this film also comes a major let-down to Hetts and E.F.,- They give up it on half of the way through its running time,- they've got another tape,- this one is titled 'Peninsula' it tells of a man who is an arsonist,- after setting the fires,-The next day he reads of them in the morning paper,- Where they are continuously attributed to a toaster oven short fusing,- Hetts and E.F, see this to be a nil,-Hetts shows Ebbey a video that he's shown to no others yet,- Hetts's own tape,- which Ebbey figures will be not much other than a simple home movie,-Goodly surprising that its features will surpass, and too make up for the 3prior follies,-The tape is footage Hetts took while in the catacombs 'neathThe White house,-thru its musk,-he photographs omens: Black cats, Black dogs:,- He photographs secrets,- But mainly Focuses on close-ups of the documents which explain UFO abduction and Hairy humanoids: This tape entertains Ebbey vigorously, He thanks Hetts for a pristine father & son evening: THE MURKIER KNOCK TURN ALL: EBBEY'S

ELLIPSIS DREAMS: E.F. discovers himself quite capable of growing anything he Desires from his own body,-starts out by doing simple things,-Such as growing fruit from his arm pits,- uniquely, some small Bananas start sprouting out of them,-He comes to discover that these don't taste any different from any others,-so they are not in any sense poisonous etc...,-He grows several more things from himself,- peaches from his lower back,- loses control a little, and sprouts a pumpkin from his anus,- Moves ahead to bigger things,- Growing(secretly) dollar bills on his inner thighs,-coins out of his groin,- smartly doing this in places which no-body will see,-so that no-one will try to abuse his power and use him for it,- Even Oddly for as far as this power goes,- he discovers,--- that he is fully capable of anal child birth,-As a typified heavenly visage,- he discovers himself fully pregnant,-Just like the average,-he carries the child for 9months,-though only sort of,-a displacing occurrence takes place half of the way through the pregnancy,- On certain days,- Instead of morning sickness,-or a badback,-or swollen ankles,- He transforms into other objects on those days,- the coldest Feelings stems from him finding himself to sometimes be Inanimate objects,-Once he was a broom,-which was completely grading,-another time he was a Venus flytrap,- The most implicit time he discovered himself as Satet,- He not know what to make of any of these assumed identities,- The latter was obviously the most congenial,- The others Were as self-ironies, and filled their parts as such,-He Juggled the 3 personas for the remainder of the pregnancy 'til transforming back into himself as he went in to labor(still a broom before that),- Had a flawless quick delivery,-hoped for the closure of this savageness,-His shifting and growing did suddenly cease,- though after planting his placenta sac.- his problems arose,- from its burial place a secular tree up-sprung,- Its trunk that was made of flesh,-and too possessed a birth canal,-too granted Ebbey's wishes,-brought them forth in unselective manner,- it gave Ebbey things from the backpart of his conscious,- particular things: A giant snail: A series of toys which came-to-life- during the witching hour And roused Ebbey awake as they chanted his name,-Once pleasantly the tree brought him Satet,-Though after a short chat she voluntarily departed,- Having found the qualm of self-growth problems,- Just a thing that she'd heard before,- His newborn Also oddly was a toy sotospeak, it's made of wood-This badly splintered his anus when delivering it,-But he was to love his newborn son,-and affectionately Name him 'Derkybee Splendor,'- While Derkybee was Probably 4 months old,- One quiet evening when Ebbey Was rocking him to sleep by the firelight,- Hetts arrived,-He walked in the house, sat down,- sprang up and began Devouring the silverware and plates,-He swallowed the Staircases and the home's walls and floors,- Ebbey Hurried out with Derkybee in his arms,- They stood on the Lawn,- seeing the house devoured,- Hetts stood in its Remains,-then walked over to Ebbey,- lifted his shirt,- Revealing a panel on his chest that had a painting of the Mona Lisa,-there was a handle on it which he told Ebbey to open,- Ebbey did so,- Inside there were was Santa Claus's Workshop,-He was checking lists,-as his elves were making Toys,-EBBEY awoke from this looking up at his ceiling,- Where he saw a large garden spider,- He took a glass of Water off of his bedside dresser,- stood up on the bed and Trapped the spider inside of it,- cuffed his hand over the Glass top,- took the spider out to the front yard to let it go,- Went back to the bedroom,-too stirred to return to sleeping,-

FIN OF CHAPTER 'C'

CHAPTER 'D'

CENTENNIAL PIPES

Receipt of plain drawn lines, under the cards,-just hours,-Under the cards,-just hours,-with my head against the bed Posts,-I see her leaning sleeping body,-petals perforate up Underneath her skin,-partake the rite of bloom there on her Bosom.-The pubic hair kept neatly groomed above her vulva Lips, too becomes tulips,-Amongst the thicket of crowds,- Where all who are there appear as if they were closing in on,-Goodly knowing when one must get away,-

LYCANTHROPY

The whistle over the coats, and too, it's graciously going Its god-passaged way on the black nights,-I saw why I Had died this long,-met---myself in the water-puddle that Gathered decently high,-I saw the sweetest blossoms in My older age,-which I oddly had taken for change in a Youth,-songs just under the cards,-be weeks,-Wednesdays,-Just hours,-under the cards,-the sweeter blossoms in their Gaining nil,-Puts himself up to great height atop the hills,-To the govern of the pastures,-letting out there,-is the Swayed freedom lose finally,-

Setting off,-to the puncture Line,-in the grinding gulf,-3 now makes a clan,-shouting in the firelight,-There's a   dither in there,-somewhere in the shortest springtime,- this world is adoringly lit with its own crown-kisses cast over the body of youth,-and on its side,-afraid of its whistle,-That nothing need be spoken,-in the toughest going,-the shouts risen higher in the blazing firelight,-forgave the best instant, the known what will be existence,-craving the holly good,-craving the holly good,-take that out carefully,-some will never know what   you've meant by that,-The freely echoes the pastoral   epitaphs then drawn in anticipated wealth to bore the   laziness bonnet,-that supports the curls in the hidden re-imagining,-All split lose,-the pass for verse reigns   acquit,-the piping is done when glanced therein on two boys who sat silent at an evening table,-All split,-under the cards,-the hours one realized them as having been   shouted,-The older tassel one finds that it remains,- Snows fluent send on the hyper weight,-foamed this   Up and coming tile matte lull,-The councils taken shelters And their homes here in the finer wood clearings,-under The thick branches sometimes,-they no longer feel The bottom to what if the trunks make the covering fall Decided in some minute of the night,-waking and moving,- Covering ground quickly,-a worthy assessment of hiding Their tracks and so in the last couple of days,-which are   Now the weeks,-after the snows,- are the months,-and then Put into the tales of the gone pasts,- The earth we cover now Will be made as the lesson for others doing the same,-I learnt from you,-to pick apart the matted grass Atop the overcovered route that leads me to a   Desire of leaving,-Then staking a claim,-is a grip On me,-the answers will be the lovers of the holly Good,-how you return later,-Clear parts are then Covered on foot when departing happens around   Dawn,-2points must be taken between,-in a certain Value,-so that we can arrive in the desired ONLY Spot prior to nightfall or shortly after,-At times we Kept moving throughout the entire night 'til the Next dawn, that day 'til its dawn,-that night,-the   Next entire day,-stopping just shortly before its Nightfall,-setting again out at the sunlight's breaking Second,- The tracks covered,-and we look back upon   Seeing how all of our time here has came carefully Together,-this journey itself is a sole entity,-This log Of it ceases on the first snowmelt,-but starts up after A unsubstantive spring,-delivers us from its start to End point of too short, yet longer than spring,-Summer,-napping 'neath the weighted down flower Petals,-bending, scraping first softly,-then much harsher,- When picked up by the steady wind,-This occurs during A lapse,-a pause before returning back on my departing,-I'm framed as if I were in a lens, in a wide foreground,-There I am in great haste to be delivered from clear view,-Moving off to some of the high woods aside pathway,-Accompanied by my sole heavy breathing,-I hear the Rustling of half remembered conversations come through the Wood behind,-Beautiful voices,-ripe faces,-A girl who takes Off her gown,-places a crown of flowers in her hair,-stands There alone in the secluded sight,-spinning,-dancing,-Not for anybody else,-they can not see how she is feeling,-I remember this as the only one looking,-could there have Been others looking too on the field's other ends,-I see her Soft fresh figure asleep there,-and I see one hundred sparkling Eyes flickering from out of the trees,-I see her soft perfect figure toss,-I see a human heart torn from a body,-stuck to a tree off to the side Of the field,-still beating,-each of its blips,-drives my focus more Directly onto the girl's body,-a succulence is reserved,-though I'm interrupted as the snow again pounces down from the woods ceiling to be there on my nape,-I step out from the high woods,-Start again quickly down the path,-This time hopefully able to move at a fast enough rate to feel as if the wind were carrying me on my heels,-enabling me to put back the fear of being followed,-and too, the hardest is if being followed then not knowing by whom,-Later I see that the springtime starts again,-and too, having completed the previous winter journey in only my own,-company,-I stand still,-the lapping the troth of the clear stream,-bursting from out of the ice which is meeting with its dissolution,-HOLLY MOSROLL-Passing down Green Dragon Alley,- a figure bounds Forth,-Spats a flame scathe,-is happy just to see you smile,-Up over high things,-surrounds people,-leaps way from mobs,-Is at the door,-Where he says he's got the beast,-lying: He's Done this to you all for the fright's sake,-tears your dresses,-Tears your dresses,- is happy to see you smile can see a Little more too,-puts himself forth to just only slap your face And bottom,-is happy to see you romantic,-Passing down Green Dragon Alley,-hisses the wildest cat in the brightest Orange dress,-flutters up to just see you smile,-nobody Stops passing down Green Dragon Alley,- I scurry over the rooftops there with the devil on my Heels,-is how I see it,-of time,-of the father who's in my Waking grains,-in Limehouse,-the devils heels,-Again I See your smugly coarse suitcase,-with so many matters Perforating its locks,-Carry it down Green Dragon Alley,- I've been down to the passed byes,- Am I home now therein The last,-We will talk, and too, for free,-The eternity of here,-It's the walls,-it's the streets of every single last city,- Where I'm relaxed when people I've never seen get together,- Go,-Go,-The rain shines on mine,-our lullaby in the front porch mornings,-Slip from where the earth is corn dusts,-The rain shines on mine, me,-I see the old rocker's sway,-the roses grew through the fine steppes where I'd fallen,-the snows shine you to colors,-it's the dismal silvers,-go better off,-When is Mother,-When is mother,-our one,-old father's got the new Loping,-where earth he's crossed is let gone corn dusts,- You had got to let it weigh dull,-They'll hold her in their arms,-The 3 have got the bounce down-patted,-I've come there With much time on my hands,-left with the snows colors to You that point the weeds from the way,-silence to take every Other man's happiness,-hey now,-hey now,-Used to the wild Holly men,-got presents got time on their hands, and too,-Their Life joys,-O' do this again,-Drawn up by the wagon in the steadily hovering speed,-says that this is the weapon that brings truth,-the thing that likes to show, to see you again,- Builds the boring lives,- and too, gets to be you,- Fog dubiously Moistens The furrow marsh,-Then I've found the strangers here In the house,-the speckle of none to care for,-the dower of the Got nothing to love,-the horses tied together tightly must be Driven with head- wind over the furrow marsh,-Is this the bigger Message that they'll deliver that will too tell of my love,-Then Take off from there,-and not care for the place there that defined me,-how I will walk from it and spoke the in-joke of its phantom like ability of changing my life,-O' do this again,-There is the spark, the ripple, the broken lamp,-Which is too, Picked up in little pieces,-

in the horseshoes,- But O' how do I know when smearing it
over me that it is lost,-and I take Off in layers,-shake it before
settling it,-to the place picked Especially for,-does not care if I
say 'don't pick at that to It",-O' here it has come,-in way,-to
Hear most clearly the sealing Of this heirloom,-When asked if
I couldn't know the lay of What has reached the affliction,-to
the fast perfected mother,-

LIKE THE HARDEST VISITERS THAT BLEND

WITH THE LITTLE THINGS WHICH WERE:

MAKES THE DAYTIME TO THEN REMAKE:
ALLUDES THE HOLLY MERGER

There's a picture inside,-The looking is to be outdone,-I am not
compatible,-yet here on the ground I'm able To really fly around
you,-for the last definite time came in The September of 1904,
but he just leaped way-far-too,-Oddly getting ready to see him,-
2wars later,-Once in a Girl's picture,-he shows up there in the
corner behind the Trees he was standing by while she was
eating an ice cream Cone,-then not present in the photograph
'til after its developing,-and once this boy tries to imitate him by
getting on a sheet,-putting springs on his feet,-but just gets
drug away for disorderliness,-maybe some other day,-I can see
that without worrying if whether it will or will not be there,- Might
get to throw open my window,- on some kind of a Date,-
Christmas Eve,-if not another,-I'll see that prancing,- I'll see
that bound and it will momentarily distract me 'til I return To
what I'd been being,-I remember the same time that all of My
few friends will be girls,-that's the way I'll have it,-and I'll Be
able to do so with out taking a sexual interest in them,- Then
thoroughly I'll sense the night is not over,-to mark it,- To mark it
some how like a map,-is that the great thing,- One in a long
black dress which is cut high up on the sides Where it reveals
her entire thighs,-up to the seam of her Underwear,-Placed
here on a continent,- with a bell flower As the reminder of her,-
moving to a different continent,- A girl,-Yes,-a close friend,-
remember her having her hair Cut very short,-I hadn't seen her
in a long time,-clipped her Bangs to one side of her face,-
While walking down the street With her, I have an asinine
realization, -this is so much better Than doing this by myself,-A

man tells that he can't see any Difference,-in what he's doing now in contrast to what he was doing about a decade ago,-I try to persuade him,-though I lose out after he tells me that he can't just chase nothing forever,- A wild kicking horse,-A springy rocking horse,-O' how they'll Both pull me up,-shake me on the scattered stones they step In the shallow stream crossings,-I am reminded of something That I've not thought of in a time,-I sat at a bar,-in the desert,- Arizona,-The walls of the bar are covered with one dollar bills,- It has become tradition and good luck,-for a patron of the bar To place a dollar bill on wall and sign their name on it,-I too do This,-and feel satisfied after stepping back out to the heat outside,-preparing for the long drive thru the desert,-Into the city which I still remember as being a interconnecting series of long strips,-I recall people on the lawns,-some small lakes,-pleasantly,-is it that I recall this 'cause it was the one time which I felt content,-peering from the passenger seat window,-on to things which I felt couldn't see that I was looking on them,-and too, wouldn't remember that I had been,- I tell the discouraged men that I come to meet later on in my life Of these things which I saw here,-though they listen,-I feel a Closure in my self worth for the fact that I fell short in giving A suffice aura of somekind of inspiration,-It is the easy Kind,-the thing I face,-is somekind of other,-that should Be done more often then it is,-and it should always have a Hold on me,-It takes a long loved time to see that I can be,- If it falls in love with just the walls here,-It gathers up sadly When it sees the whole stay was not characterized by people,- But was characterized from solitude,-One which came above Him,-as if he sat on the mattress,-and another essence rose Up to him from behind the walls,-in a native tongue it was to Speak the least funny things,-Somekind of horror,-he told Her when later reflecting,- that if she spent a night there, Then she'd surely lose something,-she sat out to disprove him,-Though as he'd believed; emerged the following day with her Hair having turned entirely gray,-and her body and face appearing to be that she'd aged 50years,-Then we'll see the sun go down,-sometimes that summer it was especially better to sit alone and watch it go down,-A peace surfaces evidently in the onlookers mind, -That summer too, -It was when I was without her and o anybody else,-I saw myself a assured again,-which wasn't strue for me in the longest time, A person who would later become a significant part of my life,-Albeit momentarily,-though he would be given off,-to what was A life not yet to've been foreseen by me in the cress of those Days, they just so quickly went,-Their pride,- and to hope to Keep them hidden,-Then they'd cause an anger,-in more Confrontations,-where I would want to stop and just say that These people could never, never see the blissfulness which I'd underwent,- I'd not let them set me up then just to knock me Down,-I'd keep the spaces between the letters to her short,- Without anything to say, and I would still write,-But I'd not Ever screamed in them the disrupting urge of having been Criticized as not being able to understand,-and then saying I Did, I did, I did,-Lost all of the ways to sign at the end of the Letters,-Take Care,-I am reminded of another thing, I stand at a lookout area,-On the rim of the grand canyon,-I walk past this British couple,-The man is trying to get a picture in proper light,-I know that A video image clouds into my mind of all of these different people grouped together yet ignoring each other,-Then I feel a set lose spirit thinking that I had to get this far,-Here to no longer ignore my-self worth,-but a bad thing too,-Though I was in that spot to lose total interest in half-friends, laying There the burial of scathing acquaintances,-those who would Too put me to rest as soon as they've got better things to do,-Then I walk slowly down to a bench where I could sit and see A lot of the canyon at close to sunset,-by the edge I think everybody who's every been here for some reason if just for a moment thinks about jumping,-or falling off the side of canyon,-thinks of what the fall to bottom would be like,- whether or not half way they'd give up on fear,-and just start preparing themselves to make their own mental finales,- generically thinking probably of all the good times they'd been through in their lives,-I know that I wondered if they'd gone through these, would they've really regretted jumping?,-HOLLY PUTTEE- "A putsch-albeit self abusive,-rings me 'WHAT',-I'm Asked as people assume the worst of my intentions", Said Rea-she spoke this into a small tape recorder,-Picking it up on certain times,-after having went through Exhaustive situations, -Holy thickets were raptured in

97

Rea's speaking voice,-She would tape her awareness of The day,-bleeding off to grounded fiction: a realism,-" to the sides of coarse surfaced road,-was a vast amount of stripped land,-We were looking for the small entrance point,-we missed it the first time by,-so we had to turn back,-drive slowly by,-Parking the car in the grass brim by where the path starts,-Mum and I start moving down it,-the path leads steadily downward,-also must've served as a water runoff,-the degree of heat greatly strengthened on the sections of the path which weren't obscured by foliage; set in direct sunlight",- Some of Rea's speaking parts she reads off note Cards,-has a secret for mixing them up together,-" Depositing of the little world, Chorus sings 'MY LIFE',- Thank the handouts,-depositing the little world,-one of These days,-where nothing matters so you've got to Believe the good byes,-thank the handouts,-you'll Think about me,-Rea plays the awkward first recordings Which she made,-labels the sides of them,-with the date That they were recorded and a code word on the tape,-'SOLELY A MISPLACEMENT'-JANUARY-10-" Apathetic frightening tickets, for the show that'll just give us a test to see if it could go on,-A tiger sprung from the back of its cage to collide with the cage's bars that are being annoyingly rung with a walking stick to entice It,-You've not yet oven seen my bad side,-look how do you leave yet,-it scares me too,- I tell me to get back to the old Rea,-The one that knows how-In-the-hell to lose",-Rea places this tape in the bottom of a crate which is crammed in the back of her closet shelf,-Hoping to the most serious sense,-that she'll not have to ever think of it again,-though there is one in particular which she is fond of,- And plays on a loop as bedtime lullaby,-

---

'RACHEL CORRENTS'-JUNE-25
-I don't lie of the smelling out of the war-
-feel the itch before the bridges-
-if you've thought I've lied of believing the dry cyclone-
-Then I felt the itch before the annotating the marigold-
-enough, enough, enough,-feel the itch before the bridges-
-In the green cloak I see the pond's reflex-
-what's this I'm wearing, enough, enough, enough,-
-to be pushed in by demons-

-I don't lie of smelling out the dower queer oscillation-
-feel the before the bridges-
-If I dld lie before the beguiling/ the standing key-
-enough, enough, enough, before annotated by Milan-
-I don't lie of smelling out the miles a way-

HOLLY IN BARITONE BROUGHT THE WOXX

"All's that we can't be sure unlost grand",-Rea wrote that down in the part of her journal that she called 'Silent Nights'-In the part titled 'Word Keys', She wrote,-"Holded down mutts, every rejecting box",-She hoped that she could splice these riddles together To form a piece which people could make sense of,-Attempted this in parts successfully,-Enough cohesion For her Mum to make sense of it?

FRACTION 1-SUBSIDIARY CANTALOUPES-

-ask for what you need, a little girl told Haless Spade-
-Just legends,-just friends of my mine,-
-two more than the havel wurts-Is there no chaos in what there is-Then I get all the while quiet,-Where I'm fostering the bigger wound,-if you don't ask the late toll-Don't you care? Then that become more out of its intention. A horrific fright it gave Rea's Mum,-who turned her back to Leave Rea's room,-Wanting not a chance to even point its Flaws out to Rea,-Rea had the whole time feared that one Rejection to this piece and her pleasure she took from it Would be gone,-though this she found to be untrue,-A Damn reaction to it,-And Rea set off again, turning back To the tape recorder with a new speech in mind,-

MY HEAD FROM MY HANDS TO CHEST TO STRIKING A PUDDING CHORD- "Becker wore the routine insane....I'll change the color of the lightning on hill when I'm inspired to her felling fax... ...fool represent the disdain of theoretical moorage fugue..but is he too kind to say it to my breasts... I've got feelings too..I've got a intuition too... I've been around long amounts to Simplify a chore boost... I'll chase the blockers from their Stalling posts near the main gate... Then matrimony wonders Why the festivals don't correspond to the annual succession Here as they do other places.. O' my she'll stand here on that Spot.. Then matrimony wonders why she's been

doused with Dollop glue... And why when she gets called foul names nobody ever hears her corresponding ..."

Rea felt this was her greatest success at communicating Displacement,-she took a short pause and then proceeded To planning other works,-While putting down the notes,-She surely saw the shrill poke of if these don't come to Fruition,-But it is not that way?,-to get them done is as always For Rea the reason for anything,-I must get them from out of Planning stages,-for the hope of further motivation she'd Put a small footnote in top left hand corner of the notebook Pages,-she'd always write a short verse,-

---

TACTFUL PARTY DRESS-
-toddle the maturation cities,-in-screwing the tribal marriage-
-Has got a leaflet left, hasn't got a leaflet left-
-then you've made your point-
-acting like I've never seen the city before-
-toddle the Immature fingers-in-screwing the hard cash brotherhood-then you've made your point-

---

STEPHANIE:THE OTHERSIDE OF HER THAT
I'VE HEARD YOU'VE SEEN:

-Those because you ask get in the way-
-Those because you ask dart to diamonds-
-Those because you ask keep me safe from the world-
-Rose 'cause the left word's safe from here to the world-
-O' baby kept the dose cleanliness-
-O' baby kept the dose cleanliness-
-Those because you ask chase her-
-Those because you ask export her too-
-O' along with the kettle-
-O' I don't mind-
-Rose on cheat's weight end up stems has never meant his chase-O' baby kept the dose cleanliness-
-Lore babble on cheat's weight ends up mending a male seam hard on its knees-
'Out of on the low lites the 55 degree spring day you say is identical to the fall of when she'd slowed and left' 'On the miss

cycle 5 days from Melvin doesn't come on darling-from my mouth to your open ears that couldn't tell in the time'
Stephanie didn't take well to the evasive roughing sort. Even back when they started, she lay her arms down to them. Refusal of confrontation; the busy shops; Stephanie had become one of the regular girls after taking up There. You'd meet a lot of fellows, some of which you'd set Off with only from curiosity-Leaving on the back of the motor Bikes-griping your arms around them, sent off in the night breeze-some particularly dis-pleasant boys had their fixings on Stephanie-This was prior to being Wed when she'd have an accepting way to give a NO-They'd wait off to shop's corner,-for Steph to lock the place up-Pull up there to her as she was stepping under the streetlight-When she'd refuse them, they'd ride along very smoothly, mumbling, trying to get her to laugh,-At least they'd give her a ride home-which they could drag out by claiming to've taken a wrong turn?

One of the only rides that she took with them did however turn Out good-not straight home but she hadn't ask them to take her Directly there,-Might as well take her chance at feeling a thrill On one of those,-Speed gaining gave Stephanie the rush which All others get even with the apprehension if they've not ridden One before,-Steady paced speed there when zipping hastily From the shop district,-spinning onto the dark quieter country Roads,-Stephanie looks over the driver's shoulder at the Headlight lapsing over the ground as the speed of bike takes Up even faster,-Dust in her eyes when a turn in the road is Taken quickly,-"To see that now while it maintains a fresh Sense there, not all a bad thing, or times that have a Broken or so confidence",-

STEPHANIE: BYE OUTSIDE HER:
-awakening finally is-
-rejection, no-
-There's I've supposed a fuss here with it-
-awakening finally is-
-proof of it, no-
-There's I've supposed time were a fuss-
-There's I've supposed a work privately, a fuss-

-rejection finally is-
-awakening, no-
-proof of it, yes-
-There's a fail I've supposed-
-that'll be shaking you up-
-if you'd had been still soused-
-awakening yes, proof of it yes, rejection yes-

"Awakening finally the sickening forbidden…I fear there's some words which relate to my behavioral Patterns…they were pinned down there in the blue map…against the contest.. cheating out to all the contestants and standing up and giving them the reverse… Awakening finally the sickening forbidden… care if I am pissed on.. care if I am snickered…what purpose will that really.. they're in to each others' drapery… Awakening finally the sickening zannoose… pinned down to their combining vines finalizing the sick nurse's effort.. "

They took her on a long loop along the roads outside The city,- It wasn't for a moment a chore,-on some of The straight bursts she realized the freedom they must Feel when they're soaring out here,-Though she wanted To go back home,-They gave her an invitation for a Place they'd be going to meet friends and where they too Planned on spending the remainder of the night,-'til Probably dawn,-She politely declined the invitation,- Explaining that she'd not preferred socializing after a Workday,- They understood a little sluggishly,-One of Them took her home,-parted their ways at her street Corner, said that she'd like to walk the rest of the way If that was OK,-He said he guessed,-but didn't say anything Of the sort that he'd see her in the following days,-Just A simple goodbye,-and she walked the short distance to Her front door,- while He anticipationlessly sped off,-

-'til too, something a bright betterment, 'til too its
to come along-
-Where's the straw that'd trusted tooth spaces in my
mouth-
-the farthest harm, though it should be so 'cause its
the safest place-
-we're under those conditions, 'til too something a bright

102

betterment, pain 'til too not trusting self made leisure-
-O' how I'll live with you, with your working actions-
-O' how I'll live with you, O' how these days I live long
 without you-

YOU & ME-E.F.'S MAGICK, NOW

Ebbey woke very late that day,-didn't properly Awake 'til 3:43
PM,-Lost the dreams he had that night As he was waking up,-
Trying as hard as he could to Hold them there in his
conscious,-Shamefully they Slipped from him,-The buzzing
which drove him out of His bed, also obscured momentarily his
transformation,-In the bathroom flushes the sleep that's
collected in his Eyes,-Looks harshly at the reflection of his face
in the Bathroom mirror,-Realizes too that his body is still dirty
Since last night,-Washes himself,-And Too, dries his body-
Back to his bedroom,-Still freshly out of breath,-He proceeds
Down the stairs to the house's first floor,-The breeze through
The open windows has grown cooler,-Looks out to see A
heavy shadow on the backyard's foliage,-He thinks the
Summer is ending?,-Sits on the livingroom couch with his legs
Up on it too,-Sees that he's the only person home,-Wonders
Where Hetts has gone,-Ebbey hopes to get outdoors to put the
Remainder of The Summer to use,-

First plans are to go back to the spot in the forest where The
magick bore him,-To see if the fragments of the events Are
there too,-Senses for a reason frOm his gut feeling,-That The
pieces will have disappeared,-Onto The country road,-
Walking the length to where he'd prior entered the forest,-
Walks on the same footpath which last night led his
departings,-Comes to the clearing,-hadn't realized how the
short the passage was from the entrance to here,-he'd never
taken it in the daylight before,-In the clearing He saw that the
tips of some of the blades of grass were singed slightly,-The
place where the pond had been,-was now just a thick marshy
spot in the grass,-This justified last night's occurrences,-They
had surely now taken place,-Though he had poor visual
recollection of them,-He mostly remembered the daze which he
was roused in after Coming up from the beneath the pond -but

103

he heavily was Sagged by the thought of the birth which he'd undertaken last night,-He thought of its spiritual value as a collage of juxtaposed shreds,-As he walked back on the footpath,-

He wondered if these signified that he'd have another Ability,-A magick which he'd only be able to half conceive,-He thought what if this might mark its emergence,-And Too, What would be the first indications of this,-Before he'd Undergone the rite he knew that if its invocations were made Real, than they'd not be the any type of generically termed Psychic visive,-He would not see the alms of these Transformations as just being handed the wish to split Metals,-Or as some would see a mental stability which Has the dis-assemblage of material objects in thought and is To enact that literally,-Ebbey knew that in time, maybe Much time, its emergence would be made apparent to Him,-maybe first it would do so calmly 'til ushering in A coherent incision of the possibilities that it presented,-

IDENTITY ON A STONE

Ebbey goes from the forest directly to find Rea,-Not completely knowing where she'd be then,-As he stepped From the last part of the forest, he crouched down to The grass and pressed his face against it,-Something He hadn't felt before,-The click made by a rainbow as it Completely forms over a city,-That simple step kept Echoing its sound in his conscious as he stood up From the Grass and continued on in pursuit of Rea,-

Rea found herself at the end of summer, in an Indoor swimming pool of all places,-one owned by A neighbor,-Rea wore a tight green slick one piece suit,-Floated on her back while the neighbor sat at the poolside,-She read her fragments of a mystery novel,-The girl would Read most of the book to herself,-but read aloud the bursts Which she'd found suspenseful,-howling them to Rea was a Way to release the tensions,-Rea's ears where half underwater,-So she'd hear the girl's passionings as a vague whisper,-With Maybe the same Echo which Ebbey was hearing in the wood,-'Round the same succession of minutes,-This caused Rea to feel a linkage point,-Knowing Ebbey was about with her in his conscious,-She politely asked her poolside friend for the time, -After hearing

this, Rea excused herself, the excuse she'd used was that she
needed to be some place which she'd forgotten 'til now that
she'd needed to be,-which was almost true,-She knew that she
needed to be somewhere, now-But she just gave a white lie
about having known before and forgotten,-
Knowing that home was not the first place which Ebbey Would
look,-But possibly he'd go to the place where they'd First met,-
Rea quickly went there,-Ebbey too as(Rea had Correctly
figured) was on his way there,-He arrived first and was Peering
at her from behind the shelf where he first hid gazing Out at
her,-The two left as soon as Rea arrived,- moving back in
Direction of Ebbey's home,-This was the first time That Rea
had been there,-The home still entirely empty,-The only change
was the shadow that Ebbey had seen cast in the backyard now
was cast even darker,-Hung like a heavy falling fruit,-Ebbey
sensed that in a way it could be lifted before nightfall,- Leading
Rea to his bedroom directly,-

A record spins upon the turntable,-Rea sits on his Mattress,-
has got a huge diamond ring on one of her Fingers,-This has
caught Ebbey's eye,- for all its pristine Gleaming,-And Too,
being that it is authentic, the likes of which Ebbey had not
seen before,-Rea takes off her clothes,-And sits in her still wet
bathing suit,-Ebbey returns from the Bathroom with a box of
Mum's makeup,-Rea smiles keenly,-Her small white teeth
sparkle,-In this golden moment which Ebbey feels could've
been lifted directly from a motion picture,-Ebbey brushes Rea's
face with a thick powder,-Paints her eyes With a blue eye
shadow,-She applies an azure lipstick to her Lips,-He brings a
box of necklaces from Mum's room, and Rea Puts several of
them around her neck,-They huddled together, Laughing as the
treble grew higher on the record,-

INDEFINITE-The shadow cast over the backyard splits,-The
sun shines,-And Too,-A steady rain falls-As his arm is around
Rea, the clicking picks up Again in Ebbey's conscious,-An
authentic rainbow has broken Over the city,-Ebbey senses this,
stands up and walks To his window where he can see it
clearly,-He Returns Next to Rea,-She takes her bathing suit
straps down from her Shoulders,-and Ebbey brings her a silk
scarf to wrap around her Breasts,-Rea, painted face, diamond

ring, layered necklaces,-Standing in the foreground of the room,-and in the background-The Rainbow laced over the cityscape,-This hooks Ebbey as if The first sign of magick's coming out is that it enables one To find grandeur in most delicate visages?,-

Rea lies down on the mattress,-smiling as the record plays,-Ebbey lies there with her,-The climatic feet for them both is The sense of each others' warmth with their two bodies nudged Snugly together,-staying like this for the remainder of the Evening 'til Ebbey starts drifting off later in the night,-Falls asleep With his forehead pressed against Rea's nape, as she lies on her side,-After awhile Rea is irritated by her inability to accompany him in the sleeping passage,-She gets up carefully with out waking him,-Goes to the window,-At early daybreak,-looks from it and sees the clouds directly,-The home itself is floating in them,-She finds this mirthingly splendid,-Returns to lie next to Ebbey,-And Too,-falls quickly to sleep,-

They awoke at 3:43 PM, just as Ebbey had done the Previous day,-And Too,-Losing What they'd just dreamt as They looked at each other,-They started the day by putting On another record,-Sat there together quietly,-As the treble Rose,-Rea changed into a dress that used to belong to Ebbey's Mum,-meaning that it'd not been worn by her since her youth,-Rea wasn't in the least concerned that it was heavily outdated,-Wanted to feel the breeze on her body that way, thru an artifact,-In the late evening Rea proceeded homeward,-Ebbey was Afterwards immensely saddened by the fact that even thru The use of anykind of magick, the unhinged reality which had Certified the atypical trove of the previous evening that he And Rea had shared, could probably never be recaptured,-

When Rea was alone that evening she juggled the similar Thoughts but free of magick,-And Too, kept recalling when She'd went to the window and looked directly into the clouds,-Wondered if she'd really been in them or not?,-She'd look forward to be up in them again that night,-But as she'd feared, only got the disappointed vibe of seeing the backyard plainly in view,-She was Not up above it.,-

" hidden... everywhere is... hidden... by my all... the hidden... emerges as the good god thing... wrapped over the ground by heath and harmful beauty... you and myself... we remember... we remember..... we capture this...as not coming from us... you, myself...we'd imagined enough that the stunning was gone...we'd shown them all the nothing...we'd... with the less that'd been took...stretch this out so far.... And Too.... Split by a shard of the holly woxx... that too which you'd scathed and feared... comes to glimpse the patter papers...."

" ever was rose up so.... far away to magick whose escapade brought it here to be cataloged in conjunction to leaping....not alone.... The obvious had to've been besieged.....what the hate marks... what the groom pox scars..... what early in the morning ... what to walk a natural carnivorous pint pass.... to take you where you want to get..... pasts... the decency... far.... way....out...no...pasts the ultra alms... there's a goner whose too bullish.... what is a scent... having accidentally gotten lucky...."

NOTE ON DECIPHERING THE ABOVE:
Ebbey-"Something exists as soon as you feel that it does.
Even without having done or seen it. If you feel it to
Be so then it is so."

A CHILDRENS' HYMN
-the possibility of planets-
-the possibility of lives-
-the possibility of beauties-
-outside of the rooms where we've spent our entire lives-
-the truth holds us up-
-the truth holds us up-
-and too is what we've not become aware of-
-and too is what we've not become aware of-
-know a few points in it-
-know a few points in it-
-anomalies to us too-
-anomalies to us too-
-will that be the first time we've lived-

will that be the first time we've felt a placing in our lives--the possible years-
-the possible month-
-the possible days-
-the truth holds us up-
-the truth holds us up-

That eve. Ebbey finds a bursting in the magick as He'd presumed was there-gave a lucid dream- A hulking play-game, Sees the Star Of Bethlehem up Close enough to see that it's constructed, has to've been Welded by somebody,-Sees it pointing straight to Christ's Birth manger,-discovers him being otherworldly,-And Too, Not in a way which Ebbey had figured it,-A figure's shadow Moves ways-back,- propositions Ebbey by signaling to him In Morse Code with the Star's light patterns,-

LEAF FROM ANOTHER: A CONTINUED SAGE

The photograph taken in Fort Augustus, Scotland- in 1934- Shows a blurry image-possibly it is on its side turning over And a fin is sticking up—Some of the pictures show rises In the water-claimed to be its humps-Could've just been Easily the water current,-the black underneath prior to Capsizing,-A series of underwater pictures, could be also Seen as failures,- Indistinguishable 'cause of their impossibly Grainy appearance,-Though one in particular details a shape, Neck and flippers-which in sense does resemble a plesiosaur,-Two other underwater photos,-show spatially flattened fins,- And Too, are entirely inconclusive,-Yet one other underwater Photograph,-Is said to show its head,-But has drawn the letdown skeptical conclusion of only probably being a tree stump,-The first photograph of every taken of it,-taken by Hugh Grant in 1933,-And Too, one of the far & few authentic Enough to probably show something which is actually an Anomaly,-Is Too, very blurred, though it looks as if it shows A manta ray skimming atop the water's surface,-All of the Promising photos show a neck, back, fins, a distance out in The water,-if isolated by the picture's taker,-some times falling To loose if we're to attempt portioning it to the Loch and surrounding banks,-

Ebbey refused himself sleep that night,-attributing this To the fact that the visage of his dreams made him feel As If he were awake,-Though he'd have figured he would Have taken a liking to this,-The part missing was the Locations,-He'd find the objects and purposes,-But not Any ground at all to stand on,- He'd found the feeling of Peering in,-or floating through,-simply distasteful,- This caused him to feel as if he were not wanted even in His own dream,-intruding his own subconscious,-He stayedAwake that night by viewing picturebooks of fundamental Works of art,-aligning himself with Michelangelo Buonarroti's 'Pieta',-Alarmed of the damage that's occurred on one of the statue's hands,-Reads in captions how this occurred whenthe statue was being transported someplace,-The photograph which illustrates the 'Pieta' is in itself luminous,- tightly lit to show the indisputable grace of the sculpture,-Ebbey does however return to sleeping, having been thoroughly caressed by the articulation that he held therein the picturebooks,-Afterwards, he need not wish himself pleasant dreams,-

---

2ND CHILDRENS' HYMN
-alley cat wide awake in the furrow muck-
-the hill moss reaps the blossoms of profession-
-alley cat wide awake in the furrow muck-
-could've inhaled the village's mistress-
-would've exhaled verdict of the shaken village-
-alley cat wide awake in the furrow muck-
-alley cat wide awake in the furrow muck-
-but O' out of time-
-but O' out of time-

A ROOM LIGHT THAT BEIGNS SHUTTLING: THEN, SOMETHING TO WRITE-

---

May 17, 1968-Wrapped therein a green canvas tent bag- Entirely unclad, other than the towel from Noble's Restaurant That was wrapped 'round her head-Two weeks prior on U.S. 25, During the rain about two and a half miles from Sadieville- Clothes not heavy enough for the weather,-The towel turns Out to be a diaper, a 'Birdseye' diaper specifically,-Excluding Noble's, -And Too, -the part of the shoe doesn't turn up,- Light blouse, Gray sweater, Short dress, hippie Hair,- It turns out Dorris Ditmar is living in Bradford,- Candace is too found tied,- And identified by her clothing,-Not her body directly,-She'd gone around 8:30 PM on March 9, 1968,-

Ebbey rises the following day again at 3:43 PM-Wanting Rea very badly,-Though lacking the motivation To contact her or immediately rush to her,-Though he does Calmly go from the suburbs to the city shops,-Though skipping The bookstore where he'd met Rea,-This evening instead of Seeing Rea in the flesh,-He chose to see something that Signifies The Importance of his bond with her,-so around dusk he walks through the city square where he sees the fountain spraying as the lights in it are growing brighter,-that is not Rea,-He looks else where,-He lets the sounds of wails and tension Direct him,-down a few streets,-he sees that in a lot a small fair is going on,-He walks in,-the lights, venders, screams of girls,- The fair is going up fully as the evening sets on,-He buys A ticket for the fun house,-after finding himself disinterested In the thrill rides,-He enters alone, it seems to be the least Popular of the fair's attractions,-the first room,-is simple,-Step on to a floor that gives in with your weight,-and a clown Pounces at you on your way out of it,-the next room is a prop That Ebbey's too seen,-a mechanical shark in a water tank,- The participant walks out on a plank, that falls with an air compressing surge,-as the shark is sent up at the same time,- Ebbey leaves this room with his excitement raised a tinge,-The next room is of colored strands, mists and mirrors,-Here Ebbey discover he's not the sole attendee,-A younger Girl,-Wearing a yellow sarong, her brown hair that's been Tinged by henna, flows down to her waist,-she smiles at Ebbey When a spray of mists comes across her face,-she stretches Her arms up from her sides,-Smiling as the streamers flow and the Mirrors that lace the sides of the room heavily distort her reflection,-Ebbey has not an impure thought of her,-He remains there as she walks from the room,-A moment later he sees how hideously the mirrors contort his features,- He laughs,-And Too, makes the exit,-

CHILDS WAKING UP HYMN

-press by the greenly panting hues that reconcile the leap to play-O' I want to know-for the one month price--press by the greenly panting hues that reconcile the leap to play-O' want to know for one given away glory-

IS'T NOT, MORES RARELY DISCLOSED

TYPEBOARD AND 1st EXPLANATION

" up here...up here.... Can't explain the world up here.... up here.... up here... here he becomes the integral piece of my life at this one of its stages... up here a scathingly damaged cognitive scatter.... The country... up here... doesn't mean none such.... here asks him to piece me up and front from the Boris scores.... Up here I wouldn't care..."

And I've been as still drawn to returning,- sat, flatter in Speckling with the eventuality,-And Too, I've not known Them further,-and if the case itself wasn't the shards to've Estimated the go-down,-never goes away,-never goes away,- It is for him to see that all this time and not once reach outward with the vain of grasping it,-the rutter stilt after the generating is sipping,-never goes away,-

" that has.... up the web.... wants to make an epoch illustrious... that has.... without over doing the wealth of wonder that its got.... that has... the lower workings... the steps on the... the cube of paradox.... One of the... the steps on them... to parody that.... Without doing over the wealth its got...."

TYPEBOARD AND 2ND EXPLANATION

He'll wake and lean to a wall,-Is when I'd begun speculation About which of these becomes the pivotal moment for him,- He'll hardly steer clearly from that right now,-Though I may Be incorrect on that estimation,-He'll wake and hear footsteps Way in back of him, lean to the wall, then he sets out from the Onset of night,-To've lived a life here where each staking Segment he saw under a cloth of darker hues,-Not once Getting the boisterous pride for the so-help of the need-be Others,-Is where I pry deeply into the speculation of what Occurs on this particular night,-Look what love does to You,-He'll lean to a wall, -hear a degrading done to a set of Piano keys,-Wants to walk 'round wisping a tulip on the Protection he gets from one or other notes,-

I remember in a room of show chairs that was asked What the requiring could be,- Yes I remember the might of When the rollers were over stroved,-I'll be honest that a difficult personality walks----in there,- Under the least laving of qualms that he'd been under for the last 20years up 'til then,-I remember the dry heat lifting the layered cotton formulating,- Comes on by a gratifying morsel of a dollop,-His scent is lapped onward to my tongue from the Roundly content of its remaining drippings,-Sets off On the carriage wisps,-His softness is derived therein,-The repute stole his vicissitude too therein derived,-Sets off again on the soft leg of the bed chorus 'til a good year,-

QUIET LAND

'Invested hymn'
-Rea tailed delirium-
-Rea tailed delirium-
-trot swerve mocks her notice-
-what can mines hopspotch-
-what can mines hopspotch-
-just glances to show-
-just glances to show-
-thank you go forth-
-thank you go forth-
-Rea tailed delirium-
-Rea tailed delirium-
-what can mines hopspotch-
-what can mines hopspotch-
-just glances to show-

'Painful verse'
It starts off, two-does it at this point, matter-Finds a group of thieves lactating in the remnants Of a bunker,-The dawn's light starts wisping,-HAS got the elite to heal,-Maneuvers the smeared Cripple's pin-bent- legs a selection of inches,- HAS a start or something,-Will feed like hogs,-Sour apples as their solid food, and their own milk Aside too,-Maneuvers the Christmas day Sun emblem,-HAS a pause,-The thieves crawl upon the bunker floor To the apples, -taking mercifully to the

bait of a trap,-

A SLICK ON YOUR UNDER ARM-

" the blood.. too... best friends... just give up... a queen... a queen... is illustrious... before she stands to her place.... a queen to a child... alive... too... shakes... too... best friends... I'm guaranteed... just to give up... a princess.... Mistaken... draws not a tinge of needed conclusive evidence... the blood... all of the ways envious... a scowl appropriated... by a incubating a queen to a child.... alive too... before she stands to take her place... is illustrious.... just give up... "

'Leaving hymn'
-told of a flurry sky comet-
-told of a leash stake-
-his pronto opens the escape gate-
-told of a cooing heir-
-his pronto opens so much that's at our
stake- -told of a flurry sky comet-
-his pronto opens the paring earth-
-told of a cooing heir-
-to the bolting mare, discontented-
-opened through by the paring earth-
FPS BOW CONTAINS-
Stoop,-I slip off her sleek red skirt,-which clads her frail Body-not the pleasing breech you'd see kneeling by a Bathing tub-in a silking suit-I clasp her vulva lightly-My palm substitutes for a rag,-momentarily,-while she's Menstruating into its cuff,-Naively, naively,-Too she Has told me to enlighten my present ignorance,-Her hymen is still intact,-Says as if I were suspecting An inclination,-"a woman's got another opening in her sex, So she's able to urinate & bleed",-
Now making the dangerous first male attachment,-Mused by the ascertained stealth of a male intellect,-Mused by a linking verse from then to here onward,-In one of two recurring plurals,-an androgynous glowing Figure motions in a solitaire ellipsis,-hay bales are slashed With a singing whip,-averted back to a woman,-Beauty skims,-My eyes gleaming,-painted like a brunette doll,-invigoratingly,-Lush,-others too glimpsed in

the same draping,-legs, buttocks, Breasts,-from only a stand back point,-the white slick,-the firmly Unsettling breech,-
Spinning a color chart,-a summary is fit on the arrival points,-
Springing the parables,-how long a place sits unoccupied,-
Surrgaever reanke dor gone feels so low,-suppose the prickles His hatewar,-pintsize criminality where does pretty dream books-Without her skin---

       -resembles the redstick-
       -its awhile forgery-
       -resembles the redstick-
       -get to town the way it'd exactly began-
       -resembles the redstick-
       -on the spindle plate there's the blew-
-color-color I know you had't now- -to town the way it'd scently begun-uncovered a side of his lying figure, mossy green growsover the bend of his figure,-his resemblance is realized on a slide matte,-a crowning manor's roof painted in the right hand background,-the larks on their play swing old amusements,-

-collect anomaly-
-all off kilter presence is the yellow lights-
-why solved-
-species why-
-why solved-
-species why-
 2-reed nozzles-2
 2-reed nozzles-2
3-is't abo't b'rn-3
3-is't abo't b'rn-3
Turns away a little hurt,-senses he's been spoken Unfondly of,-can and needs to carry himself stammering Unfondly out,-

THE BOIL FROM HERE & LEAFER

In split mind & spirit,-feeling tritely crushed at the rationality Of facing another day,-sensing another key,-feeling the link Point voids exclusion,-feeling the absolution of being lower Down then dirt that has too been speckled,-And Too, the Abolish nettles in the horizon line?,-

-and wear the terror-

-and stand all the day-
-and wear the terror-
and stand all the day-

a stave light begins to rutter,-back there is't the spacing of a
blonde army,-beginning to tell all of what too,-as if thee were
dressed in a white shirt,-does need the hindsight of the lawning
mines,-with pictures taken on all sides,-there I see having to
contemplate an invisible light,-a life entirely of nighttime,-

" I just don't see them... keeping... the breech.... Fair.... The
play model... drawn on the trottle... O' the napes....   O' the
napes... O'... taught dirge.... keeping... the breech..."

ROPING ANOAH+

-and walking into quicksand-
-and knowing how far-
-and walking into quicksand-
-and knowing how far-

"I had not tact... it's double axing... the tomorrow's
disappearance... twin layers... of light written in.... big trouble
letter... O' bought each.."

Her back silhouetted on a sliding shoot,- like a cutout lowered
Down&Up,- Creates the illusion that she's being penetrated in
Opening of her breech,-A shiver from which he's uncapable of
Disassociating himself from this image,-'causes his purgatory
Later on,-then sees her glistening busts frayed in backlighting,-
Her hair much shorter,-but still too swayed,-a black one
dimensional cutout alludes to her being entered in thru her
vulva,-Too presented a gaping troublesome unfreeing fixation,-

-Cole pelt-
-the treble 7 place-
-Texan Zebra-
-the treble 7 place machines-
-Cole pelt casts into the bay-
-his nest-
-treble 6 gulf ground highway company-
-Texan zebra as to've saved his fit-
-Cole pelt 'round the drive 'round harbor-
-casts to the bay-
-his treble 7 placing machines, my friend-

K-Nuth Pally shadowbox to the dull about daughter,-To the martyr corner,- to the silver lined corner,- K-Nuth Pally's gotten your best gay goodness,-To the martyr corner,- to the silver lined corner,-When clothing the urges, weighting them so secret,-To the reel's relished releasings,-

NATURE'S SERIES

Ebbey finds one of the strangest side effects of the Magick: his penis & testicles are extremely chilled, on Even the warmest days,-Urinating takes forever,- even Feeling that he's got to-do-so involves standing by the Toilet bowl for a long moment 'til the piss starts surging: Ebbey finds one other side effect is that the chilling sensation Increases the size of his sex itself: lit like a lily drop,-

"The blue contrast..... the lovers... daughters... fathers... sons near misfortune... reach the conclusion that he is a very ominous boy... deeply brittled... and to unhappy too and more than once wanting death...."

BRONZE PUMPKIN LACE

-the eminent dispassion-
-freely goodly ending-
-personal association-
-the relics in the embassy-
-somewhere if I'm known by them-
-then they walk away eager-
-how these images came to the hunt-
-is that the mankinding rift-
-loving a face one sees-
-only from a screen-

After Hetts, Ebbey, & Mum's dinner: Hetts immediately Took ill,-Lying first in the cot near the living room window,-Running a highshot fever,-requests an ice bag,-Looks to've Taken a Constricting illness: Ebbey suggest immediate Hospitalization,-Hetts requests that he wait 'til early morning Hours before being taken there,-unless his condition grows Worse,-At 10:00pm he seems to be running a steadily highfever,- has a stark white paleness to his face,-doesn't feel like sleeping,-asks Ebbey to tell him something,-anything,-Ebbey obliges his requests,-says in a frenzied manner,-

" one other crowd... here for a singsong.... One other crowd here for awhile... do no... give the damn... do no... give the damn... one other crowd... on & on... here for more & more.... do no give... independence... do no give... a damn.... Independence..."

A little bit of light opens in Hetts's eyes,-Ebbey obliges His request of a glass of cold water,-pours himself one too...Mum also sits next to Hetts,- she's rather silent...,-Ebbey returns To hand Hetts the waterglass,- Ebbey urgently downing his,-Slips from Hetts's sickbed with the waning urination urgings,- And Too, arriving in the upstairs bathroom, he finds his sex Particularly cold,-swollen with numbness,-In the time it takes Ebbey to piss,-Mum encounters unnatural lapses in the Downstairs,- She leaves Hetts's side to investigate the shuffle She'd heard out on the porch,-walks to the porch and can see It thru the screen door,-Sees a sleek black shape dwindling 'neath the moth-swarmed porch-light,-Arrives frightened as the shape splashes like a liquid, wetting the porch's surface,- At the same point she hears Hetts's wailing,-Returns to the living room to find him vomiting blood,-Calls for Ebbey to quickly help her carry him to the car,-

Arriving in a hospital emergency room,-Ebbey holding Hetts up On one of the far corner chairs,-Mum signing her husband in as He is spewing a thickly clotted blood from his innards,- After the Medics have made the bleeding cease,-Ebbey & Mum are told That his aliment is an extreme eternal wound,- It appears that he received it by falling from a substantive height,-Ebbey & Mum have no light to shine on this matter,-Hetts lingers thru the Remainder for the night,-dying almost once,-still alive, though, the next day,- Ebbey brings him roses,- And Too, Hetts requests that his son speak-something-to-him,-Ebbey is obliged to this,-

" overdue... rimming rolf... too dreamed au revoir.... Except the words... except the crowns pedal... off his feet... and sweep the air... expect to spend.... the month in hotlume..."

Hetts is a patient for 2more days for the safety of observing His condition,-He has a trimmed thought during one of his Naps,-
"OF AUSTUED LINES AND FOLLIES NONE LEAPING WED WE'RE HEADED WERENT NOBODY OF

ROSELY   PLOOMPACKINGS   SPINES   LEASTED
COSSET   WAS   THEE   GRAY   PERPO   WAS   THEE
GRAY   WEARY   OZOSCOPE   WE'RE   CUTTHROPED
TANGLED   LINED   BLOOD   TREACHEROUS   SKINNY
OF AUSTUED WELL SORPES VURNING THE LELP".

Mum and Ebbey offer to take him from his room to their car in a Wheelchair,-but he insists on walking out of here on his own Two feet on his last day,-The three of them walk towards the Elevator,-down the florescent lighted hall,- the corners of their Pupils glimpsing steadily the gallant dying souls in the come&go Visited rooms that lace the hall's sides,-They do not exchange Words amongst each other in the elevator ride to the bottom Floor,-When the elevator comes to stop at the bottom floor,-Hetts has a gluing virtue in his belly to the premonition that The doors won't open-but-to-the-least-they-do-so-open-Hetts&Mum&Ebbey proceed to the motion-opened exit doors-Only Hetts looks back in-to-the hospital lobby as they are in the Opening between one of the sets of motion-opened doors,- HE sees a get-well balloon which is shaped like a cloud, swayed Thru the bottom floor lobby by what little helium its got left in it,-

" pocket bell kisser from the empty sky…. High lay down… times they combed satisfaction… what's that dulcimer…. Going to be… flash your teeth as it is to defend you…"

Hetts is more than a little hungry on the drive home,-They stop at a family cohered restaurant,-Hetts orders A great amount of foods,-Oddly he only nibbles on small Bits of each of them,-Asks Ebbey something about a film That he's seen,-And passionately describes one of its lush Passages,-where a figure stands high up in the ruins of a temple, as the bottom is filled with water,- the light shining in Thru the temple's windows causes the water to shimmer as it reflects to all sides of temple surrounding the figure with abstractly patterned shadows,- Hetts smiles, pays the bill,- And they return to the car,-Hetts dispassionately fumbles Thru radio stations coming off short in satisfaction,- unable To find any music that coincides with his taste,-so he asks   Ebbey to speak something for him,-

GOT KNIT

" came to ask not a thing of you… please dear Mrs…

intending to stay together... please dear Mrs.. pass   for a
goblin... in the money scant times... plays the   fiddle for a
sardine.. came to ask to betray the stoop   ponds on the nether
worth tack.... Out of fermented   languishing.. advise the wart
pillow.. to travail....do   you core to the cinder paxx... please
dear Mrs.   Do no... do not look here hazy too.. got your name
on   It.. so something can tell you not to leave here dim.."

GURNET TIME BUYS DO WITH OUT IN TO BE SO

The Flint's arrive home,- Rather jovial after Ebbey's recital,-
Ebbey has his arm around Hetts kind of holding him up,- In the
case that he would suddenly feel weak,-Mum unlocks The front
door,-the three hadn't prepared for the unexpected Vile mutter
they immediately discover in the den,-A foul burning scent rises
therein the living room,-figuratively estimated 100hundred
pigeons are found dead,-the walls soiled and splattered with
their blood,-it appears that they've crashed into the walls in
their flurry,-the room's floor and furniture are also doused with
their excrement,-Hetts startled, figures they've come down thru
the chimney,-though he can't figure out why they'd have killed
themselves,-this took place obviously in the morning and
afternoon when Ebbey & Mum made their trip to retrieve Hetts,-
The scene is horrifically rousing,- what a thing to-come-home-
to,-the freshness of blood-on-the-wood-floor-and-the-fecal-
stench-cause-Hetts- to-feel-that-he's-some-how-descending-to-
an-uncharted-virtue-He phones the police, maybe from
confusion, just has no Other way to clean this up or take care
of it OR is doing the Normal thing that one would do in a
distilling situation which They are at a loss of words for,-

HEATHY STICK NAP HI NOW ALLNIGHT

As soon as Hetts places the phone down on the receiver after
Reporting his problem & requesting assistance,-There's a
knock On the door at that moment,-somehow the police have
already Arrived,-The same two officers that'd Earlier delivered
Ebbey home,-Though they behave as if they do not recognize
Ebbey,-Hetts shows them what has taken place in living room,-
Mum Is behaving most calmly,-Ebbey is quite uncomfortable,
being that he can't figure why the police would act as they don't
know Him when it is so soon and so obvious, -maybe just too

119

many Faces?,-It is Hetts who is most frantic,-Forcefully explaining his Shock to the officers,-Then to those two,-they stand amongst The scatter & stench as if it were not at all apparent,-   They Look at the walls of the room,- in   a humming way ask Hetts Who the architect was,-They request coffee from Mum,- Whose a bit confused,-though she proceeds to the kitchen To meet their request,-startlingly to Hetts, the two officers Take a seat on the excrement coated sofa,-they sit there Staring smugly at He and Ebbey,-One officer places his Hand on the other's nape,-the begin passionately kissing Each other as Hetts looks on,-they pause for a moment and Ask Hetts: is-this-how-they-are-suppose-to-do-this,.-He does Not reply,-Mum returns from the kitchen with their coffee,- To find them caressing each others genitals thru their   Uniforms,- Again, Asking Hetts if-this-is-how-this-is-suppose- To-be-done-?Licking the sides of each others faces,- Still sitting on the sofa, staring still smugly at Hetts &   Ebbey,-Then standing up, taking the coffee from Mum,- Thanking her,-and proceeding out of the house,- Hetts feels tranquilized,- Mum wishes they hadn't taken   Her coffee cups,-Hetts again feels faint,-Ebbey tells Him, he better lie down,- mum leads him upstairs,- Ebbey ventures to the kitchen in search of rubber gloves,- Sponges, cleaning fluids, in order to at least see if he can Wipe up the majority of the blood,-Figuring he'll have to Replace the furniture,- he's not figured what to do with Pigeons, supposedly he'll think of placing them in garbage Bags,-though that seems insufficient,-he can't think of What else to do but bag them and dispose of them Somewhere on his own,-wonders if it's an impossibility to Explain this to someone,-he proceeds to wetting and Soaping the sponge, in order to start scrubbing the blood,-

VENTILATE WALLINGS SCURF

" the fresh source... wooling off the recipe sands.... You've to've govern me all to yourself.... We splittop   The umbrella above the source that we know.....Wish luck.... Got the limpernitive right.... Wooling off The reciped sands.... You've to've govern me to'll being Within you..."

Ebbey did-the-best-of-his-ability in wiping the room clean,- Bagging-the-birds-up-for-disposal-,-he and mum trying together To Push the ruined furniture to the porch, -Mum couldn't really lend much, being that she had-to-be-at-Hetts-side-as-he-was-again-Coming-down-ill-,-so-Ebbey-had-to-alone-badly-drag-he-chairs-And-sofas-out-to-the-porch,-Then returning to the now empty Den,-to gaze imprudently at the forever red tinged wood floor,-Though next, what to do with the birds, guess call a sanitation Department,-Or put them in the earth in his forest clearing,- But getting them there,-comes to the conclusion that it's easier to let someone do it for him,-will-make-the-call-as-he-can-early-in-the-soon-arriving-day-,-Mum calls him from the upstairs,-He hurries up quickly,-Hetts has become increasingly pale,-Requests Ebbey to come To his bed side,-asks of him to give him another recital,-Ebbey Can only-do-so-,-even in his frazzled state,-He feels the obligation to meet an ailing man's wishes,-

" timed to leaving... timed to leaving from... from your reach... to be leaving... to've been summoned from the quilling dirty words... that've heard your kiss pouse utterings....to've immersed your seances... muttering the quail gallop... anybody else... sings for the fields... anybody else looking greetingly towards the sky... sings for the small symphonic mirthing rains..."

Hetts dies in the early hours of the morning,-With Ebbey & Mum there next to his bedside.

THIS COUNT I FEEL

When Ebbey steps from Hetts's deathbed,- He Steps to the walls outside the hall,-slouches down Against them,-Turns his head to attentively,-Sees the Dust particles carried thru the moldy air,-wonders what Will now carry his father,-hears his Mum weeping, but hasn't Got anything comforting to say,-

YOU DON'T HAVE TO WORRY

The Flints' have a closed/private service for their dearly Departed,-Mum & Ebbey are set to be the only attendants,-And they are glad to have it that way,-the service rites involve Hetts's cremated remains placed on a silk drop cloth,- hordes Of candles burning,-censers dispensing a jasmine fragrance,-Mum & Ebbey are asked by the priest/head-of-the-rite to each Separately say something about Hetts,-

EBBEY'S CEREMONY

" why is this... why is this.... How could we think.... Some...
we're.... We're... beck a leaf to sop... on the score... wet... to
ILIAD... one chinging... high... high... high... we're... seething
my proverb... high... high.. high... we're.... What... is done....
How we know now.... Is you..... "

MUM'S CEREMONY

" living... a.... woman... possesses a cohered... millionth....
son....   Puts gullet salt... in... .the U. Rum... living a
woman...combs a Tinter pick... son & salt & see...
wonderings... you call.... Her.... Way & daunt.. come in... in
the centennial... why &   daunt... live here... live here... live
here... live here...."
The service is brought to a close,- each of the candles are
putout 'til only one remained burning,-the censers give to
cease,-they too are removed,-Hett's urn is taken by Mum &
Ebbey,-as they leave,-Now in the funeral room, the a sole
burning candle is flicking on the dropcloth,-then putout by the
head-of-the-rite-,-Fore' folding the cloth, lowering the lights
completely,-

CREETHING FLITES

Mum & Ebbey arrive back at their stifled solemn abode,- The
hanging grief is too present,-Though the suspected Weeping
did not wan from them,-Ebbey goes to the living Room,-lies
there on the couch,-plays a side of a record Over & over,-Mum
sits on one of the front porch chairs,-Gazing off at the green of
the lawn, seemingly split & Gutted in flecks of her husband's
groomed & measured & coincidingly spread spurted grass,-
Awhile rain breaks, clouds emerge over the suburbs,- too
splitting eagerly in Mum's view as she remains seated thru the
storm,-Then proceeds to slumber,-Ebbey does not choose
sleeping,-Has gotten other planned occurrences,-About
scattering Hetts's Ashes somewhere proper,-Not-all-of-them,-
Just enough of an amount to fill a ziplocked bag,-Taking this
desired content out of the urn by using a teaspoon,-Nearing
2:00 AM, Ebbey sets out for His known place,-The forest
clearing,- There-to-procure-his-own-rite-to-them,-

A FRIEND WHOM YOU'VE NOT SUSPENSED

Ebbey slips steadily thru the residentialized suburbs,-'til onto

the backroad,-Using a flashlight beam to pick his footing,-
Though he's greatly irritated when car headlights come around
his sight,-nearly making him lose his ground,-Though only a
few cars pass,-He hurries his pace,-The restfulness in the night
air veils all qualms,-He finds saintliness in the running stream
thicket 'side the road,-He is part of the night too,-in the darkest
stretches of the road,-He even shuts the flashlight beam off,-
makes his footing on The freed gusts of intuition,-
Finds his forest-passage-entrance,-Steadily into the Wood,-
sees his flashlight beam growing very dim,-Has Got to stop to
replace the batteries,-had luckily thought Of bringing an extra
set,-changes them in the dark,-Does so precisely enough that
he doesn't drop the replacements To his feet,-knows the time
he'd lose if that were to happen,-Puts the worn-out batteries in
his pocket,-Directs the again Bright beam,-And follows the
path,-soon arriving In the clearing,-Takes the smaller-sized
duffel bag from his shoulder,-Has To take the needed content
out with one hand,-using the Other hand to shine the flashlight
beam into the open bag,-Has the contents out of the bag,-Now
onto their proper Arrangement,-Places hathor at the eastern
point of the circle,-hera at the western point,-juno at the
southern point,-nephtys at the northern point,-He places within
the circle a censer that he burns a marigold fragrance in,-And
Too, a red candle in the rightside section of the circle,-and a
green candle in the leftside circle-section,-Takes off his T-shirt,
stands above the circle as the candle flames are fluently cast
bright,-Takes Hetts's ashes from the ziplocked bag,-recites
words for his father as he sprinkles his ashes into the laid-out
circumference,-

THAT MOMENT'S RECITED CIRCLE RITE

   " stained... torn... from therein... a sleeping gorgeous
Lilith... it's your albatross... stained.. torn.. invented .... If ...
if... if.. you'd knotted... was has not chained... you'd nodded...
if... if... if... was has not hard... surfaced pasts... you'd
nodded.. you'd ignored... violate 'neath... if you'd been as
violate as the others..."
As some of the ashes are speckled to the candle flames,-They
come to a vibrant flickering, -Ebbey sees streaks of Azure shot

thru the night air,-dawn is soon breaking,-Ebbey disassembles the circle,-Puts the censer into his Bag along with the green candle,-leaves the contents Of the four circle points there on the ground,-The red candle Is still burning, he crouches down,-softly blows it out,-turns It upside down to empty the wet wax from it,-Places it back in Bag,-starts home in the dense early day's light,-

FIT GO-WAY, TULIP

Ebbey arrives home, ventures directly to his Bed,- Attempts to sleep,- During this he discovers what A hard blow he's taken in the previous days,- Seems as His whole body is aching,- the skin on the sides of his mouth is Too separating uncomfortably,- When he opens his mouth wide For a breath,-He experiences a burning irritation,-He lay there For a some 4hours, unsuccessful in ever dozing-off,- though felt He had the first parts of a dream which might have belonged to his father,- Who too might have had it in his last-days,-"is… on…a… small… inflatable-raft… the creek bed… has… risen-high…in… though a… low spot… sharper rocks.. tear the raft… as.. it… drags… along the bottom of the… creek bed… he… swims.. barely… to… a.. a.. a… grassy muck on the bank… creek bank… lying… there… is bit on… a snake bite… the swelling ..is liken to… a wad of gum stitched to his skin… at… first hot…as if it had been taken from someone's mouth… then… it…feels.. like.. a cold… spat.. wetnotch…",- Snapped from the dream as the stinging rose as if it were real…,-

I see Rea again,- this time in a gown,- smiling,-smiling,-Sniffing the scent of a bunch of roses which I'd given her,-"The lights… scents… her face… made this… a beautiful… moment…",-with her afterwards,-the top of room is shot-off,- a creaking hazel banner is stretched above us,-A red substance meant to resemble blood,-is splashed everywhere immensely,- Two cupids rise up thru the floor,- hover above,- piercing us with Soft bursts drawn from their quivers,-"requires… so less… is… a… mists… received… I'm… this… bosom… a word… makes. .sense… as a gift…",- I see Rea again,- this time as an un-violated nude figure,- discoursing an ample breech,-and what will I continue thinking,-

124

Ebbey grows more uncomfortable with his unsuccessful sleep,-
Rises looking for something to half occupy himself,-Being that
He's only half awake,-Goes to Hetts's study,- On the desk he
Sees a miniature guillotine which was constructed from pop
sickle sticks & model glue,-a Small figure that resembles the
Marquis De Sade is placed in it,-Hetts must have prepared it
For decapitation prior to his passing-on,-The blade of the
Guillotine consists of all-a-razor blade-,-The neck
of the Figure, Hetts put a lot of –give-way into,- so that one fall
From the blade could sever the figure's head from its
shoulders,-Ebbey places the figure in the guillotine,-For-the-
sake-of-Discovering-newthings-,-He counts down from 5,
before decapitating doll,-It HAS worked exactly as Ebbey can
tell his father wanted it to,-Picking the doll's head up from the
floor,-He places it next to the guillotine,-and continues about
the House, searching for other things of interest,-

CARINA MULLY: DON'T PERMISS:

I sought Rea out this time,-instead of her always looking For
me,-found her too,-but not where I knew she'd be,-I believe in
her so much,-I feel I've discovered a revelation Which I can't
explain,-which seems as it were a pretext,-The dis-conclusion
of a lifetime's wanton,-there's a shuffled Woman,-a noose-like
vermin,-a less than likable girl,-as we Come to see,-she is not
Rea,-she's no Rea at all,-

BEAUTY MARKS

The cracks of the matter,-the heart of the consequence,-The
fool-be supple smile,-Is so bleeding ugly,- An unveiled
Unattractiveness,- somehow I come-here-to-find-this-once-
Over-again,-I love the degradation,-know what the hollop is
About,- pissing a stream of blood,- ecking like a blowtorch,-
Tells heaven above to please its cut-stench-self,-Hates too,
place and people,-though at the mostly beautiful t of its
personal state of hell,-always times,-
Cuts its own noose down,-brittles its own tongue,-swallows Its
own lisp,-The indentation of this humiliating chain of events Is
one which too is therapeutic,-It defines the imaginings of evil,-
Proves that when the right instances come together at the
appropriate sequences, -that humanity can fall completely into

an abyss,-"there... is... no time... to requiem... Rea... there... is no better way... hates the sour bumpkin... I don't care...at all what you think... infecting Rea... pass that back & forth..is that the sobbing fluid verbatim...",-
Ebbey goes out of his way to keep his movings about the House as quiet as he can,-Hoping to not awake Mum from Sleeping,-She'd exhaustively been awake for most of the Last several days,-wondered what his mother dreamt,- Knew that he'd not ask, ever,-
MUM'S DREAM WHICH WAS NOT FOR HER SON & FORGOTTEN TO HER IMMEDIATELY UPON WAKING

" finds herself.. alone.. a lone... in a thickly dust soiled chamber.. there's a knock... on the chamber door.. she permits.. whom ever to come in... it is her husband... says.. he's come to get her... finds herself... on not known streets... walks pasts her husband... whom is sitting on one of the house's steps... realizes it... was.. him after shed walked past.. thinks maybe 'cause of the darkness... he'd not known her... walks back to there several times... can... not... drive the words off her.. tongue... stands by herself ... the shallow part of a lake... the water... level completely drops... she stands on the dried up...lake bottom... the fish the lake had held... squirm... attempting to flip themselves into the nearest patch of ..wet.. she sees... that the... fish faces .. mouths... resemble Hetts.. finds... him.. coasting by.. placed.. on a rocking horse... apparently propelled by a blanket of flames... he mouths... her... a kiss.. then moves past the horizon line..."

REACTOR, ROLL IN TO TOWN,-

Slide on down, the only healing female,-Exposes Rea,- The shiver dagger fish,-Wrong&Right,-I got sparkles,- I'd stated above that I felt like this bosom,-Luna,- Now, try to understand Rea's life,-She'd inserted Again,-just an act of violation,- Being beat,-split,- Peeled,-mostly penetrated,-taking the gamble on the System,-cum 'til late night,- don't be stupid OR UGLY,- The silences are as close-as-before,-Here, sees how hard She's too taken a beating over these drawn-out summer days,-The millennium tickets,- funny blue eyes,-'cause one,- I see something that I want, -it is a mess,-My Rea is the wisdom

126

Of the queening catapult,-Why are you leaving, me, come-sit
Beside,-I've never now felt jealously of her form,-las' taken
Shuffle,-I rub Rea,-I can not configure the linking between
Affection to a feminine sex, and the acting on the urge of
Intercourse with the female,-this doesn't arise with me,-
Excludes the dangerous(I hear) chemical fusion which would
stir, if Rea and I took part in a physical participation,- I too am
lost trying to decide on vaginal penetration,- Is the female ever
receiving pleasure,- I have an acute vision that in moments
the vulva only holds a prodding fever preoccupied with its own
exasperation,-The female sex forms like clothing the pad of-a
mushroom,-stretches around the male sex,-so it works some
way,-in the relation with the penis?,-

my remnanted psyche is applauded,-what if I had never met
you,-the shoulders of this girl,-Rea, rubbing them,-is like
coming 'round the back of a sculpture,-I was afraid to say that
I found the similar soft/hard to the male as to the female,- I was
asked if you can not discover a dis-similarity here,- Then jaws
agape,-Like two resting in a hole,-like two calmed Leaning
together-on,-There haven't got to be spaces,-Rea Said much of
the 'Hell of a sky',-Then the better things got,- Rea spoke of
being fucked while her sex was bleeding,- Said in her psyche
this ascertained a confrontational danger,-Then the mutations,-
The carcass of a cow, found near garbage Cans in the suburbs
on a smoldering summer day,-The flies That gathered on it,-
and the stench which rose,-I knew I'd Pissed myself,-that
stench too,-I'd not dissolved the bad marks That I should had,
of dissolved,-I, shortened the length of Sleeping-time,-but the
price was the float of crushes on my Scaled bowled mind for
the remaining morning,-and after Partially dozing and coming
off from it,-I held another fear & insincerity for the remaining
evening 'til repeating the cycle as follows, the subsequent day,-

CAN I BORROW... FOR A SECOND ASK HE AND NOT
Make me weep,-I loved Rea, I really did,-there wasn't a matter
of eating her like nice cake,-the same days when roaming I
was told the world is an oyster,-I felt the supreme confusion of
my life, here,-every step up sprung a new danger,-There's
where I was defeated horribly ,-I split the crevices of my physi-

cality apart in the walls Of the scalpel draped high volts,-Is too that those days Were the run of the iron,-the militant chastity chances,- Do we do a retake,-The most explicitly ignorant man does Come back in my thought now as not a bad man,-You want to Know why,-Because.. he did have kindness,-that is one Thing,-a thing,-I let him dabble in his false hopes and Coincidences,-because I felt he was walking with the Essence of a child,-BUT back,-he was a inexplicable Creation to have on some of his promising moments,- Every single day of his life was carried on the most entirely Primal urge,-Could he see only his own Cum,-plodding--- his Stupidity,-The beauty

was that you got to do what exactly You desired,-acting out your own paradox,-then I got tired,- As I was sulked in a piss pure bathing lather,- bite my own Words so that the opposites don't attach to my bitterness,-

---

Wish there's to much time,-I do not know why you would choose This,-what about the vomiting,-what about the confusions,-what If he.. what if he..,-he'd always stated speculation in this sense,- Not of theories but as WHAT-IF,-Everything we saw had the pricing of emeralds,-I preferred nothing,-this heart to heart regret,-What is it that you would hope I would do with these,- you are allowed to bleed here,-to retch,-to incarcerate,-all for your own well-doing,-then I knew the question became,-What is humility,-the blessed nonsense which wholly sought its gratifying,-A planet's chemicals,-in my own willing fines,- closer to when you'll wont intimacy,-this is me here,-

Rea found out about new phrases,-And Too, repeated these For the remainder of our together episode,-When the safety Shuttered,-She was the silent mouse,-but broke out of that to Ask me if I felt weak,-wondered if that's why I've had nothing to Really say in the reasonable time that anyone would wonder Too why their friend had grown to nearly solemn silence,-Rea said that the apostles were muses to Christ,-ask me what would he have really been without them,-Tells me how he knew he'd been sold-out,-tells me also that the boulder shattered to pieces,-did not just roll aside,-as was said in some accounts,-Now I do feel rather pitiful that I had nothing to add to this,-

---

something my friend had put so much of her thoughts into,-
Though I hope I at least appeared interested,-I was.. It was that
I just had a very different ailment.. I was not where she was..
though our lives had coincided,-strange how these things all go
together,-I remember when she said that,-now, that was
something that.. I.. did understand.. though I could bring
Nothing from my miserable conscious to add to it,-

PICK THANK
   " Rea... I can... not only... won't be stated as I couldn't...
I've ... not... been the... coward.... Someone's pastured   The
fox... Rea... I can.. the heart... so fast... wont.. ounce.."

HERE YOU'LL LET GO OF ME-I'LL BE STEPS OFF-O' NOTE-
HETTS'S DREAM PRIOR TO DEPARTING
   " he... moved down slowly... thru... a city street... he...
sees. That.. the.. street.., dead-ends...he turns.. to.. continue
back... the way which he came...A crowd of   seemingly
hateful people have gathered... they begin pelting   him with
stones.. bottles... other debris from the street.."

Ebbey is woken-up by the pounding,-one of those times when
You wake with exact an image on your mind,-Rea,-Rea,-He
Thinks of her,-the visage cuts thru entirely clearer than it ever
Has before,-He will set out for her,-immediately,-
And where is Our Rea,-Anywhere,-Anywhere,-Above the
Stairs,-looking down on me from atop the trees,-Unable to
Keep my eyes open,-a remarkably stupid thing,-Loving her Like
This and then not going to do anything about the dilemma,-
Know the softest scent is secreted from her glands,-Rea,-
Rea,-down deeper and deeper,-It is wonderfully construing To
hold this primary function for having not entirely physically
Knowing her,-Makes a supremacy,-when wanting to relinquish
Her more,-Primly beautiful female,-but I've stated this
previously,-
   Not desiring sexual contact with Rea,-Would that be then That
she's more of you,-
1.Interior.
Rea stands on a dolly,-and is moved on this Under the line of
the screen.-so it appears that She's gliding,-in a dark dress
that looks as though it Would be colored onto a paper doll,-half

129

of her face Is cast in shadow,-The other side lit with a soft yellowish Lighting,-A number of spiral patterns are cast around the Interior,-along with the more intense pulsing yellow,- Rea looks at the camera,-then looks down at her feet and Begins sobbing,-

It has been burst from a stone,-Why did I go,- The scales of a cumbersome serpent that has surfaced and taken me down into the azure Night pool,- The Scarlet Woman preparing to Engulf you thru her sex,-I could not hold on a Day longer,-{I love you,-I love you,- as we're Then born again as rubies in trajectory with The earth}- Rea's Heart,- this qualifies her as A Goodly grievance,-there's a cry,-A wail bellowed Outward,- Making you want to gravel,- earnest,-Nowhere, puzzled episodic rune's bell, up, up,-lies joust a surrogate-I'm none other-you've gotten fast--a facet of loved-forgave the revolutions-a facet of generosity--lies sweep my breech like none, else-A facet from the gene pool-The cream white stag slowly nay-seething none other-

THE FOOLY EMBARRASSMENT, THAT I GOT TO FACE-TO-FACE-RE,RE-ASSEMBLE, in the usual placing:

Night sonnets, when Stephanie was the no-more-words-calmly-Hearted-lover-,-Stephanie was technically living the falldown,-Alone,-by her 'Self Aquarius Trackway',-Kept however, a video Tape recorder,-in order to watch documentaries on the lives Of vicunas,-She'd left the villatic area which she'd spent the Summer, Autumn, and Fall in,-and this spring had returned to The cities,-The arrogant aspect,-whilst you,-was that she'd Believed in the facile of how underground her life had been,-

1st CITIES NIGHT

Other than flush toilets,-what it the benefit her,-Stephanie thought that she could see none,-even running water was an inhibition,- She'd not minded retrieving water,-or even a pump,-now that this was no longer,-a big space was opened wide in her day,-but not of her consent,-She may return to the shops soon,-{Heard a squelching neon light outside her apartment window- the fever like a neonblip robed her vision, she opened her window and was bask by its glare,-not a new thing,-walks to her kitchen for a glass of water, - (Maybe this is a good point?, faucet water,-)After steadily gulping the down the water,-Staring awhile longer at the neon,-coming to find the strobing a pleasant sensation,-)Returning to bed,-

'FANTASIA'

Lying in bed there,-her back is badly cramped,-moves her Body on to each side several times,-but not managing to find this comfortable,-Lies two hours sleepless,-In a puzzlement for getting used to her new environment,-Rather roughly begins rubbing her left nipple,-dampening it with some saliva,- transported from her mouth to finger,-onto her nipple 'til it becomes stiff,- opening her nightgown,- with her free hand,- placing this hand directly on her pubic area,-Taking her forefinger to her clitoris,-her other fingers on her labia majora,- brushing that briskly,-'til working on her labia minora,-The callus neon blurting even thru the drawn blinds,-As 3 ballerinas where to form, go apart,-and rouse a circular gallant formation,- A swan floating freely on the water surface thru the middle of night 'til the early morning,-Onward,-The tuft of that bird's feathers reach a quill and Rise on its back as it's shuttered by the envisioning Placed in its impeccably vulnerable sleeping conscious,-Stephanie climaxed resembling the work-in- progress of Dribble which turned to an exuberant intangible flow,- A stroll of fluids from a formerly tranquilized source,- That with her perseverance turned in its end results To a quenchable soliloquized shade-grown thoroughly Solicitous orifice,-Then speedily to slumber time,-to prepare In doing this all-over in somewhat the approaching day,-

A'CATEREST:DOSPOSELL

Mulling the toilet box flip book,-Illustrates in motion a stork Beak as it's diving to gulp fish,-when flipped steadily details A dove fluttering from the ark window and also its return Back to the ark,-when creased and flipped in an even more Feverish manner illustrates a side view of a vulva receiving A penis, heretically taking it in,- Then a boy holds a Ba-toon Ball under his arm,-leans against the corner of a deteriorating Log cabin,- eagerly masturbates himself to orgasm,-the semen Pulses from his cock, ending up matted in the tuft of his pubic Hair,-cleans it up with a page that he tears from a magazine Article about

UFO reports,-the occurrence of losing explanation Of how the last hours were spent and discovering fervid countenance to the small incisions that you may discover on discreet places on your body,-which you will come to believe were left by extraterrestrial beings,-

A toilet box of biblical proportions has an extremely averted Illustration,-Appears to be a tampon inserted into a vulva,- Smoothness 'round the seams of the majora lips,-A footnote At the bottom of the illustration instructs the viewer to turn the Book upside down,-and view the illustration a different way,- When doing this, the illustration looks like a bottle containing Maybe an S.O.S.,- half protruding from the sandy shores it'd Washed up on,-A sensory aspect of the book shows two Pictures side-by-side-,- one of a boy holding a conk shell to His ear,-the other of a boy leaning his head against a urinal,- There's a button under each illustration that viewer is instructed To push in order to hear the sound which accompanies each Picture,-the conk shell illustration's sound is of a voice echoed Thru hollow canyon arches,-the urinal illustration's sound is of a boat's mass rising and plunking down to ocean floor as its breech end descends drudged,-

"BEREFT IMBECILITY"

"..ruby fez... canopio jar... ...at...the,,.feet.. of a caryatid...there's too... replicas.. ..of... ..species.. ..of... cats..."

-Abyssinian-
-Burmese-
 -Rex-
-Siamese-
-Persian-

"...Manx ... Maine Coon.. Himalayan..."

" we're... ..searched.. ..for. ..Rea... in the paraphrased Swiss district of ... we're.. ..TOWN... ..homes.. are here too rowed in duplicated architectural... dabble.. the mappings.. we're given by Rea.. failingly.. only illustrated Winslow Homer's best works... in small plates.. where his technique is lost.. We get directed by the residents.. taking the map and leads Us to the sensual emblem of deadend upon deadend...   But the places there are similar to the places from the piece of   TOWN which we'd dwelled in.. I see... dozens or so... girls Resembling Rea... might as well then have been her... Then on a piece of the strip were the vehicle stalls.. girls There who are younger are being contested to dress and Pose as make believe Rea replicas..."

BOOK OF MAPS: THINGS WITHOUT REA :

(1.)-The inspirational tomb,-falls short on a few of its steps,- Every person sweeps a way clear,-A blue coat,- Her hair Nearly red,-Teeth shining to us from her surprise smile,- As we've waited to be loved,-lying on her back,-Pleased To have a head placed on her bosom,-Determine this for The rest of your life,-(2.)- 'CROCODILE'
Analyze a 15 minute film made by a young gay filmmaker,- Opens with a shot of wind rustled thru the leaves of a tree During the hours close to morning,-a nondescript figure Draws a chalk circle on a stone floor,-stands off camera Reciting a chant- -Mu pa telai-
   -Tu wa melai-
      a, a, a.
   Tu fu tulu!
   Tu fu tula
      a, a, a.
   -Mu pa sa-
A demon manifests in the chalk circle,-Obviously Trapped within its circumference,-The film cuts and The camera is dollying along a patio in The Fall,-roving Past the chairs and tables which leaves lie on,-The film so much captures the atmosphere of the place By using a slowly paced dolly shot to cover the entire ground,-this image ends once the camera comes to rest on the horizon line after tracking over the patio,- the film cuts to its last scene,-An older man who was presumably a filmmaker in his youth(still is/),-is interviewed in a vastly under-lit interior,-a large study laced with book-shelves and an aquarium,-He reflects on his career,-saying even after all of those films,-in which he reflected characters,-He's got no-clue as to why he still doesn't know people any better than he did when he started,-the film ends with him drinking from a coffee cup,-cutting to the credits which are drawn on a chalk board,-

---

(3.)-' QUEENLY NIGHT'

Analyze a series of short films which benefit greatly From their Pagan imagery,-the first film,-the camera Moves up a long passage,-surprisingly for a shorter Film this was shot in wide screen,-So the sides of the Passage are as well clearly visible in detail,-The smooth Walls are lit by torches which are secured onto them,- The image grows grainy towards the end of the corridor Due to the growing frenzy of the flames which unbalances The lighting,-the image fades,-when it fades back in,-the Camera is dollying thru another corridor,- This time a temple Type chamber,-The camera is moving on the walkway to The throne which will become visible soon,-There are pools Of water on ---- each--- side-- of the walkway,--The place is illuminated by the huge chandeliers which hang from the ceiling,-a number of images are superimposed over the main image,-particularly doves hovering,-A waif like angel accompanied by nymphs,-all playing harps,- Smoke rising from censers,-When the camera arrives At the throne-- it too,-continues up the staircase which Leads up to its platform,-A fully chested woman whose Visage reflects an ominous lushness,-wears a heavy Green clothe robe,-Drops it to her feet,- Is wearing a Blood red silk slip underneath,-mouths to the camera,- The lighting grows black,-When it rises up,- there are A troupe of winged serpent type shadows prancing all Over the walls of the room,-maybe the one flaw of the Film,-The woman stands wickedly smiling at the camera A red smoke rises around her,- this shot is unconvincing In the cliché of how it conveys ethereal evil,-This closes The first film,-the second also begins with a dolly shot,-This time thru a locker room,-one that would seem to Be unisex(HUH),-maybe the film's makers were hoping to Attract viewers this way,-The lush images of supple young Male and female flesh,-Are perforating in their arousal,-The camera moves out of there,-rests on the a character's Back,-we never see this man from a frontal view,-We follow Him thru what looks like an old school building,-He begins Picking up his pace a little,-As if he were running from something,-an ambient resonance loops continuously on the soundtrack,-he enters an elevator,-note that he is extremely un-patient while waiting for it,-As he steps in,- And plans to go downward,-Then the elevator starts dropping floors,-the quicker it drops,-the smaller it seems to grow,-We feel that when it hits bottom that the man will be inside something not much bigger than a small cube,- in the excitement we lose the logic of how he would shrink to fit into that?,-Though as he nears closer to the bottom,-the elevator begins returning to its normal size,-Though note that he'd been pressed in between what resembled two planks,-one to his back,-one to his chest/front,- The elevator comes to a violent crashing stop,-he and the camera are thrown with force against its damaged walls,-the camera is at a low obscure angle after the crash,--He is not visibly in the frame,-we assume he's to the side out of the camera's range,-The elevator door is however visible from where the camera is placed,-We see that it is being forced open,- men step inside,-out of the camera's range they take the protagonist from out of the elevator,- We still only see his back,-The film cuts,-The camera starts dollying behind the men,-TWO large frightening men seem to be taking our hero somewhere,-there's a struggle which is shown to us by the use of a montage of still photographs that are both over and underexposed,-the camera dollies with our hero,-As he runs down another long passage,-Enters a door,-and then he is inside another locker room,-He staggers past beautiful nude male/female bodies,- He comes to a escape door you-might-say at the back of The locker room,-which opens to a courtyard,-With high Hedges,-Jolting fountains,-neatly groomed grounds etc..,- He runs from out of the frame,-The camera slowly makes 360degree turn and reveals to us that the action took place inside an enormous castle,-the second film ends here,-The 3rd of the films,-is a departure of sorts being that it starts as a documentary,-that is a study and debate on the Thylacine,-a flesh-eating marsupial,-It resembles a Tiger, a wolf, and maybe too combining a hyena,-An Extinct species,-the last known Thylacine died in captivity In 1936,-The film states that nearly 12,000 years ago,-The Thylacines were driven off from the mainland of Australia,-maybe when Indonesian sailors brought Dingoes,-which were proven to be excellent at hunting, -It was that Thylacines were dangerous animals,-responsible For killing many sheep,-a bounty was drawn on their Scalps,-The final bounty paid Thylacine was killed in 1909,-One that was last shot was in 1930,-captured in 1933 and as stated before died in 1936,-A creature free of any affection though it had been tamed,-The last known Thylacine was named 'Benjamin',-This part of the film ends,-and does not continue the mystery of how they've been sighted,-and the clues to how the species may still be in existence,-It stops with The actual footage of the captive Thylacine,-The film makes a transition to abstract fiction ,- A crane shot lowers the camera down from the sky to come down upon the aftermath of a celebration,- streamers and banners are still hanging,-swayed a little by the night air,-the only living being,-is a young man who sits at a table,-looking smug,-Smoking a cigarette,-The camera moves in on his face,-and then fades,-to flash back to what has occurred,-Starting this strangely,-In a patch of cabbages that grows on the remains of a stone surface,-Small arm-less undeveloped(other then legs) embryo-type orbs scurry about,-the sound of scrapes on a blackboard is heard on the soundtrack,-This fades to the image,-Of a young girl standing beside a dirt-road,-Wearing a long red summer dress,-And holding a red Umbrella in tho faint drizzle,-the green of the wood Behind with the overcast half dimness conveys the humidity of the atmosphere,-She waits at the road for a ride,-though unsuccessfully,-The camera moves into her face,-Fades to the image of alien creature,-In the vine covered remains of an empire,-He lies on his back,- thru the strength of his thoughts he rises some of the toppled pillars that lie too in the empire's remains,-This fades,-and next we see the young man who sat at the celebration's aftermath in the films opening,-Now undressing a beautiful girl,- Though this leads to lying down with her as she is nude,-and not making love,-running his hand along her form,-The film returns to the image of the Thylacine in captivity,-holds this image,-And then goes to the credits,- (4.)-'QUEEN LAND'- the railing is constructed of stone,-she sits on it,- wearing a Pink suit jacket,-black hose,-black skirt stopping just under her kneecaps,-she closes her eyes for a moment to let the view of

136

the city behind her fluctuate.-MORE TO THE EYE-Crawls inside the carcass of whale,-Took off his clothes   Before entering,-took a flashlight with him,-Closes the Slit seam entrance point from the inside,-turns the light On, Begins masturbating,-turns the flashlight off accidentally As he ejaculates,-the sound of a skipping record is heard,- As he howls out his fervid orgasm,-The insides of the whale   Fill-up completely with dice that materializes in great numbers As his cum deflects from the sides of the whale,-

' TODAY'S REA '

As any other would,- The moment which I awake in the Morning I begin to visualize Rea,-I hold this image for Awhile 'til I try to block-it-out,-or cast it from my mind,- I have tried casting runes which symbolize death,-I haven't got Rea's death in mind,-Just the death of the Constant visualization of her lusciously streaming capture,-There are times when I feel that I don't want to forget her,- I await the climatic stance of her,-but it doesn't mark its Account,- I think of lying on a bed,-her leaning against the Side of it,- myself reaching down to brush my hand across her face,- I recall holding her once in my arms,-Her leaning her Face into my nape as I bent my head down,-I never want to Go away from there,-though I only fell in love with her months After Ascertaining the prosperous slither of that evening,-

'LEAVE ME TO THINK BY MYSELF'

What do I do with all of this,-A treasury of precision measured Stanzas,- When I love this girl,-Though with a void to the conventional sensibility of a romantic longing,- I haven't got a traditional relationship with Rea,-I mean it was not Ordinary,-There is a sociological penalty for not desiring the Rea's Body,-Then looking directly at its cadence,-Rea has not had an understanding to this,-only courageous mewing,-Says it is clearly sensible,-But she's truly abandoned the formative estimation of how it could progress,-

' MOVEOVER THE CLEAR DAY'

" tangent... skunk... muses.. we're choked up... hardly bottle necked Rea... only a tribulation.. you've got what... is took... got to've feasted... wool...The departure.. I hope... the roots.. the lasers.." -what are the things that I know--what are the things that I know-

'RE-CAPTURED'

Rea walks to the tip of a diving board,-when she gets there,-She turns around,-So that I am directly in front of her,-I have Got a camera and I'm preparing to take her photograph,- She drops her bathing suit's shoulder straps,-reveals her Bosom,-Though she frowns,-I Get my wished photograph,- She covers her bosom by rising the bathing straps back over Her shoulders,-Turns around,-tells me to please step from the Board,-I do so,-And she dives into the water,-I will no longer Look at the above photograph,-

SEDNG FEELINGS OF A CROWDED BARRAGE OF FACES-

Stephanie scuttled thru the city's streets,-She'd not Set foot her for what she'd estimated as an eternity,-She sees how much was destroyed that was built back Up anew,-She doesn't want to search for familiarity,-As If knowing it's better to let it just go,-There's Some things That should never be brought back up,-Several of those Actually,-what is the point of thinking of all of them now,- Stephanie thinks that it is actually entirely normal to not Want to seek any old familiar people,-She doesn't go Even to see the street where she'd grown-up,-Knows That a star explodes on the thought of that block,-See How easy this can be if she just remains unknown,-Not Letting anybody know that she's come back,-Hide from Them if she sees them coming,-Hopes she'll have time To,-After this long they'd probably not recognize her instantly,-Even her parents,- she did not inform them of her return,-She's answered none of their letters in the last dozen years,-Had her fill of them,-she hates to put it that way,-BUT she's got no other way to figure it out in her mind,-Though she does feel sad that she's got no contact with them,-but that is by choice,-Maybe because she knows the difficulty of re-entering someone's life after such a large amount of time has elapsed,-Thinks that it would be funny if they saw her and did not know who she was,-She knows that she wouldn't say that she's their daughter,-If they came into a place she was working,-that is another thing,-if she had a name-tag on,-something would have to resonate to them,- But maybe not,-

'Cause hopefully they figure she'd have never Chose to return to here,-If she hadn't got a name tag on,- Maybe they wouldn't know her,-Then she thinks something that Turns this around and somewhat saddens her,-What if her Parents are hoping that she doesn't return,-what if they never Want to see her again,-Can't understand why this saddens Her,- Maybe because she does like them,- Is just not yet ready for them,- needs time to first organize her life,-then appear to them,- OR she wants to punish them by not letting them have a part of Her,-BUT if she does never cross paths with them again,-she would hope that they'd remember her as she was,-It is sort of that-- she-- does--- not--- want—them- to- ask- her—to explain the last years,-Hopefully they would just be so glad to see her,-that they would not ask anything about the years which she's been absent from their life,- And what if they'd looked every where for her in those years,-What if they expected the worse things had become of Their daughter,-Stephanie had also a husband that she walked from,-taking with him their daughters,-Who would be about 9 & 6years of age,-Probably don't remember their mother,-Though Stephanie would at least like to see them,-just a picture Of them,-Or if they've got someone else that they considered their Mother,-would they have to be told to even remember they have a mum That went off a ways back,-Stephanie hopes that maybe that is the case,- That she'll not have to know,-Then Stephanie figures she'll have to take steps to solve all of this things,-She cannot just take easy steps out of situations for her whole life,-She's fell guilty of this before,-And feels that she needs to some-way recompense for it,-

---

HE PASSED NEARLY THE PAST

Rea, another reminder of how you made me feel,- pass where you are leaving your home,-You do Not notice my presence,- I follow behind you down the street,-Why were you happy to meet me when you turned around,-I thought of your ass being visible when you bent over wearing This short dress,-Then cruelly revealing your open vulva to me,-As if this notion was done to scold me,-It Resembles a starfish To me,-I thought too when I saw it,-that somebody is one who Will see how far the momentary whim can get him,-I'm not he,- Then   to the oddest prank that you've set for me,-I once discovered your nude body entirely encased by grasshoppers,- There was not the shadow of a doubt,-I tried to brush them off,- Though as I did so more came in swarms,-I thought when they Departed,- I'd find your body moistened by a semen green film,-I'd visualized us making love,-Too entirely encased by Them,-Attempting penetration with them attached to your majora,-AND them crawling under the skin on the end of my prick,-I will stop,-AND proceed off from that supposed distaste,-

'MID-DISINTEGRATION'

The picture is supposed to show the Thylacine,- Showed a creature from a side-view,-its face was not Visible,-The back of the creature,-Stripes, Stiff tail,-Must've belonged to that creature,-Though the animal Has been sighted on occasional direct view for a matter Of seconds in direct sunlight,-"A Red Hare... makes... His... appearance on a dirt road... has been pushed Out... to...the.. water... lies in it... reacting.. 'A Lady' 'A Lady'.. the capsizing wood vessel... Has Clung to The post... of a bridge... she'd... passed.. under.. .... Quickly back... thru.. the fields... the Red hare is dampened." "To let go... of that feeling... missions... I won't go nowhere.. Then from the distance from across the field to the road... she... plainly in... view to any... one.. sitting on the porch.. she's gone half way over the field... half way... over she's.. Gone... her children are out thru the field... with hopes... To've found her.. Onto the warm spot on the earth... they heard maybe Her voice swelteringly.. echoing... about the... surroundings.. then that too ceases..." "Also as...she'd .. gone.. to retrieve... water... from.. the.. well.. a.. Night... in the winter...didn't want to return.. leave footprints... Just end at one spot... ceasing in their steps... she's not be aside... them.. she had to've.. been taken up in the Sky..." "The huge bird.. nailed.. to.. a wall.. Six men.. Stretch their arms out.. fingertip.... To... fingertip.. Across.. both.. of.. the.. bird's.. wings.. ..nowhere does the photograph... turn up... I remember.. A rendering of it.. that looked as.. if it... were a colored.. plate photo.. I took it to be.. real... have fell to falsehoods..." "The red hare has got... a.. streak... of.. joy.. thru... sadness... Then.. in.. a... new.. place.. it begins.. does

things... returns back.. over a foot bridge.. at the composure...
of sunset..."

ONE WEEK LAUGHING: TO A GOOD HELLO

2[Nd] What Stephanie dreams on the second night-

Her home street,-Looks downward from her bedroom window,-
A figure appears in the half darkness of the streetlights,- Wears
A tall hat,-A white coat,-And pants to match it,- Looks directly
up at Stephanie,-Who realizes in the dream That she is maybe
only 13teen years of age,-They make Direct eye contact,-
frightening to Stephanie,-Who draws The curtains and returns
to her bed,-Shifts,- Again back to The window,- The figure
appears again underneath the Streetlight,-signals her to come
down to him,-She is Frightened,-Draws the blind,-Returns to
bed another time,- After a succession of moments(in dream
time),-she gets Up from the bed and walks downstairs,-out the
front door,- To the street,-the figure is still under the light,-She
goes to Him and a flickering comes in front of her eyes,-He
takes her In his arms putting her in his coat,-She is next aboard
a train Coming into a station,-Seeing her reflection on the glass
of A window,-she sees that she's now again an adult,-
Inclination Makes her take her bag and step to down from the
train to the Platform,-looking to her right she sees her former
husband,- He helps another woman down off the train,-this
woman seems Have the exact likeness that Stephanie had
when she'd met him,-Stephanie pauses there and then
awakes,-

Nearing morning,-Ebbey Flint,- Fully realizes the discontent
of his father no longer being with him,-waking to a large silent
House,- has an unpleasant feeling unlike no other that he's
Known,-and then thinking that every day will begin this way
From here onward,-After about half an hour,-he usually goes to
Wake his mother,-Knowing that he's got to do this,-Or she'll
stay in Her bed the entire day,-enters her bedroom and sits
beside her In the chair next to her bed,-Where his father had
always sat in the morning,-Ebbey thinks that it is unfortunate
that she'll sleep only in the bed that her husband died in,-
Ebbey knows that has got to hold another feeling of grief,-And
without any sanctuary other than what he can offer, -Which

these days is very little,-He hasn't yet known what to make of his life,-For time's Remainder,-Has he buried the magick that was in him,-Hardly,-It is sucked up in him,-Prying on the moment that It will dispense,-Though maybe Ebbey's disappointment was That the magick didn't rise him over grief,-could it only Assist Him,-not remake him,-At least not the core of his existence,-While he sits in the chair before waking Mother,- Every a bad Thought lands in his mind,-They're constructed layer atop Layer,-Disappointment,-Distrust,-Dislike,-He flinches to free Himself from them,- not wanting to let them cast down his day,-He set small altars up,- casting runes of death to these Damages,-Lit the Altar candles every morning as dawn Broke,-Then he returned to sleep after deconstructing Them,-Sometimes he'll wait to let mother wake on her Own,-even if it means sitting in the chair by her for 2to3 Hours,-While waiting,-He tries to project pleasances,-

'IMPERFECTIONS'

"Arms… that hold.. you what.. else… there's got to be… the Arms that hold… you what… else.." – It is up to you, Rea,-Free me,-Free me,-"It is said that you get up… and.. That… you… go.. on…"-Rea reenacts this too,-

(1.)-'HIGHER'
looking at the reactions that Rea has gotten,- It begins where she is dressed in a kimono,- The print of the image has been badly damaged,- Her face is hardly visible,-Just her body dressed as The picture skips,-Also a monochrome print,-Except That when she enters a room of fruits,-They've been Hand tinted,-The next print is of much better quality,- Just Rea in a pitch black room,-Where the only section that Is fully lit is her face,-And the lighting shifts from either of her hands, occasionally,-The blackness of the image is altered as a yellow seeps over the frame,-

(2.)-'NECESSARY'
"The Red Hare… does… not.. wait at all. thru any of the parts of the eve… doesn't need any help in that way…"
"My appreciation… the haze… Green forests… rhapsody… type… meadows… ponds lined the sides of the dirt road in…. the… day… suddenly… came… mechanics of the

142

ease... a hideaway of   capable gapes... I..."-Enter Ebbey flint, again-   Preparations   for   a   casual-though-valid   day   of His life,-Starting this after he wakes mother,- He decides to contact Rea,-Easily he knows where To look for her,-But what if he wants to make it Difficult for himself?,-"Knows... that... if... he... waits..For... her... she'll.. probably... not contact him... She hasn't made the first steps before... so... he.. Puts... aside.. waiting for her... going to... directly.. Find... her... today.."

(3.)-'PLEASURES TO KNOW, PLEASURES TO NOT KNOW'
        -look for Rea-
        -in a Rea garden-
        -look for Rea-
        -look for Rea-
        -find her in a Rea garden-
Ebbey will figure to just walk thru the suburbs and hopefully bump shoulders with her?,-After that's unsuccessful he will plan other routes to rediscovery on the spot/'The way Ebbey wrote these as notes after each phase of it'
        <1>
-first by chance search for Rea-I walk down each street-Not looking at the faces of any of the passers by-Want to just keep walking? Without Even hoping that Rea will show up-She Doesn't Come My Way Here-Maybe The Point That Never Ends Is That WE Haven't WANTED her to Ever come a long a way Remember Clown don't be afraid-The minute Rea Fools me I start my dispute all over My Veil-Make the world fold-Your Apprehension-Want to just keep Walking? No hope to foresee Rea-Here's what you gotta say go past Even if you do know her-and the Best is that the chances are that You will not know who she is-All of Pointless dowitcher worries and scuffles   Were for the point of nothing-Want to Just keep Walking? Want to just keep Walking?
        <2>
-gone from home-To town and no Rea-How many sweet virtues remind You of her lateral secretions-Get back There -I went to the shop windows and Hissed at how they

distorted my appearance-I heard them aside saying-you know you'll Be altogether-gone from home-To town And no Rea-Then you do see her-Walking Early back to her home-Grope her from behind- Run your hands over her ribs-coming to her breasts- Pitching the nipples-Then just leave! If you hate These lusts that you'll notion for notion confront Her with-Rapping the valor-recognizing the squirming Blush-All you've got left is the way past where you See her-to go off from that-

'REA DISCOVERY ROOM'

While he'd scraped the street in His imaginary search For her,-Our Rea sat alone at her home,-As If she Were on the verge of breaking in-to tears,-But Was Holding back,-She didn't like feeling a sadness for no Reason,-Seemed to her that she was waiting here for Something,-She'd have to leAd herself from these unpleasances,- She wouldn't waste this afternoon,-So she set out,-not in search Of Ebbey but in search of setting something off inside herself,-

     -REA NOTE-
       <3>

I quickly fled the fay questions-Thru the adventure That turns on the danger draw-how do I insight this Abnormality-flaw for flaw-I'm draping satisfaction-The relics which were saved are of the most tiresome Vulgarity-not 'til they let me see a new way to a weary Likeness-We'd used to've jotted down the contending Vouch-My silver sin-My silver sin-We're the same person-Let Us Be The Same-So you've not got nothing too unattractive-O' that ugly face-The blemished and raw visage-Just to let out-We're the same person-

THREW OUR OWN VISIONS

A Self explanatory Rea Verse. What do you think Rea will care about?

       <4>

-not about a way or leaving a place-not either about ruins-about here is what she's up against-here is what she's under-heard you call it oppression-is that the phrase to've coined it-

       <5>

Rea shall doubtlessly run a course into Ebbey's Would-be kind words,- The desires of Rea's Goal Change quickly, -Felt a burning,- "LOOKS FOR E.F."

SPOILED, SPOILED, SPOLIED,

'How We Came Together'
         < 6 >
-definitional, their bodies pressed up against each other-her breasts against his thin flat chest-appear as two walls of barrier prior   to   merging   to   coitus-"torn...   shivered... appearance... smashed over so many times... 'til... gain... the... layered... proportionate... textural... summary... of what they.. contain...",-not dull in the least-two friends have taken off-

Too,-The Magick brings itself back thru Ebbey's sex Completely,-like it was to reemerge in the ripe of his Climax,-" has... he... got.. any.. thing... for.. me..",- Jolted out from his orgasm,-Lies next to Rea,-Who smiles Right back to his strain,- The room where they lie,- Is itself Pried from its steady base,-to be pushed up to situate itself On a rotational axis,-when it is flung back down on them,-They caress each other out of other jitters,-"then... there's...spoken... to... be.. much.. pleading... then there's... some.. kindred.. plasma.. cuddles.. the soul's core.. even when sanctioned as... physical...",-
-ascertaining a slow mountain-
-I see the day right-
-I see the day right-
-hold me up alone-
-hold me up alone-
-ascertaining below the mound-

RE-FINDING WHAT TO DO

Ebbey felt the Magick's burst as it was released,-Knew it from the extra sting which it leaves,-Its fire etched ripple rolled over & out his veins As if it were patting his bloodstream each step Of the way,-what to make of the Magick, again,-He would have to go back to how he'd intended To proportion its powers before it'd hid down in him,- Re-surged the rite to develop him above his heart,-

STOP GIVING LONGER

Ebbey Doesn't however   leave immediately for Home (can pause before setting out to use the Magick),- Stays for awhile with Rea, instead,-She ask him to paint Her toenails,-He obliges to do so,-Holding Rea's outstretched Foot as she lies back and directs you on how she wants this Done,-is to say the least an incredibly pleasing experience if You're one of her lovers,-gripping her foot steadily,-kissing It several times after proceeding from toe to toe,-See Rea's Head leaned back, and smiling,-A beautiful daylight shines In and obscures that image of her,-Slow dancing with her, Wearing nothing but underwear,-To rub your fingers over the Seam line of her underpants,-feeling her soft skin,-is too a hymn,-Again back to sex with her,-This is as exuberant as you'd Liken it to be,-If you were very much in either Lust OR Love For her,-when making love with her I'm reminded of the image Of a jewelry box opened on a dresser, with a swarm of bees Flying out from it,-Then I don't need an explanation?,- Ebbey exits from Rea's late in the evening,-Arrives home Long after dark,-He was delayed a dozen or so times on the Way To Home,-He kept wanting to go back to Rea,-He'd Turn around and start walking back to see Rea,-he just Wanted to have to never leave again,-But was pulled by Something inside,-as if it were telling him that he had A mission,-that he had something waiting for him to discover It,-so he was to proceed home,-and not that night return to Rea,- AT home he finds mother asleep upstairs,-does not wake her To tell her that he's here,-he just heads directly for his bedroom,- In the a crate in his closet he stored something for this occasion,-The occasion of when the He Felt The Magick blister in its full force,-simple things actually,-A book of transcribed spells/ chants,-also a piece of red chalk,-he takes these and proceeds to the basement of the house,-Doing this both on Whim and inclination,-On the stone floor of the basement he Draws a circle with the red chalk,-takes off his clothes,-and kicks Them aside,-turns off the lights so that he is standing in absolute blackness,-with a lighter that he brought down there with him,-He ignites this in order to read quoted chants from the book,-After reading some of them specifically,-he hears a crack like thunder,-sees a powder fluffed smoke cloud start to fuse in the circle's bounds,-this fusion rises up to a little over his own height,-sees a unbearably crass visage staring out from the smoke,-It flashes its eyes,-A yellow flicker,-

which sends Ebbey to his knees,-Quite crashing,-it feels as if he's fallen from a building,-sees a depthless pit swirling down in his psyche,-Seems that his skin is ripped off his body too,- Though that only In his mind,-Falls,-back up to consciousness,- sees still the scathing therein the circle,-that which he must diminish quickly,-Its cast enough light that he can quote from the book,- Though he Stops first,-Thinking this might be a misjudgment,- Now seeing only a swab which he must utilize to his own advantage,-He rapidly quotes a passage from the book,-Which shrinks the fusion,-to where it tends to evaporate,- Ebbey rekindles his blessed self,-

CRUX<1>PLACED AHEAD-(to Rea)

He cannot take away immediately the impression that I Sufficiently assessed throughout my existence here,- Who is he if for so he believes that in the gentile lurch Of his dialogues that my poised effectual rivets will Swiftly fall,-I will not be told that I did not care for you,-

Rea,

It's true that a person's life can in the end leave them With absolutely nothing,-Less than they've ever thought They could live without,-Also there's some big hits That you'll never regroup after,-I remember a person (not-myself) who was rid of they only possibility that   they could ever see for themselves,- They just went on living,-But the sparking was actually entirely gone from their eyes,-They could find nothing else that was worth seeing to them,-And when they Had what they were a goner with-Out,-they hadn't even been clear on the measure of its Value,-SAD, Sad,-My friend Rea, I never want you to be as they were,-

Rea,

Sometimes I don't know a thing about Love, Hope Or Any shining light for the matter of that fact,-Then I feel Nothing sunk into my heart as I underwent living,- I hope you do think that,- Other days I seem to want to get up and prove my life,-'cause I know   who you are,-I won't believe that I underwent your friendship and didn't learn at all where you stand,-I feel 'by your side',-

Rea, 'The Exuberant Daydream'-start with me being lent advice thru people who are strangers to me-Then living in one of those high up Houses-omens of badness are placed   On my doorstep-I receive visitors all Day-who remain in silence-when the Backyard pool isn't frozen over-it's   Inhabited by gillmen from the fear Driven tales that were told-then I Come to watching them in the water-Sure bet entertainment-whispered Exposureless view of spending a   Life with-Out communicating with you-

You Got The Knack Of Making Your Eyes Flicker,- That Cuts Directly Through My Body,- There aren't lies that you tell, Rea, you don't Tell any that are about living,-When You're Placed Away Too,-There The Unquenchable Lust For Time-To-Sleep Begins All Over- What Will You Do The Next Time Your Spirit Is Free- How Will It Differ From What You Did The Time Before-

COSMOS NAUGHT

Adios eternity,-does a Rea come to me,-This fineland time,-Here, How Rea's discovery of herself got to where she was Feeling that she'd never be aside of any groups of thoughts,-I... letgo her to what's a sin,-

We're having a goodbye with a person that we're close with,-Wait, had been close with,-Though for a lot of time we'd been estranged from them,-We've dreamt of this goodbyo,- Though...Though... Why... We've expected to findout that they've left us On the next morning,-"His... Magic Hands... don't feelup the Afternoon"...,-Seems as though what he wrote before,-Being Held by him,-his masculine Bear grip around your body,- That epochs childhood warmth,-Why coming from a hardened Man,-Though.. Though.. then he walks to his car,-Is drove away And he halfsmiles,-preparing for him not wanting you to miss him,-have you seen the face that I am speaking of,-

It's a trying naughty visage,-as too he steps away... As too he Steps away,-a prickly red hare appears to me again,-And Yes Also I'm riding down with it in an elevator,-Has got a shuffle of Magazines,-I'm hoping to see their contents,-Some person Has got to say,- "I need something too",- "Not plain old safety",-A prettier girl,-Dressed in a frock,-Sits by the railing with her legs Folded, -I keepup at her, -trying at her nerves with my fingers

brushing behind her ears,-The irritation cuts to a smile,-"Here...
is.. how.. I would have hoped you'd have.. Trusted Me",-
-can you see-
-can you see-
-can you see-
-if.. you.. can.. not..-
-if.. you.. can.. not..-
-whats.. the use of you-
-whats.. the use of you-

BUZZLE HEAP

Rea had(as I said) set outward for proof,-This I will say is how
she comes into her own on it,-first,-She was the one who
wished everyone to do their bests,-Then she thought that if she
gave them that,-then what in eternity could've defeated them,-
She,- keeps with saying never give up, She,-Keeps with saying
words are just words,-Until you learn a damn thing about their
undercurrents,-Here goes the proof that Rea needed at that
point,-Knew that she had the capacity to have love for a lot of
people simultaneously,-Too knew, that she'd before relied on
only herself,-so she figured thru all this, it's herself who holds
her together,-and not somebody else,-never has been anyother
people,-Wait.. forsaking the times that she'd put all her beliefs
in others,-it was the fact that she believed that they were
saving her,-That their choices were what held her up high,-then
she gets to tell herself,-that you must know that they really did
nothing,-It Was you.. It Was you..,-Is that.. Is that.. a badpiece
of news,-Like a sweeter mother,-Rea wouldn't bury this fact
away,-Thought Too that as long as she's going to everyday
stick with it,-Then she's got to grow from it,-Says also that she
can still be there to love people and gather an assessment of
self-worth from what she'll share with whoever,-Yes, seeing
this,-This way,-Has got a potential that was prior unrealized to
her,-Felt like She saw things that she was capable of,-It's
amazing when you Feel like you could do anything,-Walk and
be anywhere,-Then you disregard a fear that usually follows
that feeling,-I wish I could literally be you,-When I cannot be,-
That's then why I don't hope to see you again, ever,-unlike my
mistaking,-Our Rea will not want to be another person,-just her
now,-This is the time that she's got to herself,-Does it mean a

lot if she does something outward with it,-What does that validate,-If she uses it all to imagine things,-Then it is just as justifiable,-Then I am Re-reminded why I love this person,-Her strength for burying Peoples evaluations of her,-When she doesn't want them,-And has got to be this time,-Disregarding a predictable future,- Must just be a riddle,-Then Rea,-Right away,-Another time you Were as alive,-

"YELLOW ENCHANTER"

"Were.. Rea's.. fingers and hands.. as slender as I thought them.. to.. be.. I saw them grasping the binding spine on.. A blue book.. which she proceeds.. to open and.. read.. aloud passionately.. it just must be her lovely dramatization is that why I want to be hearing her... Or isn't.. It.. Just.. That.. Then I needed anything that kept me alive"   "He speaks the demeaning verses.. in order to only bring you down.. by.. him.. these.are.. ..the.. humiliations.. that.. I.. would.. not.. Verbalize.. even.. If.. I.. could.. what is.. the.. point.. of.. the.. hurt.. I.. Get.. from.. this person.. unbelievable.. that.. it.. is.. as.. fresh.. As.. if.. it.. had... been.. presently.. jolted.. out.. at.. me.. Hater.. a.. hater.. then.. too.. I.. draw.. a.. respect.. for.. The.. beauty.. marks.. on.. him.. but the worst rips draw On me.. I want to rid time.. I.. I.. come.. to.. the.. rescues.. Of his scene"

CROCK-NOTES-TO REA 100

<1>-Everyone's source seems to notice my anomaly,-Not that they scathe who I am,-Rea, I wanted to just remind you of wall, barrier, distance, call it-what-you-will-between them and I,-You know when first find out what sex is,- ..I guess it's all the more confusing,-trying to understand that normality is expected of everybody,-and already then you can't live up to it,-and you know it,-you really know yourself already,-and you know what you can never be like,-aren't I like that,-I am,-getting farther away from them,-I won't put you in there with them,-I kept you here,-It's closer still,- I have pride for it,-that not a soul could take out of me,-<2>-What if you would travel from here to your heart,-almost the whole world and find not much more than what you had when setout out on the trip,-Rea, if you came back, would you just be content to have average things for the rest of your life, - 3>-In

fairness,-I hated once or more over,-every single person,-and when I was doing that,-I forgot about you for a time almost longer then the time I'd known you for,-Then I wanted not a thing,-There's things I could do well with,-but I did not desire them enough to seek them out,-To actually seek them out,-To actually make them a goal,-And also there were stretches so long where they were the last things on my conscious,-That I guess that made them mean extremely little,- I did ever after that want them at all,-My conscious point Became to never want them,-Then I think importantly there Were those things that made me spiral down,-But at this point were I've begun to-want-to-tell you of them,-I have put them all aside me,-what is a person anyway who derives their lustfulness from my displeasure,-Rea, should we even concern ourselves with them,-I've been told both ways,-That it's an important thing,-And,-That it's not,- Remembering the displeasure that made me,-As much   As the leasances,-I know there were plans and plans of Awful things that I wanted to act out,-Though.. Though.. As sank,-Those I idea went downward with me,-The time That I spent fused against what I believed had caused all Of this,-This way of living that I hated,-I saw after that,-How I let it make me nothing,-It had also been what I Had put into it,-that I think made it worse,-I was done With that,-and.. then I remembered you,-But not like I had before,-All that I had put into disliking,-had taken a major portion of what I could have put into an ideal of you,-<4>-Am I saying how selfish I was,-Yes I am trying to explain that,-It's falling farther luckily,-No, then it's close back to me,- strong enough that even after hiding it,-that even if I need call upon it,-Then it is freshly awakened,-New,-   Rea, unfortunately, I will never be fully rid of this,-I hope   That you can understand that,-

I, LAST, STRAIGHT ON

"Made.. worse better.. worse.. possibly.. I may have.. been not slowing.. someone.. straying.. you were told.. you were told.. give me a change of what I reel over" "Again that Rea.. I remember her carried home.. near dusk.. the greenest fields.. Oncemoreover them.. I'll go early from home.. not faking any Choices.. right.. way.. to.. lose.. your.. hard goods.. ON" WHY

HIM, OF ALL THESE PEOPLE Amuse to it,-The colder person eats the bigger number,-Then Says bye,-It should be something other,-It's cruel for you equally Not to,-by-the-way-very-moving,-come back here to fly,-Now They form,-Thanks for waiting,-I am followed down for taking a Possession of his,-It is found after I disregard it,-it cannot be Likened to me,-Though.. it's clearly obvious,-he parts Too,- Not at all angry,-Sees this sketch of things,-I asked that the Ride be blocked,-and that we'd have to edge our way past the Object that they place by the entrance,-Remember what I am Asked by him,-to analyze this,-Which I hold,-over papers Partially typed and written by hand also,-Oh, it is her,-Why?,- Does she stand as the crux of this non-sequence that was Pulled out-of-hand,-I know who I told be there,-Down inside You,-somehow,-<5>-Rea, don't include me as having been a faithless person,-I thought of good fortune,-I handed you beauty that I thought You could do more with then I could,- For at least that says Something to me,-I think you've forgotten,-It is just trouble Everyday,-and more tensing, though,-I know that we've Experienced disassociation with being classified according To our sexual orientations,-THAT, of all things is the loneliest memory I've YET had,-PLEASE, we can't write ourselves off as THAT,-Then what would we be clinging to,-Just plain old reluctance,-You'll get torn,-And I'll stay the same miserable wretch,-We'll live this way,-See you continue your life as such,-Then of all things closing out inspiration,-And that, of all things, when I'm onward to freshground,-

---

THERE'S SILENCE MIXED ALL AROUND

"I Give You Mine" says Ebbey Flint to his mother on the first FallDay,-Handing her a book on 'The Gardens Of All Things',-Explaining the PassPoint between the eternal spirit and the Land, Earth anywhere,-She smiles at her son,-She was feeling A bit better that day,-After a LongSpell of dislocated sleep days,-Ebbey got his wish of waking her from those permanently,-She remembers that when waking from the LastLongSleep, That she was roused by carousel music,-Possibly coming up From the basement of her home,-She never asked Ebbey for Any explanations of this,-Was so happy

that this was the day where she wanted to try all NewThings,-
Knew how long since she'd felt that,-Ebbey Too felt the best
he'd felt in a time,-He wasn't sure what to entirely attribute it
to,-He new better what to, however as he saw steam rise from
the lawn, while peering from the kitchen window,- "A Gift.., A
Gift From Time" says Ebbey Flint, waving his hand up,-Can it
really hurt if ever having to bring It down,-
May-
   -17-2001-
    -Che Elias-

PART 2. 'IN A TIME OF GIANTS'

Dear Emily,

Remission when I stood on those porches, I wasn't lifted From familiar places. I'm not believing my extension. Maybe this is the wrong place. I want to think, I've thought For a long while that this current era for me is meant to be one of Subjection. My cruel aloneness. The hour manages its recompense for my time to be judged as a lasting accomplice. Why do matters not last, right? I have before forgotten steps I have taken that have led me swiftly to tasks that I might soon Conclude. Certain faces of people that I was assured meant very little, returned to me in dreams. I learnt in time to daftly rethink my waking hours spent in their company. Even those with whom I shared an enmity, the hate stopped. Progressed itself backwards to its origins framed at the rise in a girl's brow. A younger girl's face blurred behind her, as she knelt in the dusts blown across the dry earth. I mechanically speak their dialogs. These two friends, their words transcend my grief.

Sincerely,

Monologue 5

'Nora Serip'

Starrigotta Windser owned nearly all of Pine Cove. Laurels, peaks fountainesque in natural construction. Emuneel Lurry kept watch there daily, saying she would make this better for Starri . To be relieving some of this pressure, after all the time that Starri had to keep cover of Pine Cove entirely by herself. Satrri said she digest a humility out of the tense calm while wandering over and under these hillsides. These forests stretch in her heart , then listen in on some surrealness, bluish English forests when cropped become exotic to Starri. Emuneel had spent the main years of her childhood more in Africa than America, used to the big rustle crossing vastness.

Emuneel-"I'd walk to a distance , I would sit and paint
Animals .Now, I only can tell them in pictures."

Dear Emily,

I did not send you a present on the anniversary of
The day that marks a year from the time that we last
Saw each other. Much to my surprise when this day
Occurred I felt congenial ! You probably assumed that
That I would feel a twist inside me that you hoped at
Its best could calmly put my belief aside, for a
matter. I didn't have that, I didn't at the least miss
you .Please do not think that this is the end point in
our association .With hope I think my not wanting you
will cease, eventually. And you will return yourself
as a visage.
Sincerely,

1-Monologue

'Checker Board Apostles'

Though, I think it's just as if my parent's left it-
Nor-nor-This girl/Abigail –she said that she always spent
Part of every summer in England
        / Around early 90s/
She rode horses in rainstorms / she made a point
For a matter to ride these horses – She rode them
Bare-back and entirely nude(without any clothes)
She says whether weather apostles hang those
Decorations and lightly when she rides on those
 Horses "she thinks of oil fires and of bombs being
Dropped"   So , I'd suppose she wants to nudge me
So that'll I'll think of the 'GULF WAR'
Her, She rides, ..rode … rides –HORSES
Nnn+naked "Her hair is a jet black and
Her Hair dangles down to her waist" "I see her and those
Horses and *** her wet hair covers her
Breasts – her nipples are brownish and erect
'Cause o' Rain – 'Cause o' rain' / I held on calm in
Moors, by myself and it's just staggering but it
Should be calm "RAIN COULD BE CALM"
                    I
                    HOPE

Monologue-2

    'GRAPES'

Codel=As ferr-He was the most beautiful/Male.
Doris had ever seen with her own bare eyes.
POUR Doris-the delicate lighting, the flash, and
The deletes-
Codel=Hover on such ornaments-I stood on the balcony,
5:30AM-Two pots of leaves by each of my ankles-
Warm crusts on the bayonets-
        'HELLO DORIS'
My coda will bloom if tension ferments/
I consider you a must and tenderness I appreciate,
That I glimpse its ovals/ When I will meet with you,
 Doris I will by regiment hold-"NO"-"NO"-open all
   Doors.
     "DORIS"!!!
I will close all windows
       Doris,
  DARLING

'HIS PICTURES'
1. 'LE VALMON'S Tropics
My dearest Theodora,
The piano will gradually be the underbottom of
Your trials – where you keep all phone numbers/
The little postcards and my friend's pictures –
Theodora , Stay visible (PLEASE)

My grand knockings which forwards The heart swarm/and
I=I=ME –"Will on top of Pretend castles that I keep get ready to
give It all the way .My heart and my soul will be
The wounds of your dilemmas"
     Theodora ,
  Remember at certain private times I was proud of us .

2. 'Office in City'
The family heirloom stood round-I wept at the window
where I had clutched Emily . I found the opening in the
hallway wall where lie hidden trusts which dissolve. The family
dibolt horribly bloomed but then stopped as It just was before-
A PILGRIMAGE –Then marginally It declared its nationality.

3. 'Cubic flamethrowest'
I took Emily for the carriage ride in the park at nighttime.
When she slouches down in the seat of the carriage , I feel
The cleft of a gallant cloud .All tiles, all spiders and in
Particular my own beheading .

'Velours'

Marsh over the outsides / Inwards.-others.
Abigail washes her feet in a bowl –every morning-
While she sits in the reclining chair, she's still wearing her
Night gown . As we find her(secret) , the sleeves are short
And she feels goose pimples on her arms . She keeps
Kerosene lamps barely burning – their flames kicking
Around a pulse – "It's better to watch the day break this
way" "I mean – being barely lit" Abigail, out of humor
takes a pin from the ceramic vase on the mantel. Which is also
filled with coins. With the pin she pricks Each of her toes
individually – On the left foot , she Pricks them biggest to
smallest- On the right foot, She pricks them from smallest to
biggest- She flinches As she pushes the pin into her skin- She
pushes it In just enough to draw trinkets of blood- Each prick
Will leave a small discoloration after she's wiped away
The blood-The wounds are not severe enough to form
Scabs .

Abigail-"A lot of other things…a lot of other things "
Abigail- " He did a lot of other things , besides these"

There, she stops there in here entirety .
If she's to stand before these trophies –
Then she's to want to walk-OUT- or we
Think –SILLY-if nothing-LASTS-

Abigail-"I felt free"
Abigail-"I swear"
Abigail-"And I came"

'LETTER WITH PACKAGE'
(REVERSABLE)
 P.S.
NOT REPLACEABLE

My
Sweet,
I own the lights-Least you've of forgotten-BABY-You were my dream-I'd have – DREAMT-I'd be talking – TAKE LEAVE-when you'd of waited-I have the smells-and-SOLENTS-From intimate Features (Yours)-I KEEP THEM-in hoists of Small bottles- according to the zodiac –
    "THE SUN ENTERS MARCH 21ST"

I take a teaspoon and I rap on each bottle and I Conjure your scent-like I'd have put a catheter in You(Gross?) Each teaspoon rapping(CINDERELLA)!-Leaves a tender crack on the glass-BOTTLES-and parts of your scent seep out Into the air-The poet would say - " Aroma of flowers", The narcoleptic would say " Fuck the aroma of hours", When today counts and tomorrow matters,- Aren't sparks the hand on your cheek?
    - Yours truly-

A doll with a pale white complexion And rosy blush- came wrapped in red tissue Paper – and a green ribbon-

Abigail-"I were lucky"
Abigail-"If I were lucky?"

When I held Abigail – SERENITY-
Aroused me to smash the face of her doll
-THIS DOLL- on the posts of her bed-
 So,
As I smash the doll's face-
The porcelain disparagingly
Turns to grains –

Abigail used the strength of her right arm And I do mean forcefully – to hold my face Down to the pillow- straining my neck-She digs through the inside of the head of the doll-Which-is clear due to the obviousness of the smashed- face-which-I- turned to grains-PROUD-

She finds cotton candy dressings –A think blot- A father's clock, that you'd of kept on a chain in your pocket-AND-Abigail finds in the bottom of the doll –one of the bottles(which the teaspoons rapped) – She counts each crack-the bottle contains – A

        Wasp(Hershey)

   +

This stinger/ thorn
She takes from the bottle-
  She grasps the Stinger/Thorn
  In her thumb and forefinger /
    NOTE-if her fingers were to sweat
  -then the stinger/thorn/ is a goner/ HER/

I turned over with my face right back-
I had her place the thorn , which will now be
Known as the spool –NO- a spoor –
In the pocket of my –EYE-

Abigail-"The marbles are gone"
 Abigail-"The pieces of glass were the shreds In snows, and
        mirrors –YOU   – wanted Flowers but I can't have
        gotten your name"-

Tropic 5

'Convergence'

Dear Em,
I had for at least several months- January, February, March,
April and until the 16th day of May/ Your glass hippopotamus,
The one that you always kept Dutch chocolates in/ In there – I
Kept for those 4 1/2 months – January, February, March, April
And until the 16th day of May – In there-I put the photo of Doris,
That prior to your departure I usually kept in my drawer , and
in A heart shaped locket that I broke the chain of a long time
ago And never got around to replacing it .By placing the
picture in The your hippo I don't mean to hurt you and by no
means Should you feel that it is my way of forgetting that you
held That object very precious – to you it must have
symbolized our Once endless nights of intricate privacy. I
placed the photo in The hippo 'cause both of you are gone.
You did not depart by choice but by manners of the
Circumstance .

Doris(where ever she may stand as I press this pen to the
New paper) left us both without ever mentioning what it was
She hoped to make of her life. I remember that we laughed in
Her room as we sat on the floor and we went thru the toy chest
From her infancy(one to me that was all the more relevant after
I recall her cryptic adolescence) .When I took all of her toys
From the chest and we spoke to each other about each toys
Significance , we spoke also of what a darling Doris was at that
Point in time. I sunk into you as I cried ,I thank you for how I've
Always felt most comfortable crying with you. Crying is
Something which I've never felt comfortable doing around
Anyone other than you. So, it was not by chance that I placed
Her photo in your ornament , it was to place you both together
Again. Juxtaposing emblems of your endeavors .
I say this honestly , you need not gull up your heart as you
Read. Emily , I'll see you and I look forward to that
More than I can now say.
     Sincerely.

Tropic 6

'The Calling Of Hemase'

Starting by gently rubbing its hands over Emily's ribs, pressing underneath her breasts with its thumbs .

"THE SELFISH PRESERVATION"
          The Sun Enters June 22nd

Emily-" 'Cause we stayed and the proof"
Emily-"Or the proof-That… -I earned . That … I'll suppose was
          Nearest My calves –I would staple them-
          That..- proof of a basket – that.. It came in ."

Emily's Account Of Thursday The 21st
Friendships are gonna hold me as lovers, As failures As spheres that I cross and I put a tiny star in their center, which I keep as a very brown with a caption of costs . The soaps in the bath think twice with the second chances lost. {sparks in her eyes}
I'm at the window-WAIT- now, I'm on the middle of the staircase .I look for a minute at the plate on the step which has an illustration of the crusades. A Knight held the stars to the rising finale and I always liked the reverse of when he greeted me(to me) by saying he hadn't a contest.
Wait, top of the stairs.

Emily-"Speaks-mate-the caskets empty.
          Fine-speaks-mate-Answers the enemy."
Emily-"The flown has shortly ordained the proclamation."

Wait, I'd settled at midday outside of a rectangle

164

Tropic-7
   'Rose Shattered , and Rose in love'-

Ticed the pier and caused all of them
Ticed the pier- Across the water(sea)
If your gonna pass looking out-There
Was Thames – proud on the Mass –
He means it-
-Nicol Thames –

Nicol-"T'was the bright –wh're The sailors spoke the captains
Name and they casts 'is shadows-They'd tied em to the mass-
and There'd em sirens-fishern-screamin-In the water –he's a
say-Dorn't plug My ears –I'll of heard't their screamin.
-Nicol Thames-
Actually, Thames would have never Spoken that way- he had
been thru   Universities-but he did not credit them with
his thought and speech –

Tice the pier –

The children scurry and the old man   Screams something
which Thames Can't understand –
            'JUSTA GUESSED YESTERDAY'
There's a crack as the ship docks – moments before they dock,
Thames would like to see himself leaping down to the pier and
throwing Everybody out of the way and drowning himself – He
calls these thoughts parallels(once over)

First foot on the pier-CUT- Second step-
Fade-truth –we'd plowed for that-

Thames leads himself (while laughing, Silently)past the
upheaval of the children- Past the old man , whose screaming
Thames Has likened to that of the " FUCKING
                        DEVIL" –

Off the pier
        -(allow)-
Nicol-"I keep the scroll under my pillow and in My thighs I got a
map of the world-And there's a serpent in every sea-A serpent
in every sea"-

Thames carefully crushes each flower With his steps. He
purges thru the townspeople .He comes to what was waiting for
him .Or "What I crossed ta part of tha Ocean ferr"-
-twilight till dawn you get to plan the clock as starlight –
        this is who I loved-
        this is who I loved-

Thames,
        Each times a diamond-

At last I seen what the people gathered for-
A stone, er a- statue-not flesh –not real-
And I'd a camed all this way-

There in the town up above the town's
Fistsfalls-Thames kneels burning within
His body –I le stops the birds with the stone
Bust of Athena –

Thames-"I will nail er face(Pulls)"

Ticed the pier –it don't get stolen even
Though it's small, so loud we are here-

Tropic 8

'Cleo'

Thames,
Doused the cress.
-reverberation-
This has seemed as weeks –er- months on water.
Thames, much as he's used to never seeing land.
He stands failed to correlate any radiance.

Nicol Thames-" ..which breaks over something , kind of ordains
it and then it's another which completely pulls the
same thing down."

Thames ,
Tomorrow when near the end of his bewilderment .
His urgency will be bridged at a time and where he'd stay
-LAND- at least .

Nicol Thames-"To feel something steadily underneath you.
    I'll put entirety to rest , I'll re-emerge
    Re-assured."

The ship again docks,Thames will watch the other's flee to
The port .He'll watch them out ahead of him. He will stand
-THERE-Happily Alone- Rest and then he'll(alone) walk those
streets. Guided towards those lights in those high winds .
-Earthly Creatures-

THE SUN ENTERS JULY 23rd

-The Promise-

Nicol-"Bareable-I feel for the increase –I will the next time
I step off land –TO-ship-Have lapsed In physicality."

The Rounders, how Thames refers to the other men. They'll fill every bar, purge every brothel, copulate With every whore, in their minds they'll grope each brothel madam .The pockets in their eyes will "MELT LIKE THIS", sides of their mouths turn up for the number 2-5-Hundred.

All Thames sees of them is a shiftless flesh, A red form .A currency will hardly float away until the moment next morning . Depending on whether Thames awakens alone or next to female form . Thames would preferably awaken from a night of purging Male harm. Think of the burgundy the sailors pillage while They spend months on the ships .The rite of masculinity. The sensuality Thames has felt indefinitely . He most proudly In a boyish coyness did not feel indifference .One day or night With a whore , Thames would never feel to them as that. The sanctuary of the petals Thames spread with his fingers many Times before entering Once he's in , he's lost until he explodes Withered in a maze of heat . A spiral catapult thru forests returns Music boxes that play always on the dressers of those lovely red Rooms .Thames always repeats that familiar tune as he moves out thru the night .He is always good for one brothel , but no more is he good for a bar.

Nicol Thames-"The clogged shreds – They are not merriment.
            The clipped waves approximately are somber.
I don't shrug their pull – the shreds I wouldn't
Be merry drowning."

Thames, his escape thru land tonight will find not company Or aloneness . The apocalypse of the hellish madness That thorns around .He will by knowing at heart turn this into a dearest a self lesson . Himself, tonight his thoughts are his blessings .

Tropic 9

'Hell's Normoanen'

The orchid was at its most charitable for then a sad, sad Emily .
For my Em as the days shortened they were becoming their
most lonely – For my Em to want company, this was not a fable
– Pretense .

The Roving Of My Em And Her Abigail .
THE SUN ENTERS DECEMBER 22nd

The wait that my Em felt and without laughter .

Em-"Not to change the subject   –excerpts necessity-
        If I were to find a girl that I cared for in the way that
        I've cared for a boy . I guess people have told me that
     if I were to , it would stop short at a point . It wouldn't
     reach to where it reaches with a boy.

What my Em told me of her first times with her Abigail.

My Em – "The place, our place by the rocks . Where   me and
            you used to go . I'd given off for too long – So I went
            without ..- I was never supposed to tell you-
            Remember you never wanted me to go there
            without you- You said if I did , that what I'd find and
            feel –Would make me not need you . I WENT-
            THERE-OK– Probably the second time or 3rd time –
            I peered over the water and I saw a dainty little girl.
            I felt that I should not refrain from smiling
            at her , 'cause no others gleamed our place
            during the colder winter days – and it came to
            be the fourth time I saw her that I decided to
            approach."

My Em- "Dear cold morning?"

Abigail-"(softly ,- taken back by my Em's immediacy and
      consummate warmth)-The cold's upon me dearly –
      Data-Yes I always come here by myself to –
I'd have to find another but I've felt prominent
discouragement when it came to the chances."

My Em placed her smile-and put her hand on Abigail's
shoulder .

Drifting,
   -This to me-
My Emily and her Abigail now sit side by side in –TWO-Red
chairs –Em particularly looks at Abigail with a sort of sideways
glance for a time . Then , Em's glance changes – Her brow
lowers as she no longer needs defense . Abigail looks down ,
presses her hands on the wooden seat Of the chair . Then,
Abigail looks at my Emily .

Emily-"I'll show you this- I want to."

Abigail-"You can-I want to also – I'd like for
   you to show me anything."

Emily led Abigail to her bedroom that was lit by The dismal
dreariness of the winter light – Emily did not open the curtains
preferring to keep the room under lit .My Em always preferred
the forms of secrecy .She sat Abigail on the bed , she
crouched at Abigail's feet –Abigail wondered what Emily was
about to do- Emily reached under the bed , under Abigail's feet
–She brought out a small wooden box with a lemon pelt cover
out form underneath the bed . Emily sat down next to Abigail, a
beam of light shown on the tone of Emily's skin as   her hand
flexed to open the box . Abigail's eyes widened , my Em
revealed   to her some things that belonged to me . She
revealed 3 possessions that she knew were dear to me . A
ruby, a ring with a blue jewel in its center(belonged to my
mother) and a stone sculpted in the form of an infant's foot-This

I once gave my Em because I knew she would need at some point an object that would be the way of remembering that she had known me .

Emily(holding the ruby)-"He said the red signifies
           choices he made that he
           wished he could take back."

Emily(holding the ring)-"Down by the rocks/water (our place)
           he took this off his finger and placed it
           on my smallest toe . I recall that when
           he held my foot he said "No more than
           this" . I think he said that , maybe he
           said nothing ."

Emily(holding the stone foot)-"He said hold this to remember
                         when I put my ring on your foot
                         and hopefully for neither of us
              will this call on what you know
              the ruby means to me ."

 - After That-
Emily and Abigail sat on the bed motionless They waited there till the winter's light was gone and the bedroom became the why of darkness .

171

Tropic 10

'Burmanchuss'

Towards if like a dart, yet still when hanging. The small moments which alter the balance of voyages as wholes. These moments have a purity and honesty all to themselves. Thames keeps a log of them when he can. He wishes they would happen daily. There are times filled with great pockets of disdain and misfortune . But he will read his accounts of past occasions and feel wisely about his choice to have jotted them down. Nicol can remember two months before and two years before .If he would have to, he could pull back perfect recollections of instances that occurred more than a decade ago . Nicol has wondered how others can't even remember so much as the prior day. He has kept anger when concluding that the moments that spell out his exhilaration aren't even counted by others. Nicol reinforces their importance by concluding that because they are his and his only , that they now mean more than anyones valuable times. Sometime he'll make this, sometime he'll… Nighttime, the men sleep on lofts . Nicol has chosen considerably ever night the lower bed. He's chosen the lower bed since the night when he awoke with his wrist shattered, clinching his teeth, biting his lip. Blood from his lips doused his yes and while he felt terror in the darkness after falling from the loft saying "God, God, my wrist is in pieces and I've lost my sight" . Back on the lower bed, tonight Nicol lies awake and listens to a man's body toss on the bed above . Knowing that a substantive condition that would arise in the water could also send the man above him crashing down to awaken in the same horror that Nicol found on that night . He's lost this or it's pushed back, away if the water's currents were to pounce his chest .He gets up from the bed , in the darkness he walks to The ship's deck.

Nicol-"What'll find but to not yet realize later Is captured .
         What's found ?"

Tropic 11

My Birthday-A Time In November –
'I Spent This Time With Emily And With
Doris'-

I would have spent my birth night alone. I would have also liked
to have spent the next 9 days alone. I tell you this to indicate
that the girls presence was originally unplanned. Though,
because of my fondness for them –Spending This time in their
company did not require any kind of exception in changing the
plans –'cause I clearly love them.

THE SUN ENTERS NOVEMBER 22nd

Clear to myself, out of tradition at 11:50 PM on each November
22 –I stop whatever I may be doing and pause in silence for the
next 13 minutes. I was born at 12:03 AM on November 23 –
This occasion to me is of far greater importance than the ball
being dropped on New Year's Eve in Times Square . This night
to me is obviously the start of a new year of my life . I see this
as the time when I can put all of the things I've done in the past
behind me. At 11:25 PM on this night (Nov 22) I heard a knock
on the door, while I was sitting in the kitchen . It came as
unexpected, I was eager to see who this was . At first I did not
unlock the door but pulled back the curtain that hangs over the
door's glass pane. My eagerness was even more encouraged
when I recognized the familiar smiling faces . Emily and Doris
and only a door between us . I opened the door . I did not really
need to greet them . I saw them so often that for the time I
considered the two my apparent sisters. Doris was wearing a
short blue dress and black stockings. She had painted her eyes
and lips for the occasion .This night, she considered it to be
mine, my night . She knew that I thought her face when
painted had fondness, it was sometimes my inspiration. Emily
wore no make-up .Her usual clothes, long pants and a plain
shirt which she buttoned all the way to the button just below
the collar . She had her hair tied back . The fullness of her

features , her face was lush . I can remember it as if I were looking at a proof sheet that had pictures of her face taken from every imaginable angle . We sat down at the table . Doris was blushing , Em spoke for her "She's been bugging me about giving this to you for the whole day, so we won't let it wait" Em turned to Doris " Go on.". Doris took a small package from the pocket of her coat that hung behind her on the chair that she was sitting on . She was still blushing as she handed it to me. Figuring that is was something of exceptional importance to her, I opened it carefully. I made sure not to tear violently into the paper as I usually did when given a wrapped package .I did not wish to shatter how tender Doris seemed ,I was starting to relish that . What the package contained could not have been more unexpected . A diary, not a new one but Doris's own diary that she had already filled completely with her thoughts over the last several years . I opened the cover of the diary, I felt a strange intimacy unlike any other that I had every felt before . I still consider it peculiar for someone to give a person their actually journal . Was Doris wanting me to see a part of her heart that I had never seen ? But a journal at least to me is a private thing. Doris looked directly at me .I did not know how to respond to this gift , I couldn't use words. I reached across where Emily sat to where Doris sat next to her . I gently took Doris's hand . I held her hand tightly . By doing this I meant to imply nothing other than what Doris had implied by giving me her diary and the only way that I could do so was by this gesture . It had a grace , a silence . a kindness and a warning ! In spree that had ensued in my heart due to their unexpected arrival , I realized that I had missed my annual moment. My 11:50PM to 12:03AM . This was the one birth night that I lost , the only one where I could not immediately have a new start.

Tropic 12

'Here & Elsewhere'

1.If my lips would wish to stutter – I would be shot out from Doris, pulled down from Emily-Made to dare in poise – Seeking missionary descents – I'll not strut my lips –Where I hither , is where I'll try .

2. Doris-"I've loved time, I've tied very much a loop."

3.Emily-"Presently tame each other, course presents".

4.Early Afternoon, because of the position of the sun-these are our hours . All of us ventured down to the rocks –The pool- Our place- Mine & Em's –I realized how much I enjoyed standing back and watching both of them at a distance .Doris's thighs are milk white , lay rose suckles her breasts . While she wasn't looking I etched a coda to her In one of the stones at the water's edge . Accordingly the coda read " You, a beauty who in this land at her fairest will find me always repeating this."

5. Doris-" Light traces upon and on top. What has been built and abandoned I consider self -fulfillment ."

Monologue 4

'Tonal Epitaph'

The perch L. Hudson built at Grace Park, its wrath shimmers more or less as a prophetic arc in headland hearing me unclear. Kittiwake held at knife point. The old and the new . Laity characterized as piercing ladder back . Doris, I saw her by lamplight . She was landed magic . I will have a truce with her regiment of necessary arrangements. Every time she let me down , she resurfaced In laitance .

Dear Emily,
I have not been well. These days I am ill In mind, body and most certainly spirit .It is in the latter that I have a most unusual pain that I have never had before. I grow tired and more tire . It's as if there is not such a thing as rejuvenation. I can only gather myself when YOU are the goal involved. To see your photo , read things that you've written and remember the films that you loved . Though, those films I don't personally recall because it was the expression on your face while you were viewing them- that I was watching. Your face to me was the only cinema i.e. a dream that starts when the curtains open and the lights are made dim. I will always remember you as the best thing.

To just be together and not change ourselves,

Sincerely.

Dear Emily,

I can never make a rightful evaluation of a persons courage or cowardice . As you once said " I feel no attraction to situations that I already know the outcome of". Strangely, in some of these situations it's one thing, a minute detail that gives me so much to go on . I believe this intuition was brought on by all of the lessons that you taught me . You not only gave me an idea of how to read people but also an idea of how to read the spaces in between their lives. You said how being bound to one's surroundings can make a person disburse into predictability and other times it might cause them to capture themselves on the very brink of the standard of living which they have set . The ease you gave me by not wanting me to be part of that , is in sorts a burgeoning alienation tinged by grace .

   Sincerely,

Monologue 4

'Isochron'

Abigail, irresoluble .
Abigail, irresolvable .
In land I will do all .
Please come isolable .
Preamble on wishing the presence of
Belongings , there is destiny which predetermines .
Abigail, I predicted that he would come , I knew
You would both yield and glow .

Dear Emily,

I see myself standing on manna grass in an isolated place where I manipulate time while I wait for you . I thought of a very dismal play called 'Life Performed By The Human Beings' . This play begins and ends with the sun rising . So, other than that it's set entirely in an interior . The interior I've envisioned as being a room designed by what I guess I'll describe as Japanese architecture . The plot deals with a family . A mother , father and son .They all end up killing themselves . I hope to write it , not that I've any hopes of it actually ever being staged but just to give it to you. I know that death is a subject or factor as you would say , that interests you . You felt that it was most comforting to play this subject straight instead of storing it away. Oh, what did you really mean when you said "There are people that I want to know now, only so that I can later hate them". . I've still never really got that .

Sincerely,

Dear Doris ,

You know phone calls that are barely a minute in length and the caller only calls because he or she has a brief point to make , their motivation for calling is that they believe they can get something from you ? I no longer take or return those calls . Later now, I visualize all of your senses being activated as you sit in a room filled with candies, perfumes, art, gowns and jewels. You're sitting there wrapped in a red blanket , you're blindfolded . You're not reaching out to feel where you are, you just sit still taking this atmosphere to yourself . Each piece of it, one by one minus sight or touch. I hoped the vision would turnover after that into a collage of sounds . Maybe, nighttime in a forest , wind chimes, your laughter then your voice repeating awkward questions .

Love,
Sincerely,

Tropic 13

'There is a book of haste'

Emuneel-"We're the passengers, we're the few who came in.
        The way covered by us, complete . In a stride we're
    over silk caves . We're to've known in very, very
    dried lakes a type of mirage can fuse and is there for
    us, her pact. Come with the followed succession,
    we're to've sought her till we can corner and plea .
    We're to've gathered each dream, for her to've
    made them true. A count backwards from 9 to 1 and
    in a puff all's gone. Does that all reappear again in
    perhaps the mirage? We're to've said to the next
    successors, we brought her hands forward, No !!"

Doris-"I began each letter with a poem. Entering into verse
    After The coma placed after Dear Emily. I tempted her, I
    hope. The tradition to remunerate her, it's obvious that's
    always going to occur. In parentheses I would write
    "Lesson one, Home Drama"-In which I transcribe a
    series of phone calls, wherein a damp solitude? She'd
    would not ever note that I'd understood , even after
    I'd been apart from her, and so long. Everything I gave
    to her mattered to me then, but was not in retrospect
    what mattered. Verse has an inability, it cannot bridge
    our gap. Neither can patience. I will even if backing out
    of this, leave with positivity . I leave at the point before
    her arc nullifies."

Tropic 14

'There is a book of meddles'

Starrigotta-"I see Pine Cove mostly in a jest. I see it
as it is in the geomorphology , figuratively.
I know there are spots where people have been
where they shared kinship. I come upon those
places and I only share a gesellschaft with the
litter they left."

Emuneel-"I will belaud Pine Cove by seeing it in terms of the
Hawthorne Effect. Here two might lie down in trust,
though the same two might irrupt and leave here
irremeable. May we nail to each tree a sign that tells
that here mishaps can vanish."

Tropic 15- 'There is a book of magic (Emuneel reflects)'

Emuneel bends over the railing, her feet in the air. When doing so she always hoped that she'd be able to reach them, that they would come close enough that the tips of her fingers could brush their skin. The time spent observing the tembos was an epoch to Emuneel. She came always on her own. On the tembos occasion friends were not thought as affinities. She wore a large white hat, a silk drape came down from its brim, it served as the veil which shrouded her face from the evident sunburn that one with light skin was certain to acquire if they were to be out for hours in what this time of year was a seemingly harsh sun, whose strongest hour typified in this season where it stretched from moments after dawn until vanishing ordained on the whim of brisk dusk.

   Emuneel would watch them on some days till very late afternoon, some days till evening, other times for less than an hour. Except for weekends. She had set in her mind that if she were to view the tembos on Saturdays and Sundays that it would become more so a task and she wouldn't be able to structure her weekdays around it. At home her room has colored drawings of the tembos, pieces , plain and stellar situations she has observed. On and on these could have been taken. They were likely to be exorcised extremely from her on days where clock time dispenses on for her to create the way through. Regardless of the technical average of her drawings, an extent in the grandeur to keep a thing that's very much herself. A cache she's to give another(her child?). The color overlapses within the plain drawn lines of the figures, shirts, pants, shoes. It becomes mixed, perfectly turns to an unwanted shade that she'll except. She does not value the concern of keeping a single drawing until put down as exact on paper as it looked when it lingered in her mind. STOP-all summer-START-It's last summer's parts that she'll draw; real summer vanishes. The urgency of collecting expanses not wasted. Now, after those are gone on their way. When she tries looking at them and feels the expected cringe, But a relay in hanging hurt, they were even then drawn. COLORED PERFECT!!

Tropic 16- 'The Play Of Sound And Light'

Remaining footprints quickly filling back up as the snow fell swiftly. I ran beside them willing to leave my own mark in step with theirs. I wore a dark red hood, its seam is tucked tightly under my coat's collar. The breeze carries on. If there were a coy subvert in my nature my dance through the wood that night was not a doubt of it. Going in patio lites, stove fires, steaming pots, I trove the front door. I've kept three keys that're identical in appearance. Two unlock the upper and lower locks on the front door. The third opens a chest in the house, where I put objects when it occurs to me that living amongst them has a private idealism. I place them in the chest until I might farther examine them. Closing the door behind me, taking a towel to wipe the dampness off me. I alone scurry to the den. Stocked on shelves are board games, records, books, letters and magazines. After bracing myself. In thought I will take a record from the shelf, place it on the turntable, take a book that I had been reading off the table and start where I previously left off. Till the end of night, then complete sleep to redo me. I begin anew starting someplace else. The laughing float coils supremacy churning by trying to reach here, new. I dress, step out of home, sparring the typical hours of preparation. I will walk, you'd ask where? Old places feelings our children walked before, here. I do remember watching them, beautiful, vulnerable still at that age. As said, this all does take time till when the sadness, I miss them, searches orders gave. I don't completely dress, I just pull the fur coat over my nightgown. 'Cause I'm tired of robes not keeping my ankles warm and stopping at my knees, leaving ankles chilled .I cover more books in silk. I place them in the private chest. These same books were taken good last night. Supplement one, A little girl pranced by herself. Her parents threw her, though they watch her together at a distance. The little girl pulls herself half over the fence, catches, tears her dress. Perfect danger, pictorial enlightenment, the girl hanging there still. The parents run over , pull her down , slap and scold her. Forgetfully the footprints more hollow after much of last night's snow was melted by today's winter sun .

Tropic 17
        -That Witch-
            -I Can Name-
                -I Will-

Thames's hand touches water. Between having slept and
being determined, beside a debacle. YES! No matter
what you say. YES! There is time. Harken, Thames would.
He leans against the face of the wet stone wall. Looks at
The water. The force it falls with rallies Thames. A myopic
foresight-the shreds of water abound in their thrashing.
"If-you-could-have-seen-what-occurred-in-the-past-you-would-
surely-see-the-importance-of-my-doing-anything-You-would-If-
you-would-have-seen-where-I-have-come-from."

    OK,
Thames walks out from behind the waterfall. He stands
shirtless, soon foreboding a sun burnt back. He was mostly at
peace-SURPRISED- that again having found this peace, He'd
sworn to've heard a succulent ringing coming from the
trees. This ringing grew tense, it came first from
their long brushing branches, it was also present in the water's
gushing spray. Thames thought the ringing dilated in the ether.
A bargain, a chorus sung with perforating warmth, somebody's
Sonata-"Riches are strewn through their fingers, till they've
seen half enough."

    The ringing sound shifted away from Thames.
He heard it carried out, back farther and farther.
He saw the branches on every tree forcefully sway upwards.
When he squinted he could see the hazel tinged ripples left in
the wake of the ringing.
    " A compromise to've made. I care about misery, I think
    It should scurry forth."

184

Tropic 18
    =wicked=hetta-1=1

Doesn't matter how far we've been, Emily-always calls to attention your purity. You've not dis-vowed my chances. Emily-you're to've filled in me. Warmth will be an indication-we'll be back Together-in such a way-restored-no-matter-how.

Emily standing most still in the dell. Both sides of the valley rise, they wrap like Wings in both directions, wrought aside, -Up-she with her elbows bent clutches a white purse, she holds this tight to her chest. Small, resolved in that place on the earth. She'll shine full to my face. Emily knew what she'd come here for-but more That she did not know.

Emily-"The street's stones-where I have in the past
    Been-caught-passing-them-now-achieves
    Vision-wise-in-breadth-cloudy-I once told
    Told him to keep a small lamp lit in the front
    Window. A miniature delicate flame will stay
    Steadily 'neath the side of the curtain that's drawn
    Open, when he asked if there was anything he
    Could do-the stones on the walk to the front door
    Tend to separate, peak at this point. Not good?
    Knowing that home is empty-the flame prevalent-
    The entire house rests, lit only by this. Even though
    I have kept a door key, staying in tradition-I reach
    Under the doormat for the key placed secretly for
    One who has been locked out-Filth that has collected
    On the key from years of lying hidden, makes its
    Way into the lines of my fingertips-At home, not
    Needing to disrupt and refigure the rearrangements
    Done with time-sitting for moments prior to leaving,
    Writing a short note, and placing it next to the
    Lamp, so it will be known to whoever is next here,
    That After years I returned-though they'll wonder
    Why I didn't wait."

Tropic 19
'Lurdane'

-Please tear out this page-'Cause I fell into the ideology of soaking in merriment-and I now feel guilt-Obviously she directed me because I was blindfolded-But I could have led myself by feeling along the sides of The walls-and by following my ears to the sounds of the Crowds jeers-She put her hands on my shoulders at the top of the staircase-and told me not to move from this spot-She said that she would yell up from the foot of the stairs To indicate to me that she was ready for me to take off my blindfold and make my way down the staircase-I'd heard her feet go down each step-I knew already that she was wearing a long dress-a ball gown- knew this when I heard it brush along the staircase-The restraint of my peripheral vision and the thunder Made by the crowd made seconds of anticipation Into a lifetime's-To brace myself I envisioned her flowing form inside The blackness of my blindfold-As she finally commanded me to take it off-There was a silence in my heart in between the time it took to tear it off and first bearing the sight of the surface of her world as she wished to present it-Rainbows, bent streamers hung about the vast room-The party guests were divided to two sides-A deep red lit the left side of the room where one pack huddled-A burnt green strobe lapsed continuously in the joy of the guests who merged to the room's right side-Abigail stood in the room's center-Cast by spotlight-Pure white neatly ordained her-Her hair was rolled in a crown of rosebuds-She wore a silver mask which as I got closer showed me I lacked in needing myself-This was flashed in the hundreds of small mirrors that lined the mask-I did really know then just by dancing with her, I Could assess myself, I now believed to be worthy Of doing so-She is such a countenance, that while holding onto her for a night-One finds a whole history –Though of most importance, I felt that the history of myself was resolved-

"I-DON'T-NEED-WAITING-AS-THE-TIDE-TO-CAST-AWAY-SCARS".-BUT-"I WILL NEED THIS OTHER THAN HER-I WILL KNOW THAT SHE WANTED ME ON THAT NIGHT-yes-IT MEANS MORE THAN IT SOUNDS LIKE I AM SAYING IT MEANS-IF IT IS A LOSS, I WANT IT NOT TO BE MINE BUT HER'S ALSO-IF IT IS GAIN THEN THE TIME WHEN IT TOOK PLACE WAS FOOLISHLY SURMISED."

Tropic 20
   One who sits or presides

1.Do give attention to the blur of hedge ranges
   Till the central staging of pleasure where
   They confirm their truce

2.Your potential was written above and to
   the right of the cartouche.
         -So, what can't you-
         -Count on-
         -So, when can you-
         -Count on-
         -And may vary-
3. The next bridging is executed much more
   successfully than the "DREAMING" done
   by the swept latter

Tropic 21-A construction point for point-
The paper which I first held-TITLE=FESTIVALS-In where a cliff side above moss, water-in secret titles-fountains hidden in their rises, folds in jagged edges,-Tips spray out beauty circles timed by one's hand-Gorgeous doused by a fresh gust-TITLE=CONSTRUE-I'm dragging the tissue paper sheets down her unclad body-I'm wetting her breasts with damp red cloths-Her eyes slowly open-shining/silences-Momentarily she came as the girl drawn on a matchbox-I peer from behind the bedposts-Her facial structure framed by gold finished metal bars-I felt coldness brush past but it quickly vanished to my impression of the legacy of her life as she held an album of photos on her chest, resting her nape on her pillow,-TITLE=BRANTE WANGERED-He smashed the room's objects

as fast as he could-Throwing me over. Taking not a thought of if I would land safely. Striking downward from atop in sharp blows-Splitting my nose bridge-Trampling over me, dragging himself towards the hindsight ranges-TITLE=SUMMER'S DAY-Understood that-DAY-From where I was sitting was all dazzling-Leaves-Cinematic Clouds-Spread-Away-First 2 girls back-Then her occurrence again-I saw her and have kept seeing her unclad at this appearance-She was walking about the borders of a pool moments prior to leaping in-Leaves-Cinematic Clouds-Spread again together-Cover this view in width of all which it gave. I've not impostors nor impossibilities.

Tropic 22
  "To
    Not
    Take
      Away"

-I am sure-
-I am more than sure-
-The colossus/The prohibition-
-Far back-
-Followed and here sitting-

'The Wanting'
THE SUN ENTERS SEPTEMBER 23RD
Comma-the moon begins fading in-Pause-one-Emily in her life pleads everyday that all matters Should have their by-regiment-dress-rehearsals-"THE BIG PLAY"

Emily-"Take 5 Fridays, I'm dreaming up those Fridays On the Thursdays before them. I think of laughs. I think of how tomorrow-FRIDAY-I need to see People and be at places." -NOW I HAVE THIS-
        (A)
     -PREDICTION-
    (IN SYMBOL VALANCE)

-A dried starfish-
-Sunk to bath water-
-bubbles go forth in its breadth-
-turns out again-
-it is alive-
-A fairy shining over the stars in me-
-cold bottom 'neath the earth-
-I'm figuring to do just one of the things and the others
Will be as alive as acts or a vision in my head-in trouble I find
not the head or the start point for either-the act that beckoned
and the vision are now the same-though they have changed-I
sit on rocks, my bare feet in the leaves-without water for the
starfish but running my fingers about its 5 points-each are now
rethought as the visions of drastically different starts-

Tropic 23
Albatross and aversions

No bout less delamore
-TIME-
In which she was pasting stamps onto the greetings of mare's
tail.
    -TIME-
She, as the mare liberum chorus of rites. I reverted to the
traumas she caused me early on. I was prepared that she
would grasp me, again. To've first sunk to her folds and now –
THAT-PART- I feel just uneven with –THAT-PART-

Tropic 24-What I read about Neptune-What I read in A Book of
superstitions-

1.Day.Exterior.Water.
-The episode starts as one of major importance-The little girl
drowns and a swirl of roses trim the outline of her swollen
floating body-I enter the pond to pull her body out and write
'Crown of thorns and prose' on her eyelids-
-CUT-
The book indicates that when
Preparing the spell of love
One must have a strand of hair
From the person of his Fancy-

Then he'll burn this hair
In a chalk circle with
Lava
Sparks
Feathers
So his loves come to
Him by ten-fold azure
Assortments-

2.Interior.Half/Lit drawing-room.
In this episode of lesser importance
Gods in water
I was told pulled back the sea
I was told that's what waves were
Rises folding in search of loss
-Cut-
The panel of clear glass
Her face glistening in the
Sunlight shining down to
The casket-
To return by next guiding
From the book
'Spell of the risen'
-FADE-

Tropic 25-Faux Pas-(Emuneel's Songs)

-Medley-
Were satyrs to play bort flutes in ringing to spoil eka.
-Medley 2-
'Wampum Waltz'
Oh, I wore lavala
Ah, that I bought for a pound
It's what I'll wear in every misfeasance
-now mzuri-now mzuri-
The short rains have their place through all of November
 -and lala salama-It was my treat to see pierrot played by couples-now mzuri-now mzuri-
The short rains have their place through all of November
-and lala salama-

Tropic 26-'At Heart With Malador Crotesha'

Dear Emily,

ECK-ECK-Unity-part of love is in process with being bound. You cannot just give all the time. Guide to the first floor-She is beginning to fade farther and farther from memory-now I could only Recognize her by her facial beauty-Though only then for its youth-A thought that to others may seem sexual-This thought should despite its beauty be the exampling primer in voluntary celibacy-Stephanie's Frigorific skirt, a split in the dressing of its seam revealed subtle flesh-legs ample in beauty-thighs formed to be photographed in the new prime of her twenties-Sharpened in disciplinary means-When sketched by me from memory that on writing paper folded and was sent to anybody at random-Remind her drawn from the waist down-Though sordidly kept for files-this is that unity-it can't partially have remorse for when once loving her-purely in scenes-later in omnibus book forwards, anyway.

Sincerely,

Tropic 27
'Hyssop'
The arcs cry a comatic rattle. Starrigotta ceases hold of the arborvitaes. Phalaropes reawaken. The rheas that subscribe their existence in Pinecove will be given proceeds by Starri as a thanks for when they played subrogates. All things that have the flow of life in their veins subjugate Pinecove's main ploys. The limit includes pine drops. Starri's rebellion was characterized by sense of her swinging at a pinata supposedly to pilfer its candies. Her rebellion totters like a windmill and wraps down in a pinnatifid formee. Though Starri is fallen wide-she finds a choice place by off reeling this theorem. Having authority in Pinecove has created a wanton. In this age she feels vowed to being preservationist. For all good intention the horizon savors the link Over Pinecove which keeps sync on generations.

191

Monologue 6
'Flounce'

Oh,
Emily was here again- Permanently forever-
-flurry-flurry-
Oh,
Emily with not a price
This, we're put right
In the flurry that abides
The time I sacrificed
In just being myself
Without you to be that
For.
Oh,
Emily-FACED-

Dear Emily,

Have You gone forever ? Does that mean that these plans
won't ever be formed-and so what I hoped for won't fit-Now
when I think about..-I feel a colonization of paralysis-and guilt-
and a wide open end-that it seems will forever remain in that it
currently is abound throughout fear and loss-We won't have
any more put-ons-I will either have you or not have you-OK-
NOT-OK I will not correspond to you- I will cease to sending
these letters but I would miss the tassel on the act of capturing
images to tide you over-PLEASE=PLEASE write- you've
provided the means of encouragement in your own sense up
until this point-WHY=then have you not responded to my last
letters-if you should choose to close me out-then please go
about that by proper ways of indication-I hate this misery of
being strung along.

Sincerely,

Tropic 28(the filling of tropics 1-4)

-'THE LAST NIGHT ON EARTH'-

"AMBER"

-MEDLEY ARC-

A crystallization is posthumously
Issued in hypallage infancy
Burn't And't-does wait across
A strewn't lining four't table
Whose occupants flemly lent
So'ght thro finds a bride in easiness
Manger becrofts packed manx cats
Carri'd better opon manque in Zodiacal
Code-
"GOODLY-IT-FINDS-THE-CATHERINE-WHEEL-AND'T-HAST
GONE –OFF-"

1.VERA'S WISHES

Icarus rant the olm in one fullness
His feet widely proportioned
Took more in each in every stepping
He found his stance at the end
On a pinewood plank
Icarus there glimpsed the breadth
Though he turned backwards
His covered distance in more
Moments .

Staying in home delivery
Out reached 3 red chalices
-Their suffice-
ONE-for't onus
TWO-for't ink
THREE-for't trouble's

Palm fought too hard
All again
Icarus
"THE NIGHT"S ROOM"

Its cavity a displayed lamp
Which olmer red glow
Holds OT' the rummage
INT' fury
Heavy velours hung the
Push
They're painted in stars
They'd forebode thist'
Somnambulist int' hist'
Practical sleeping day

Icarus feels the weeks pulse
Int' stands all In for't buzze'tas
Curls rhythmic seaman

Roall came'd round-TA-
Icarus takes pardon
In her singing table
Manners, bed chants

Roall's figure hisses
As if't were a siren
Her breasts god knew
Rapped in a pre-Raphaelite
Manner
"MY CHILD I'LL TALK TO
I WAS MOVED IN AN IMMENSE
FORCE BY HER HONEST
AMUSEMENT."

Icarus lowers her down
His hands now dry
Loose grip on her shoulder
Blades
Climaxing as if two leaves
Sway'd off their edges
Scrapping opon the gate's
Brickwall-

2.OH, You

Icarus in stroll
Blasts the 'PONTEF WAY'
Scents accosted by spider fish
In the mantis of the wake
Of the PONTEF'S riverbed
Their aromas foretake
Arousal in the earnest
Of our stroller.

Icarus steps coldly in front
Of an AltarFountain
Lapping viciously its
Diminishing substance
Only fought hist' phallic
Revery.

Icarus enters
"EARLY CHILDHOOD"
By its front door-

"EARLY CHILDHOOD"
Is placed architecture
By way of 19th century
Manners
The walls ignited by oil
Lamps, hung paintings
Of a woman's figure
Between-TOO-worlds
Of royalty, Icary skims
Their beauty in hindsight
During his waterfelt
Lurge to the resting place

The cadavers sit
Opon the pedestals
All photographic
Clasp drinks in hands
Lifting them as accord
With a soldier's march.

3.MORE

Icary ducting downward
In mist of the resting place
Caught first glimpse of Mollana
Her tinge seemed as one
Of a sent creature
Glitter lit her high boned face

Smiling, head tipped downwards
Eye color obscured by frigorific lashes
"YOU KNOW NO-ONE"

-Mollana-
-Near would-
-Be depending-
-On others-
-Mollana-
-Was remade-
-In one's own-
-Trusts-

Inside Mollana something
Is given away to Icary
Who's only standing there
And't-now the urchins ignite

Icarus-"Karibu"
Icarus-"Habari?"

Mollana-"Mzuri!"

And't-sadly for
Icarus

Mollana says " Kwa Heri".

Ic(to himeslf says)-"At last-
Asante sana"

4.Dilemma

In my head forever
Those few hours which
Bow before the harvest
Stephanie, you would have
Had to have been there

I can't get over with those few
Hours onward in me
How passionate I felt your
In-counted steppes
I didn't forget
At first I very badly took
Hold and most significantly
Was redeemed by you
I slept however short
But coming here in comfort
You would seize my nape
I would merge against your
Bosom
Neither of us really saw much
I whispered how clear you've
Been to me
We saw enough and we have
Very much gained our rest

Sincerely,

"AMBER"

-ARC-

-Opon sipping barafu maji-
-Opon deeming I was thinking of hearing problematic voices-
-Looks like I saw so much of that-
-Still, maybe to say the least received by not distilling this
Sense of loneliness-
-Whose urgency as you well know exist in the sprayed mists
Opon fields-

-LALA SALAMA-

Tropic 29
'The strike when approached from behind'

LISTEN-Che-"He can be left slowly-Out- they love him for sake-They share his Application/ Education-And't-so too"-

Stephanie-" 'Belle's-life-IS-mystery-So-other-Times in through cracks, rain-seeps, Lapses-unsaid-damping-the-heavy-blankets- Atop Belle's sheets"-

Che-"Streaked-hazel-footage-Belle's-father-filmed-Down the street that leads Belle out of home -And't till the projective misfortune-Belle, there -only on wings of his(SELF)thought precious -directions could have led him."
Stephanie-"Though-before-the-illustrious-night-times-Were the advising-----foundations-reel'd-for-Anybody-searching-some-of-the-Blemishes-The---wall's-plaster-----releases-Belle-He-had-a-funny-puzzle-OH-The-Walls-simply-Looked-as-if-cake-Belle-bit-Down on his tongue, leapt the distance-from his bed to the cornerwall-----And't---stung-his-fists-And't-his-entire-face-in-the-dough, butter And't--ic'd wall-When-Belle-fell-back-out-certain-dialogs-Situated in 'em-Che said every time we Lie in bed awake in comfort-He-Remember'd-our-comfort-came-from-our-Silence-Too-Che-had always with his nape leaned back on his pillow- KINDA TRICKS/TWO-MEN'S VOICES"
    "For moments he referred-to--Their-conversation-as-a-trunk-pulled-Out-by scholars, wherein hidden the Best pictures of him moving away from His reliance."

Tropic 30
'Is this a stunt, of somekind?'

Stephanie-"He falls,he leans-
　　　　　Done,abound-
　　　　　Seems that they're
　　　　　Crawling out of home-
　　　　　And the large pyramid
　　　　　Screams his life
　　　　　The ambiance is
　　　　　Time to time recalled
"AS PAIN PUSHERS LOOP,ALLTIMERS"
　　　　　Oh, Arrest beginnings!

Che-"I will never have to wait 'ta' Sunday
　　　I'll jump- great, great cries-
"IF SO THEY"D BE GRANTED"

Tropic 31-'Peace, I think of as luck-when I rarely but on this occasion realize that even recent disappoint which steadily brought rage-was for the better'-ENTRY-1-FEBRUARY-7th

I was deeply frightened at how things seemed to be turning Out-Though I just feel that I Had't--to've seen them from this distance-It seems assuring as I recall last week- Wednesday- A thing or two out on those days-My my lites have Been a'certain- One of my loves good NOT(I Feel), so todiefor- Maybe that love really shouldn't be-Really shouldn't At all be on ground where I love its posting I really do feel my time with Stephanie was the greatest Help to my heart And't--body-To just walk with her And stop, placing your arms around her- -CUT-The promise of natural surroundings crystallized Like a little wing waved gently by a slight fanning The tightness of Stephanie's image, can And't-- is Played over And't--over-it is a moment that I've Only borrowed still felt beautifully its pressing Between she And't--I---And't felt as if not an'other Soul need understand- I can overly relinquish this Realm, it's still sharp in a physical presence Just counting her steps, being held with her good Byes-those are both separate blows- Stories Opon stories-WELL, DO, LOVE-But is mostly A coincidental dislocation in having been anywhere With her- Watching her sleep as an expressive Version possible only as where prominent religion Would put her as verses of sanctuary- I will not Fall asleep-to linger the presence of a still, still Soul-Is holy comfort, gathered tablets, 100 Tales spun into a buried concave, grave calmness A cobweb spun with the wisp of hope-Wherein the Squirm of the caught fly-moments before the spider Scurries up the web in urgency of his devouring- -AS CHRIST where to arrive as the black witch, Who crouches opon Stephanie's chest as the Paralysis-Then over plays her being alive every moment, Even 100 years gone or before, The Crowning Nocturne, The darkest achievement , making the Hours prior to sun-up the feasible account of day Time failure And't--accomplishment-"THE SUM EQUAL SATISFYINGLY-DREAMT-WONDERS-REINFORCING-A------- BELIEF IN MAGICK AND'T--A BETTER LIFE" –she's sung off to dreamland-

201

Tropic 32
'To look into your face, saw something which said that you're
going to finish the things you're set on doing.'

IN MUCK-How's 'cause he's dancin' around That's how he'll
stay And't-he very well holds
Off living-
Stephanie-COME ON-closer-that's the certain
Trigger of't-my cognitive thinking skills-She
Wears a fluff'd red sweater-NO Brassiere-
Stephanie comes about And't-the wool of't
The sweater shreds my eyebrows-with
Her running her sleeve over my head-
She's fascinated-In't the way-she behaves
Isn't that she doesn't use 'EXCUSES'-

Stephanie-"The boat ride in-wasn't a
Very good time at'all HALF the boat tottered
On the water-Even though, it were-A calmday'-
Tha'day happily
With its being over
I manage to avoid the crowds
And't-scurry-my'self to the
Rooms-
Quickly picturing my dressingup
Oh, come on you weren't understood-
In that way then- "SOME OF US" tried
Anyways.
Going down then, the meager roofs of
The huts, caved in, many of them-
Outstretching-I began to hang over
The scene-Re-catching the time peering
Outward-"FAINTED STICKS PEERING ON
EVERY WORRIERS SHOULDER"
So much of this is remembered in the aura
Of a'fusing my idenity-'Cause when
Everyone's masked And't-not expecting
Me to take them as their real selves, it's

This stable caring , I had And't-I got it for
You too"-

Stephanie-"lamely, their is just/ME STANDING-
NO big, big affirmation
Plenty of sight, of visual re- occurrence
It was't-peering over this slot
That was't-embroidered with finefinished
Wood And't-journeymen-
I looked in there, you know
Half of my face-
I think was shining And't-I think if
You'd have seen me-NO, from if
You'd been seeing me(I, seeing this)
In aid of a looking-glass,
"IT'S-A-PORTRAIT-TAKEN-BADLY-WITH-A-FLASH",
And't-every imperfection is noted-not only in my complexion
But in the framing of the picture on the wall-Which-
CUTBACKTO-what I see-
Is a toll taken on'over my life
A hundred butterflies in there-
Just laid on planks-
And't-I was burning empty-
"I WANTED TO KILL MY OWN SELF"
Scenes facing me over And't-over
Not sparing me From loathing-To be at a place And't-which
Was-Splendid-GOD-to-find-a-little-little-imperfection-that
Triggers-these-Complications, stones that flare on from
"HEAD TO TOE".
AH, really blood spil't-and't-maybe,
Maybe will be beautiful 'cause it's
Cued from years, years where the
Source was love's…-

AH, really blood spli't-and't-pours
Lushly ast' if were irrupting fire
'TOR' chopped holes int' storage
Wherein's 'VINES".
 -CUT-
 -To-

203

OUR, OH,
-His FREENESS-
1.Interior.Morning.
On the dresser-LIE-lipsticks
And't- Stephanie dresses in front of the
Long, long mirror, the walls are-
READ-,A LITTLE BOY sits on a chest
In right hand corner of the frame-An
Image of water currents is barely at first
Imposed above the main image-
She(Steph)tries oufit after outfit-and't-3
Times at the screen's bottom appear the
Words-"TOMMORROW'S FORECAST,
SELFENEMIES, SELFENEMIES-THEY DON'T GIVE ANY
BREAKS, THAT'S THEIR EXPLANATION FOR IT".

Tropic 33

'When Spring Is Dawn'

-A SONG-

-MEDLEY-

For't thoughts to've remembered
'Cause AN evil year, is't too,
Remembered

And't-therest a stop...
Jus' when I believ'd that I
Found na'thing

'Cause An evil year,
Therest magick..
Therest else...

A brightnight, he saw for/ever
On a BRIGHTNIGHT, he saw
For ever: There's where we're hardly
At a piece-
-trust-
-cuttoo-
-the finale of loudsongs-

"THE 5-POINTED INITIATOR SHALL
MOVE PROUDLY THE QUOTATION"
-'til-
"THE SPHINX'S INBRINGINGS"-
"MY DAILY HEART"-

As knew what would've been 'APERFECT MOMENT'
, if he was not so sudden

, if he was not so solely diminished by their
confinement…-

And't- if not knowing them, 'VANISHING', And't-
If not 'REALLY','REALLY'=Whoelse could've
Vanished in he ?

That's dor-mid- And't- they've managed to celebrate its
Specialty,
"IN A HARP'S STRING MINUTES"

All knew the greatplace OR no,no the place that
Earlier=GREAT,GREAT And't-shadowblankets
Covered the moon that will refer to He And't-cross
Terrifyingly shatter, He, wager-

-

RATTA-,
-RATA-,
-Tatter elms evol-
-fortip-
-toliv-
-jus'toliv'it-

'THEN ALL ROADS, THE ROADS PEOPLE
VENTURE OPON AS THEY GOABOUT PICKING
THEIR SEPARATIONS , THESE, THESE ROADS,
MAY I GRANT THEM TOO,"

Q-you,would so/say much-YEARN/ON-
Seemingly persistently sure?

-EPILOG-
-BREADLINESS-
" THE SPECTACULAR
DEVOTION"-
"IN GIVING HE A GIFT FROM MY
OWN ADORATION"-
"ABHORRENCE"-

"THE SUN'S CHANNEL AND'T-IF THERE WERE
A SON, WOULD HE RUMMAGE AS ITS PRISM?"-

"THE SHIPS WOULD CARRYOFF HIS INNOCENT
PARDON"-
"MY PHINILLA"-
"AND'T-BIRDLY PARAKISS"-
" THE CASTLES OF MYOWN SHORTCAME AS
 HIS"-
"MY SON'S TORTURESHIP"-
"AND'T-NOT LYING TO THEE"-
'AND'T-APPRENTICESHIP THAT LET THIS
SON, AH SUCH='horns bursts'.

Tropic 34

Stephanie-"I did not understand why they did not
Want me to have love/life-In my
Imagining(maybe)I knew they'd do all
In their power to take this from me."

Entry-February-13-01

-FOUFIRE-
We're getting all we wanted
-This time is returned to this way-
As it was given-MAGICK, suppose if
I am all for running thru my lack of encouragement
This time-I would stage my disappearance all to myself,
=LIVINGSCREENS=

Stephanie-"At their feet-marks-Guards who never
Budge and seem-to/be-Statues-They're
Dressed in silk blue cloaks I report my
Disturbances-They reply to me by slowly
Communicating that it makes no difference-
They act like the idea of me even trying is one
That congers complete outrage-Congers
Complete foolproof disbelief-cutback-
The guards gave (blue) at first, granted
Permission-
It was in this permission that I believed that…
I began to believe that all this TIME was going to
Payoff."

Entry-February-14-01

To dream mercy all'of'thaday And't-reap
Its nightpromise-Strange to me-

-A PLACE-
-A TIME-
-BOTH-
Can never be suffice-
-BOTH-
Will be only clear if I am never asked of them, later-

Tropic 35-'Explicit'-"How I survived my summer,last"

Stephanie-"Should'of expired its case=in symbols-
That's how, it should have=BEEN
Told with symbols-then-TOWN-
All inhabitants, they're scared, aren't
They scared?(PAUSE)"
-CONFIDENTIALLY-
                    (" I guess so/YEAH…
I…guess, SO/EASY-for them to say-
GRANTED that'll be their purchase/
Letting me down-Caused in falsehood-
OUR structured guest, he says=He,
Made no issues about these sacrifices
When it was his turn to be-
EXCEPTIONAL-They made clear that
In amiss colony, there are not reputingly
Whimsical margins ".)

POINT 1. 'VS' POINT 2.
(The-oblivious-will-now-feel safe- Wherein the entire course
and In a pried-book-You-are-either-inhere-or then you are
either out-)-If you- want-to-be-the-type-of-individual-who-feels-
strongly-for-the------ reasoning-of-saving-themselves-Then-you-
might-think-very-----hard-about-looking-elsewhere-for-the--------
holding-to-one's-rites-----
CONFIDENTIAL-

Tropic 36
'Then…, be different'

Dear Che,

It was to typify in a very unorthodox chain Of thoughts and feelings, a light superficially Cosmic-Though rather intensely it will burn out and Rest as a blanket of ashes over any wide sea- I would hope to at that point tell you of how that Would reinforce my hastily torrid en-captured Nihilism-A viewpoint that can never at this point It seems break free-Rationally, we both believe in still trying To show our dis-believers that the loss of US was THEIRS, Entirely-We start out by planning a way that would make them want us back- Then(remember) we hoped that we'd honestly prove that WE needed nobody-Obviously, that time is over and I'm telling you that I think that there is no longer any point in keeping that inside of you- Hence how so, at any other day I would have usually told you to keep going on in that direction but now I hope that I've made it clear that for your own betterment you should cease your interest in that struggle.
LOVE,
Belle

Tropic 37
'WHAT, the place. We called that, HOME?'

Che-"To tell you-there are no destroyers-
 Then, I can't say there isn't safety,
  Not there, I don't think."

Che-"I was suited for the situation-
 I will come back opon its meaning
  And surprisingly this is still tender!"

-FADE OUT-

210

-FADE INTO-
1.Exterior.Fountain/Park, with my hearts put-on.Daytime.
A red tint is visible over our central image-A LARGE
FOUNTAIN-which appears to've been long since active- A
weather/aged statue is still in the fountain's center-CUT TO-
Families of insects swarm about the ground At the foundation
of the fountain-Cut TO-The sky above the fountain-That is now
being seen From a low-angle, turns dark-Storm clouds are
Heavily sharp, about the farthest from if you'd
Previously to the storm's start have hoped for a
Gentle rain-The clouds scrape into the frame from
both corners-A dangerous sense resonates to the
point where it could tear the sky apart-And then we freshly
breathe out to emerge having now returned to before the
storm-CUT BACK TO-A clearest sky, void of all clouds-The
fountain Looking now as if the final stages of its construction
Were completed just yesterday, The statue stands
Drawn on one leg-A stream of water is dispensed
From its stone penis into the many lilies and reeds
That artificially line the fountain's wishing pool-
CUT TO-The statue's ejaculation, sotospeak- Over shoots and
is now becoming the steady Center of muddywater that caves
a figurative Distance deeply into the soil-JUMPCUT-
The small maturation of the bright details of An embryo forming
in the earth beneath the wet Ground and then making a clichéd
metamorphosis Into the now living replica of the statue whose
more than willing lovestream caused its fertilization.
The statue/boy stands amongst his rite, the sky
Now as in the start of this, is scraped with
Darkness, giving forth the start of the heavy rains-
Tosaytheleast.

Tropic 38
'MYSECRET'

-STEPHANIE-

Intellection Hops about the Colonization of real reason-
Aura, Castle, OH my small light, To me is just her red light
before lavage

Che-"Pond, pond and where music is. Hands pressed in
arthritic claw shape, Useless at moving away stones.
I, then was tracing up the stream-That as so'much narrowed,
widened-And--dropped-dried-completely-in-places-----Where-it-
could have very well been a Footpath- squatting at what when I
counted My steps back-would have been if not the
Half point of the stream-least a half point In my conduct of
venturing up it.-SITTING OPON STONES-Its end was a wall
that obscured any sight over It, to forebode still seeing where
the stream's origins lie. The small thresh of the stream first
seeps, it seems silently under a slit where the
earth caved down barely underneath the wall's
foundation. I, placed my head at this spot and
formed what I thought just over the wall was –A lone harp
player- one who plucked strings Endlessly. Though: I, wanted
the sad feeling of Thinking the notes fell short in every attempt
At clearing the wall."

-STEPHANIE-
Deliquescence happened on the rite/away
Jus'to'you-though I cleverly sent an Imperial
Moth in place of a carrier pigeon, with a small
Card attached-"STEPH, IMPORTUNE I WANNA' ALWAYS
BE MISSING-I HOPE TO DANCE SO'S I'LL
ALWAYS BE LOST.-ALWAYS BE LOST-
     -ALWAYS BE LOST-
          ...ALWAYS BE

Tropic 39
'The Dragondays(to children)'

(GAVE)
Me,
This part is now not about pasts-
(GAVE)
Me,
This part is now kept clean of referrals-

Glanced out'a car windows was a string on
A wind blown dragonkite, bright red mask,
Cloth ribbons were wings-
Formerly an open spaced not crimson-
Dramatized stealth, exquisite now that you
Mention 'IT'-

Meredith: I remember her name-

Meredith: I think I couldn't ever place her face-

Meredith is leastly' never to be a goodchance-
Only does she-
The reminder of nothavingfun-
The complications in the preclusion's
Of absent happiness-

"THE SERVICE OF THE FINISH"

This disclosure: is why I didn't spend rest
In an attitude of being short for time-
Every answer didn't let me gape-
Draw heavy breaths-MY-MY-and
I will come not close to even settling with
Respective insights, as becoming a failure-
-QUIET-
So, I will..
I will hope not that anykind attempts

Standup, sitting long at the mercy
Of the test of time-
"HE IS NOT HAPPY"
-BELLE-
SOME THING COULDN'T FLATTEN HIM
ANY MORE ALLEGED SPEARS, THOROUGHLY
-pleasecut-A SHINING FLOATS ON, SPITTING
HAIKUS-TURNING HIS PALMS WET-YOU, I BEG
FOR YOU TO NOT BE A STAIN OF YOURSELF-
I LIKE WHO YOU WERE AND WILL BE-
-pleasecut-GOT SCARED IN MY PRESENT'TENSE
STONESQUARES, LOOK ABOVE AND
SIMULTANEOUSLY KEEP YOUR FEET IN THE
WATER DESPITE ITS TEMPERTURE-ALLNEEDED
IS LEDCONTEMPT-CONTENTIVELY WASTED
TIME-IS, I WANT YOU TO MANAGE IN THE SIGHT
OF ACCEPTING-

Tropic 40(fails miserably in letters)
'ENTRIES, FEBRUARY-23rd-FRIDAY '
Pre
Script,
EMILY, Oh who represents
The transgalactic CELIBATE- Amiss
The landfills bores and giants?
-DEAR EMILY,
Oh the cities peered toply beautiful
Your burning transexamines perversity
Your poor murders, transposed unfactually
Stance:
If your earthly times over, who are?
They, least they'd respect you
Oh only thought hating: forms
Spent life chasing
-CANTHAVE-
-CANTDOTHAT-
-LEAST LIKE YOUD BE, OK –
-TABOO-
-SLEEPSCIENCE GOT TO
TURN TO RELICTION-
Che-"Belle had the problem of putting himself down
About paper, Understood: what's wrong with him being
This close to me: nothing wrong has been done by this: If
Wrong actions were to be carried-those could surely
Not end us, not here."
 -STEPHANIE-A HOLY ROLLER ONWARDS SPOKEN A
MADRIGAL, A VERSE IN THIS IS TO SCANDALIZE
ORGIASTIC RITES-WE'LL HAVE MADUROS AND SIT
TOGETHER ON A FATFORTUNE- I WILL LOOK BACK
FROM UNDER MY POKE BONNET AND POIESIS SHALL
OF BEEN LISCENISED AS A DECKOFCARDS-pleasecut-
JUS'WADE TO TURN M'WAY-
              .   –STEPHANIE-

Tropic 41   -Nymphaid-
                -an' come on down to me-

'KEY 1 OF 5'

Emily- "Sagging out, from dragging a tale on who-back to
        Destiny-Who-roaming? A useful protectress, whose
        Intentions brought a suffice collective of them t'gather,
        Another up artwell "NA" , "NA"(back to walking wayfare
        From status)-Before we came on him last-
        PLEONASM+a gemmy sky sat upward.
        Each other road, take either.
        Believable(Sole) at these measures. Here,
        Two paths fork, and starts(each)-godlucky
        Strumming crippled by the time we're...
        He still(we hoped) managed someplace,
        Though, hopelessness the while-we turned
        Nothing new, bottoms gaining nearly all of
        Other bottoms!!"

Tropic 42
-CURVILINEAR-
KEYS 2,3,4,

2. key
Doris-"Doubtitude in the distances of a sole gram of
Regimented speech-EXAM..-"My Apologies,please"
Exact'as "My Apologies, please" hints as you've
Fallen on'ta something pleasurable&somehow a
Universal feeling that chants on, it's about a phrase
That glow,glow, glows.it does metaphorically take a
Coward to tie the lack of spite without verification of
Presence in the reasons comingover you as a
Blackprayer –A calendar with a shadow for each
Day, shadows that though are cast by living forms,
They haven't got any person givin'em'off,
NOT(pause),rightnow?"
3.key-Che-"Q.What--_you wanted him to've been
Something Which he is not"--_A."a cue, go on
Wait."
"Q.apprehensive"A. a little rhyme took place-
A garden kill't by Winter , the happyfaces wish it
Back, Summer"Q. breezy failure, comment on
Scurrying to her bed in 3 weeks of weekdays&
Sundays(2)&missed one"Q.'member leepin' off
Without thinking anything's wrong
"A.18days inall"A-Che-"I don't not care for a reminding!"
4.key-Stephanie-" the altars created quickly, makeshift have

You-a redtallcandle,a lessheavy
Greencandle-two lilywhites-a'storing
Offerings-cracked Fall leaves in the
Kneelingcircle, been brightened in
Reason, in length of knowing to make
Haste the requiring of the purpose,
Committal(secondly tradition)

Overshadowed that, a satinshaw
Overtop rotates slightly palms

Glidetense. There Amber sat on
A blanket she'd brought with her-
She'd grown drowsy, nodding quickly
Backover a surf's lapse-Drizzle-
She'd rolledover in the sand ofta'
The blanketside,coverd, her with a
Towel.

'Void sun's light, she'd awaken humming to wetsand
Meshed in the corners of her mouth&the corners
Of her eyes.Drawing the towel backover her head.

She again slept, hours-Now diminished-that extra
Skin sagging 'round her belly-and infant's eyes
Roll directly to her breastbone, they shut'miss'd
Directblurr, awhile feeding from her breasts."

Tropic 43
-A pockmark assures-

Key 5. Che-"Sat, stiff, straight-assumed leaning, can't
Help not smelling a graveltype scent after
Sleeptime's been thrownout-You've heard,
Gettingup subsequent times&I liked promising
The uniqueway to forward these unrests,
Its, "CRIME", "A BADDREAM, THE REAL
FIRST TRY"-
Q."HOW TO GO ON LIKE THAT?"
Stephanie-"NOT ONE&NONE AT ALL"
"OH lord, What a horridtime!"
SCREMING-stepped-down-to-just-
A-continuous-rambling. MY throat
Went hoarse-drenched in a hot muddythick
Syrup-My belly musseled, distrusts the plight
Of my-way-over to tell you I'm love-with-you
I held on to this till it actually emerged here."
Che-"I'd of led you out hand&hand"

Stephanie-"That is your best advice, thus to this point."

Che-"You've made yourself, acutely ill in
Preparatory stages of psychologically
Readying yourself for this venture over."

Stephanie-" So it's was better to've been said here,
Now"

Che-"Not a thing other to do, than to only fall,
Or is there something else?"

Stephanie-" What of a short song, is that the best?"

Che-" That isn't in the question, best?"

219

Stephanie-" Rather you've been letdown in your total
Defied self-assurance, leave it to your own
Faults, But Then love?"

Che-" If I were self-afflicting, I'd tell you give that
Its needed time."

Stephanie-" You hope I can walk off here, with leaving
That & void we're to've looked back there."

Q. No, down about this time, here they've
Showed. "PIGS!!"

Tropic 44
'If she wants doom, than it's doom which we'll give her'

" -STEPHANIE-
-SMOKE BLENDS AMONG THE HEARTSHAPED
BALLOONS-
-WHICH HELIUM TEMPORARILY SITUATES
A'TOP
THE CEILING-
-STEPHANIE, THERE IS ROOM FOR ONE WHEN DYING-
-REKINDLED SPATS OF BLEEDING 'ROUND A CHILD'S
MOUTH-
-HEADS PRESSED DOWN HEAVILY 'TOP
PILLOWCASES FREELY OUTED CHANCE'S
SITTINGUP-
-STEPHANIE, HOMESIGNAL THRU WISP
NAME EXQUISITIONS THRU PRICEFREE
LASTS ENTIRITIES"-

ENTRY, the first day of March-2001,

SINGS-"If I only knew"
SINGS-"Everyone is entirely uncorrect"-and then blocks out
flights of mistrusts, the last being-"NONE SEEMED TO
CONSIDER THE MOST INVAUABLE OBSTACLES", proceeds
thru taking the fisrtdeep pride of His time at the risks of having
had the privilege of naturalistic evils serve as that which linked
him thoroughly within the Winter anomalies , draws over the
xerox of a girl's back-she was wearing a corset and had her
hair tied-up-
    SINGS-"for your excellence"
    SINGS-"In thanking your perfectionary examples"

Tropic 45
'MIRA'(an overtly brief historical account of celibacy)

-Mira waded 'bout the outscursions of
LOURDES DREADFUL MANOR-
Cast over her shoulder a 'rikitirakiti' ICE LANTERN- She once
walks the firststeps casts from Hell&HEAVEN-
Permanently earth is purgatory? OR Permanently earth in
justso entirety?(and) Mira SANG-" sat about a day, I taught me
one thing Obey blindlanguage"

To let her haveway the morning, Friday
This life an'her
TO REALLY MAKE LIVING
(and)
Mira sang-" I learnt a charred rocket,
I learnt the one in your highness
Passes on your keys,
Jacob when passing the keys, let go
OH the angel"

The prejudice 'gainst the girl
Her keeping in favorite
A virgin
(and)
Mira sang-"Naturally not kicking missus-
            Naturally go a part"

Her hair bonfire red
She takes her advantage
Back tolerance
Back compromise
The 'itchycage' smoothes things
'OVER&OUT, OVER&OUT'
Not
Throwing a thing at'MA

Her hair bonfire red
Pleasure

Her, red burn

She, in a nameless country
Carrying the brass's trio
-evil speechless-
-evil sightless-
-evil soundless-
(and)
Mira sang-"if I were a pigmy signaled
By the civilization of the westernworld's
Witchdoctors.."

JOURNAL,
I wanted to-
I'd give in-
I wanted to, for 'em-
(and)
Mira changed-"gonna banish children?"
"gonna banish swans?"
A rose from right'up
Creation-OH-AH..
Polaroid brown /yellow
STUNG 'MA'

Her hair 'gain call'd bonfire red
MEMORY holster-

"THE FIRST GIRL IN TOWN WHO LEAVES THE OTHER
GIRLS LOOKIN' WHOLEY PALE, LIKE THEY'D OF CAUGHT
THEIR DEATHS!"
(and)

Mira sang-" in a brightburn ruff 'low the sheltermantle
The boys stayed close durin' all the stronger
Rains, them boys stayed free of spiddle
Jetting out the frothing cronurn in trophy
That appeared as 'a waterdemon,
It was them boys who put their chairs
'gather'

Journal(Mira writes and smugly smiles)
-the weight, the bristles that earn a body
its freerites,the chance, gonna need to
rise more&more, the weight, the chants,
the spinsters, that earned a body its freerites,
(Mira tightens up closely to the end of the page)
-the-can-not-be-here-will-niffly-get-at
this-body's freerites-

ISBN 155212872-5

9 781552 128725